It was clear Taylor was waging a battle with herself.

Maybe she needed some inducement, Russ decided. He settled his hands on her shoulders and brought her against him.

She remained stiff as a branding iron, refusing to relax the way he wanted.

He could kiss her; that might help with her decision. He settled his chin on the crown of her head and felt some of the fight go out of her. A smile twitched at the edges of his mouth. He'd known she would come around once she had time to think about it.

"Taylor?" he whispered, lifting her chin so he could look into her eyes. He expected to find sweet submission, perhaps even a hint of desire. Instead, what he saw puzzled him....

Dear Reader,

The Silhouette **Special Edition** selection has seldom been more satisfying than it is this month. For starters, beloved **Nora Roberts** delivers her long-awaited fourth volume of THE O'HURLEYS! *Without a Trace* joins its "sister" books, the first three O'Hurley stories, all now reissued with a distinctive new cover look. Award-winning novelist **Cheryl Reavis** also graces the Silhouette **Special Edition** list with a gritty, witty look into the ironclad heart of one of romance's most memorable heroes as he reluctantly pursues *Patrick Gallagher's Widow*. Another award-winner, **Mary Kirk**, returns with a unique twist on a universal theme drawn from the very furthest reaches of human experience in *Miracles*, while ever-popular **Debbie Macomber** brings her endearing characteristic touch to a wonderfully infuriating traditional male in *The Cowboy's Lady*. Well-known historical and contemporary writer **Victoria Pade** pulls out all the stops (including the f-stop) to get your heart *Out on a Limb*, and stylish, sophisticated **Brooke Hastings** gives new meaning to continental charm in an unforgettable *Seduction*. I hope you'll agree that, this month, these six stellar Silhouette authors bring new meaning to the words **Special Edition**!

Our best wishes,

Leslie Kazanjian
Senior Editor

DEBBIE MACOMBER
The Cowboy's Lady

Silhouette Special Edition

Published by Silhouette Books New York

America's Publisher of Contemporary Romance

For Irene Goodman,
agent and friend.
Happy Birthday,
give or take six months.

SILHOUETTE BOOKS
300 East 42nd St., New York, N.Y. 10017

ISBN: 0-373-09626-7

First Silhouette Books printing October 1990

Books by Debbie Macomber

DEBBIE MACOMBER

hails from the state of Washington. As a busy wife and mother of four, she strives to keep her family healthy and happy. As the prolific author of dozens of bestselling romance novels, she strives to keep her readers happy with each new book she writes.

With *The Cowboy's Lady*, Debbie Macomber is beginning another miniseries. For more about love and life in Cougar Point, Montana, be sure to read *The Sheriff Takes a Wife*, a Silhouette Special Edition available in bookstores this December.

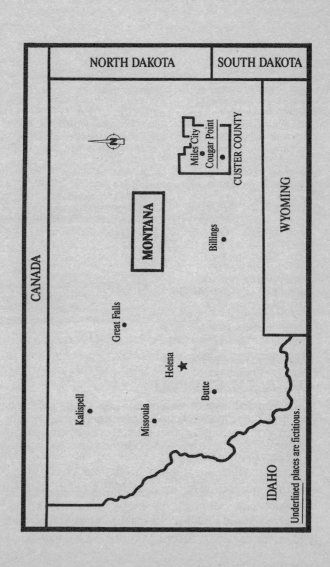

Underlined places are fictitious.

Chapter One

Everyone in Cougar Point, Montana, knew the bowling alley had the best breakfast in town. For a buck ninety-five they served up eggs, sausage, hash browns and toast, plus all the coffee a body could drink. Russ Palmer was hungrier than a bear in springtime, but food wasn't the only thing on his mind.

He needed a woman. Bad.

There was a cocktail waitress Russ knew in Miles City, but driving all that way just to get laid was hardly worth the time or the trouble.

"Mornin', Russ," Mary Andrews, the lone waitress, called out when he stepped inside the restaurant. Her greeting was followed by a chorus from several other ranchers.

Russ removed his black Stetson and hooked it on the peg just inside the door. Although it was only a few days into

September, there was a nip to the air and he'd worn his blanket-lined denim jacket.

Sliding into the booth with a couple of friends, Russ picked up the tail end of what Bill Shepherd was saying.

"Pretty as a picture."

Russ's interest was instantly piqued. "Who?"

"The new schoolteacher, Taylor Manning," Harry Donovan answered eagerly. At twenty-three Harry remained peach-faced with fine, blond hair that he couldn't seem to control even at the best of times.

A schoolteacher. Russ's curiosity level sank several notches. "Taylor's a funny name for a woman," he muttered, reaching for the menu, which was tucked between the sugar container and the salt and pepper shakers.

"The missus and I met her yesterday," Bill went on to say. "She rented old man Halloran's place on the edge of town."

Russ nodded while his gaze scanned the menu. He ordered the "special" every Saturday morning, but he liked to see what was offered in case something else struck his fancy.

"She moved here from Seattle," Harry informed Russ enthusiastically.

"Then she's a city girl," Russ said, and a hint of sarcasm slipped into his voice. The kid had it bad. Personally Russ didn't hold out much hope of the new teacher sticking it out past Christmas. Seattle was known for its mild climate. At best Taylor Manning could deal with four or five days of drizzle, but he'd bet his ranch and five hundred head of cattle that she didn't have a clue about what a Montana winter could do to a body.

"Whether she's a city slicker or not, I couldn't rightly say," Harry said with no lack of fervor, "but I do know one thing. She's real pretty. I swear she's got the bluest eyes

I've ever seen and dark, silky hair that falls to about here.'' He gestured with his hand to a point well below his shoulder blade. ''A man could see himself running his fingers through hair that thick.'' Pink tinged Harry's cheeks as he stopped abruptly and cast a self-conscious glance in the direction of his two friends.

Russ laughed outright. ''Hell, Harry, she hasn't even been in town a week and already you're sweet on her.''

''I can't help myself,'' Harry said, and reached for his mug so fast that he nearly spilled his coffee. ''Wait until you meet her yourself, then you'll know what I mean.''

''I'm not going to be mooning over no schoolmarm,'' Russ informed the two men. He hadn't gotten to the ripe age of thirty-four without marching down a church aisle to be taken in by the charms of a citified schoolteacher, and especially one Harry Donovan would moon over.

Bill and Harry exchanged glances, then Harry snickered loudly, apparently amused by Russ's attitude. ''You just wait till you see her yourself,'' he said.

''What do you mean I can't use my American Express card here?'' Taylor Manning demanded of the clerk at the small retail store. ''I could use this card in Beirut!''

''I'm really sorry,'' the round-faced older woman said, ''but as far as I know, no one in town takes American Express.''

Mumbling under her breath, Taylor pulled her Visa card from inside her pigskin wallet and set it on the counter. ''I'll use this one instead.'' She pushed her chocolate-brown hair over her shoulder and glanced around her. This situation was getting to be downright embarrassing. Taylor had used her meager savings to rent the house. She'd gone shopping for several small items she was going to need, thinking she could use her credit card and pay for them when it was more convenient.

Glancing around, she was grateful there were only two other people in the store. A cowboy and his daughter, no, Taylor decided on second thought. The teenage girl was too old to be his daughter, but too young to be his girl-friend.

"I'm very sorry, but we don't take Visa, either," the clerk went on to say.

"You don't take Visa," Taylor echoed in shocked disbelief. "*Everyone* takes Visa."

"No one in Cougar Point," the woman said apologeti-cally.

Taylor smiled blandly at the fair-haired woman. "Then what do you take?"

"Cash would be convenient."

Taylor rummaged through her purse, drawing out a checkbook. She looked at the meager balance and sighed inwardly. She wasn't exactly flush at the moment. "I don't suppose you take out-of-state checks, do you? Don't an-swer that," she said quickly. "Anyone who doesn't honor American Express or Visa isn't going to take a check from a Seattle bank." She stared down at the few items long-ingly and made her decision. "I'll simply put everything back and wait until my printed checks come through from my new account." She'd also have to wait until she'd de-posited her first check two weeks hence, but she didn't think announcing that fact was necessary.

"I'm really sorry, miss."

Taylor nodded. "No problem," she said, and even managed a respectable smile. She turned and nearly col-lided with the cowboy she'd noticed earlier.

"Oh, sorry," she said, scooting past him.

"Just a minute. Did I just hear you mention Seattle?" The tenor of his voice was deep and masculine. Without giving her a chance to respond, he added another question. "You wouldn't happen to be Taylor Manning, would you?"

"Yes. How'd you know?" Not that she should be surprised. Folks had been introducing themselves to her all week, telling her how pleased they were that she'd accepted the teaching assignment in their town.

Setting his black Stetson farther back on his head, the rancher explained, "The kid mentioned something about you this morning over breakfast."

"The kid?"

"Harry Donovan."

Taylor didn't recall meeting any youngster by that name, but there had been so many names and so many faces that she'd long since lost track.

The cowboy smiled, and their eyes held for a moment. The brief exchange, at least on the part of the rancher, seemed to be filled with curiosity. For her part, Taylor had no feelings one way or the other. Oh, he was good-looking enough. His head was covered with a crisp black Stetson that all the men in town seemed to wear. His dark hair curled along the nape of his sun-bronzed neck as if he'd delayed getting a haircut a couple of weeks too long. He was tall, easily six-three, and clad in tight-fitting blue jeans and a plaid shirt beneath a thick denim jacket.

"Mabel," the rancher said, looking past Taylor. "This is the new schoolteacher."

"Well, for goodness' sake, miss, why didn't you come right out and say so?" Without a second's delay the clerk reached beneath the counter and brought out a tablet and started listing the items Taylor had wanted to purchase.

"Does this mean you'll accept my American Express? My Visa? My check?"

"No, I do feel bad about that, but most of the commercial people in these parts don't do credit card business with those big banks. I'll just write down these items here and send you a bill at the end of the month the way I do with most folks."

"But . . . you don't know me." The woman hadn't so much as requested identification.

Mabel weakly waved her hand, dismissing Taylor's concern. "I feel terrible about all this."

Taylor turned her gaze to the cowboy once more. "Thank you."

He bounced his fingers against the brim of his hat and started down the aisle toward the younger girl she'd seen him with earlier.

While Mabel was writing up the sale, Taylor watched the exchange going on at the rear of the store. The teenager was standing beside a cosmetic display and was gesturing wildly, clearly frustrated.

"If you could just sign here," Mabel instructed, turning the tablet around for Taylor to pen her name. "I can't tell you how pleased we are you've come to Cougar Point. There won't be much of a social life for you, but we have our moments."

"Yes, I know," Taylor murmured. She hadn't accepted this teaching assignment because of the potential nightlife. She'd specifically chosen the backwoods of Montana in an effort to give herself the necessary time to heal after her disastrous affair with Mark Brooks. She'd moved to Cougar Point to involve herself in her chosen profession, and deal with the emotions and the bitterness of losing Mark. A year from now she'd leave Cougar Point rejuvenated and whole. Her family, especially her father, had assumed she'd taken this job on impulse, and God knows her personality was often a spontaneous one, but for once her father was wrong. The decision to spend a year in Montana had been well thought out, the pros and cons carefully weighed. She was taking this time to mend a badly broken heart, hoping twelve months in the country would do what six months in the city hadn't.

"I want a second opinion," the teenager cried as she rushed toward the front of the store. "Excuse me," she said brightly, holding out her hand. "I'm Mandy Palmer and this is my brother, Russ, who happens to be obstinate and stubborn and completely unreasonable and the worst male chauvinist who ever lived."

"Mandy," Russ threatened in a voice few would challenge, "I said no."

"That's just too bad," the teenager returned. Tears glistened in her green eyes while she valiantly struggled to hold them at bay. She was a pretty thing, petite, and wore her thick blond hair in a long French braid down the middle of her back. It swayed when she jerked her head toward her brother.

"Mandy," Russ threatened again, his voice as strong as a steel cable.

The girl ignored him with a defiant tilt of her chin and looked at Taylor. "When a girl's fourteen years old and going into her first year of high school, she's old enough to wear a little makeup, isn't she?"

"Ah..." Taylor hesitated. Mandy was staring at her with eyes that were charming enough to make her a poster child, while her brother was glaring heatedly in her direction, silently demanding that Taylor mind her own damn business. "What does your mother say?"

"Our parents are dead," Russ said gruffly. "I'm Mandy's legal guardian and I say she's too young to be painting up her face with all that garbage. She's only fourteen, for God's sake.''

''Were you wearing makeup when you were my age?'' Mandy asked Taylor, the appeal in her eyes desperate.

''A little,'' Taylor admitted reluctantly. She clenched her purchases tightly to her breast, not wanting to get caught in the middle.

''Mascara?''

''Yes,'' Taylor confessed.

''Blush?''

Taylor nodded, ignoring the fierce scowl being directed at her by the girl's brother.

''How about lip gloss?''

''I was wearing that in junior high,'' Taylor said, gaining a bit more confidence. In Taylor's opinion, although it was clear it wasn't wanted or appreciated by the male faction of this family, Mandy should be allowed to experiment with a little makeup.

''See,'' the girl cried enthusiastically. ''And you turned out to be a fine, upstanding citizen, didn't you? I mean a little lip gloss at fourteen didn't automatically turn you into a lady of the night, did it?''

Taylor couldn't help laughing; that was the most ridiculous thing she'd ever heard. ''No. But it was close. It all started with too much mascara, followed by a thick layer of eye shadow. Before I realized what I was doing, I was into perfumes.'' She hesitated and lowered her voice to a mere whisper. ''The French variety.''

Mandy gasped for effect.

Taylor couldn't help a smug smile as she continued. ''From there it was a natural descent. I found myself standing on street corners . . .''

"It's time to go," Russ ordered. He gave Taylor a look sour enough to curdle milk. "We've heard more than enough."

Still amused, Taylor left the store. She hadn't made a friend of the rancher, but Russ was being more than a little strict with his younger sister. It wasn't like her to take sides in something that didn't involve her, but Russ's attitude had struck a familiar chord in her. Taylor's own father was often hard-nosed and outdated in his views. More than once the two of them had butted heads over the most illogical and ridiculous issues. If her mother hadn't been there to run interference, Taylor didn't know what would have happened. The crazy part was, she thought the world of her father. They sometimes argued until the cows came home, but that never dampened the deep affection they shared.

Till the cows come home! Taylor paused midstep. Good grief, she was already beginning to think like a cowgirl. If this was the way her thoughts were running after ten days, God only knows what she'd be like in a year's time.

Taylor was walking to her car when she met up with Mary Beth Morgan, another teacher. They'd met earlier in the week during a staff meeting. Mary Beth was in her mid-fifties, friendly and a country girl through and through. She was the type of woman who made sure that what everyone said was good about small towns was true.

"You're looking pleased with yourself about something."

Taylor nodded. "I just met Russ and Mandy Palmer. They were debating whether Mandy is old enough to wear makeup and somehow I got caught in the middle. That man is certainly opinionated."

"Mandy can give as well as she takes. I once heard Russ claim Henry VIII couldn't stand up to Mandy when she truly wanted something."

That sounded exactly like something the cowboy would say and, despite herself, Taylor discovered she was smiling.

"Russ has a good heart, so don't judge him too harshly," Mary Beth said as they strolled down the sidewalk together. "He's raising Mandy on his own and genuinely cares about her. His views may be a little outdated, but he tries hard to be as fair with her as he can be."

"What happened to their parents?"

"Actually Mandy's his half sister. Russ's mother ran off when he was little more than a toddler. I doubt that Russ even remembers her. Fred Palmer took his wife's leaving him real hard. I'm sure there are two sides to that story. Fred could be as ornery as a saddle sore and was as pigheaded as they come."

"Russ must take after his father then."

"He does," Mary Beth said, missing Taylor's joke. "Most folks around here would rather tangle with a grizzly bear than mess with Russ when he's in one of his moods. I suppose that has a lot to do with his living all those years without a woman's influence. Thank God for Betty."

"Betty must be Mandy's mother?"

"Right. To everyone's surprise, Fred up and married again. Russ must have been in high school by this time. Betty was the sweetest thing, and just the right kind of woman for someone like Fred. She was gentle and kindhearted and as good as the day is long. Mandy arrived a year later.

"Fred and Betty were real happy. I don't think there was a dry eye in the town when she died. Not long afterward Fred died, too. The doctors may have a fancy name for what killed him, but I'll tell you right now, Fred Palmer died of a broken heart.''

''How sad.'' The wit and humor drained from Taylor. She couldn't help being affected by the story.

''Russ reminds me a good deal of his father when Fred was around that age. What Russ needs is a wife—someone like Betty who'll cater to his whims and pamper him with love and a gentle heart.''

That left her out. The thought startled her. She would no more consider marrying a rancher than she'd entertain thoughts of riding a horse. She was sushi, soft rock and lazy bubble baths. As far as she was concerned, cows smelled, hay made her sneeze, and the sight of a horse sent her scurrying in the opposite direction. She was as suited to country life as a goldfish swimming around in a glass of fine wine.

''I'm sure if Russ said anything offensive...''

''He didn't,'' Taylor was quick to assure the other woman. But not from any lack of desire. Judging from the look in his eyes, he had wanted to spit nails at her. If there was ever a man who longed to put her in her place, it was this formidable rancher. Unfortunately, or fortunately, as the case may be, it would take a lot more than one cowpoke to do it.

Mary Beth and Taylor parted ways at the corner, and Taylor made her way to the grocery store. With a limited budget and a distinct lack of imagination when it came to cooking, she headed for the frozen food section.

Without much enthusiasm she tossed a frozen entrée into her grocery cart. The local supermarket didn't carry a large selection, and it was either the salisbury steak or the country fried chicken.

''Was that really necessary?'' a gruff male voice questioned from behind her.

"The country fried chicken?" she asked, turning to face the very man she and Mary Beth had been discussing.

"I'm not talking about your pathetic choice for dinner. I'm referring to my sister. She's going through a rebellious stage, and I don't appreciate your taking her side on an issue. We can settle our differences of opinion without any help from you."

Taylor was about to argue when she spied the teenager turning down the aisle.

"Oh, hi," Mandy greeted, brightening. She hurried to Taylor and her brother. "You're not eating that for dinner, are you?" the girl asked, eyeing the TV dinner in Taylor's cart. A horrified look spread across her face.

"It seemed the least amount of trouble," Taylor admitted. She'd spent a full day unpacking and cleaning, and dinner, even a frozen one, was more appealing than being forced to cook for herself. As far as she could see, there wasn't a single fast-food place in town. The nearest McDonald's was a hundred miles from Cougar Point.

"I've got a big pot of stew simmering at home," Mandy announced eagerly. "Why don't you come over and have dinner with Russ and me? We'd love to have you, wouldn't we, Russ?"

Her brother's hesitation was just long enough to relay his message.

"It's the neighborly thing to do," Mandy prompted.

"You're welcome to dinner, if you want," Russ said finally, and Taylor had the impression it demanded a good deal from him to echo his sister's invitation.

There wasn't any question that Taylor should refuse. But something perverse about her, something obstinate and a tad bit foolish wouldn't allow her to do so. Perhaps it was because she recognized the same mulish streak in him that she knew so well in her father. Whatever the reason, Taylor knew she was going to enjoy this dinner. "Why thank you. I'd be honored."

"Great." Mandy beamed. "We live about ten miles east of town, and our place isn't too hard to find."

"East?" Taylor repeated, twisting around in a full circle in an effort to orient herself. She wasn't entirely sure which way east was, at least not from where she was standing in the grocery store.

"Take the main road and turn left at the stand of sycamore trees," Mandy continued. "That's just past Cole Creek, only don't look for any water because it's dried out by this time of year."

Further directions only served to confuse Taylor. Heavens, she wasn't all that confident she could tell a sycamore from an oak. And how in heaven's name was she supposed to recognize a dried-out creek bed? Usually Taylor followed directions that said she should go to the third stoplight and take a left at the K-Mart.

"Why don't you just ride along with us?" Mandy suggested next, apparently sensing Taylor's confusion. "Russ can drive you back into town later."

"It'll probably work better if I follow you," Taylor suggested. "My car's at the house, but it would only take a minute for me to swing by and get it."

"It wouldn't be any trouble. Russ has to come back later, anyway. Besides, I wouldn't want you to get lost once it turns dark. You might lose your bearings."

Not for the first time, Taylor noted that Russ didn't echo his sister's suggestion. The temptation was too great to ignore, and once more Taylor found herself agreeing to Mandy's plan.

"My truck's parked outside," Russ grumbled. He didn't look very pleased by this unexpected turn of events. But then he hadn't looked all that thrilled about anything from the moment they'd met.

Russ's truck turned out to be a twenty-year-old dented Ford that most folks would have hauled to the dump a year earlier. The bed was filled with a variety of supplies. Grain sacks were stacked against one corner, fertilizer in another.

The front fender was badly bent and had started to rust through. The license plate was missing, and Russ had to completely remove the passenger door for the two women to slip inside. Once they were seated he replaced the door and latched it into place.

Taylor squirmed around in the bench seat, searching for the seat belt.

"There aren't any," Russ explained as he slipped in next to her and started the engine.

The seat was cramped, and Taylor was forced to dig her elbows into her ribs. Her shoulders were butted on each side. On her left from Russ and on her right from his younger sister. It had been a long time since Taylor had sat this close to a man. At first she tried to keep her thigh from rubbing against Russ's, but it was nearly impossible. So their thighs touched. Big deal.

Only it soon got to be.

There must have been something in all that fresh country air that was adversely affecting her brain cells. Without a whole lot of difficulty, Taylor could actually find herself smitten with this man. *Smitten!* Oh dear, her mind was doing it again, tormenting her with this country jargon....

Everything was going along just dandy until they turned off the main road and headed down a lengthy rut-filled section that tossed them around like Mexican jumping beans. They'd hit a dip, and Taylor would bounce off the seat as if it were greased. It was all she could do not to land on top of Russ or Mandy. They apparently were accustomed to this thrashing about, and each managed to stay neatly in place as if it were a perfectly ordinary thing to do. Taylor, on the other hand, was all over the inside of the cab.

Every time the truck hit an uneven patch, some part of Taylor's anatomy came into intimate contact with Russ's. Their thighs stroked each other. Their shoulders butted and rubbed, their waists bounced together. Again and again their bodies were slammed against each other.

Taylor couldn't help noticing how firm and muscular Russ felt. She didn't want to acknowledge that he was all sinew and bone. Nor did she want to experience the heat of his body and the warm muskiness of his skin. He felt solid. Strong. Virile. A host of sensations, long dormant, sprang to life, assaulting her.

Not once had Russ Palmer purposely touched her, and yet Taylor felt as though his hands had caressed her everywhere intimate and private. Her breasts had never felt heavier, and they tingled in a way that was embarrassing and unfamiliar.

Hot blood gushed through her veins until she couldn't stand it any longer.

"Would you mind slowing down just a little?" she cried, hating having to ask.

"Why?" Russ asked, his voice filled with amusement.

"Russ," Mandy cried, "Taylor's not used to this."

For whatever reason, Russ slowed the vehicle, and Taylor went weak with relief. She could feel a headache coming on, but she wasn't entirely sure it had anything to do with the skipping, hopping and jumping she'd been subjected to for the past ten minutes.

They arrived at the ranch house a couple of minutes later, just about dusk. The first thing Taylor noticed was the huge red barn. It was the largest one she'd ever seen, but that wasn't saying much. She knew next to nothing about barns, but this one seemed enormous. The house was sizable, as well. Four gables stood out against the roof of the huge white structure, and the windows were framed by bright red shutters.

Taylor climbed out of the truck on the driver's side after Russ, not wanting to be trapped inside while he went around to remove the passenger door. It took her a minute to find her legs.

Mandy bolted ahead of them, with an energy reserved for the young. She raced up the back steps that led into the kitchen, holding open the door for Taylor. "The stew's cooking in the Crockpot."

Taylor noted that Russ headed in the opposite direction, toward the barn, probably to see about unloading the contents of the truck bed. Her gaze followed him, and she wondered briefly if the close confines of the truck had affected him in the same way they had her. Probably not. He looked a lot more in control of himself than Taylor felt.

A thin sheen of perspiration moistened her upper lip. What the hell was the matter with her? Groaning silently, Taylor closed her eyes. She knew what ailed her, and she didn't like it one bit. Not one damn bit.

Taylor Manning needed a man.

Chapter Two

Russ remained silent for the majority of the meal. He didn't like this schoolteacher. But he didn't exactly dislike her, either. She was as pretty as Harry had claimed, and her hair was as thick and rich as any he'd ever seen. A couple of times he'd been tempted to lift a strand and let it slip through his fingers, but that would have been impossible. And what she did to a pair of jeans ought to be illegal. On the ride to the ranch he'd purposely driven over every pothole he could just because he liked the way her soft body had moved against him. Damn, he needed a woman worse than he'd realized.

"You're from Seattle?" Russ asked. He'd been trying to ignore her for most of the meal, not because he wasn't interested in learning what he could about her, but because—damn it—he was as taken with her as Harry had been.

Taylor nodded, smiling. "I was born and raised in the shadow of the Space Needle."

"Ever experienced much snow?"

"A little."

The thought of her creamy smooth skin exposed to the elements knotted his stomach.

"I understand winters are harsher here than in western Washington," she said stiffly. "I came prepared."

"I doubt that you have a clue how severe winters can get in these parts." Russ had seen too many cases of frostbite for his own good.

It was clear that Taylor resented the way he was talking to her. He didn't mean to imply that she was stupid, only ignorant, and he didn't want her learning harsh lessons because no one thought to warn her.

One quick look told him he'd raised Taylor's hackles. She seemed to be taking several moments to compose her thoughts, then she set her fork next to her plate, placed her elbows on the table and joined her hands. Staring directly at him, she smiled with deceptive warmth and said, "You needn't worry, Mr. Palmer. I'm perfectly capable of taking care of myself. I've been doing so for a good many years now and will continue to do so. I may be a city girl, but let me assure you, I'm both intelligent and resourceful."

"Do you know what happens to skin when it's exposed to temperatures below thirty degrees? How about the symptoms for hypothermia? Would you be able to recognize them in yourself or others?"

"Mr. Palmer, please."

"Russ," Mandy cried as her outraged gaze shot from him to Taylor and then back again, "you're being terribly rude to our guest."

Russ mumbled under his breath and resumed eating. Maybe he was overreacting. Perhaps his motives weren't so lily-white. Perhaps he was more angry with her than concerned about her welfare. God knows she'd done plenty to upset him in the past few hours. Taking Mandy's side with that makeup matter hadn't set right, but that was hardly an issue after the way she'd been forced to press herself against him during the ride from town. Sweet heaven, but he couldn't get the feel of her out of his mind. She was as soft as a newborn calf, and damn if she didn't smell like wildflowers and sunshine. That thought led logically to another. If she smelled so damn good, he couldn't help wonder what she'd taste like. Like honey, he decided, fresh from the comb, thick and sweet. The knot in his stomach tightened. If he didn't curb his thoughts soon, he was likely to end up kissing her before the night was through. The way he was feeling now, raw and hungry, he wanted to grab her right now. The ache in his loins was surprisingly strong, and he nearly groaned out loud.

"You're an excellent cook," Taylor said to Mandy in a blatant effort to lighten the strained atmosphere.

Mandy beamed with the compliment. "I try. Rosa and her husband retired last year, and I talked Russ into letting me do the cooking, and really it's worked out pretty well, hasn't it, Russ?"

He nodded. "There have been a few nights best forgotten, but for the most part you've done an excellent job."

"She took over all the cooking at age thirteen?" Taylor asked, amazed, although Russ had trouble figuring out why. He'd long suspected that city kids didn't carry anything near the responsibility that ones from the country did.

Mandy nodded and eyed Russ. He knew that look well by now, and it meant trouble. He bit his tongue as she opened her mouth to speak.

"It seems to me that any girl who can rustle up a decent meal every night is old enough to buy her own clothes without her older brother tagging along, don't you think?"

The way things were going, Mandy was looking at being sent to her room without finishing dinner. "That's none of Taylor's concern," he said tightly, daring their guest to challenge his authority with his younger sister.

"Isn't it?" Mandy pressed, looking at Taylor.

"Ah..." Taylor hedged, looking downright uncomfortable. "I have a self-set limit of answering only one leading question per day," she explained, reaching for another piece of bread, although there was already a buttered one resting against the side of her bowl. "I don't think it's a good idea to get on Russ's bad side twice in one day. I might end up walking back to town."

"Russ would never do that."

Want to bet? Russ mused. Okay, so he wouldn't make her walk, but he'd sure as hell hit every damn pothole he could. The problem with that was he was the one most likely to suffer.

"What do you honestly think?" Mandy pressed.

"I think you should eat your dinner and leave Taylor out of this," Russ ordered harshly. The girl would be the end of him yet. She had turned willfulness into an art form.

"I...your brother's right, Mandy," Taylor said, lowering her gaze to the steaming bowl of rich vegetable stew. "This is something the two of you should settle between yourselves."

"Russ and I'll settle it all right," Mandy responded defiantly, "but he won't like the outcome."

Russ didn't take the bait. "More stew, Taylor?"

"Ah . . . none, thanks. My bowl's nearly full."

"When did you start buying your own clothes?" Mandy asked, clearly unwilling to drop the issue.

Russ's gaze collided with Taylor's, daring her to question his authority a second time. She glanced nervously away. "As I recall, I had the same problem with my father at this age. I got around him by taking a sewing class and making my own clothes."

"When was this?"

"Oh, about the eighth grade or so. To this day I enjoy sewing most of my own things. It's economical, too."

"The eighth grade?" Mandy cried, casting Russ a triumphant look. "You were basically choosing and sewing your own clothes when you were only thirteen, then."

"I don't think it's a good idea for me to get involved in a matter between you and your brother, Mandy. I did earlier and I don't know if it was the right thing to do then, either."

Russ felt a little better knowing that.

Mandy's shoulders sagged once again, and Russ was pleased to note that she was gracious enough to accept Taylor's word. Finally.

"I didn't mean to cause such a scene in the variety store," Mandy murmured apologetically. "All I wanted was Russ's okay to buy some lip gloss."

Russ set his napkin on the table. "I wouldn't mind letting you wear some lip gloss, but you insist on overdoing it. I walked past your bedroom the other night and I swear your lips were glowing in the dark."

Mandy glared at him, her eyes filled with righteous indignation. Dear God, what had he said now? Before he could ask her what was so all-fired insulting, she tossed her fork and napkin onto the table and promptly rushed out of the room.

"Amanda Palmer, get back here right this minute," he shouted in the same steely tone that sent his men scurrying to obey. When Mandy didn't immediately comply, he stormed to his feet, ready to follow her.

"Russ," Taylor said softly, stopping him. He turned his eyes on her, wanting to blame her for this latest display of pique.

Taylor sighed and pushed aside her bowl. "Give her a few minutes. She'll be back once she's composed herself."

"What did I say?" he demanded, sitting back down, genuinely perplexed.

Taylor hesitated, then said, "It might have had something to do with the joke about her lips glowing in the dark."

"Hell, it's true. I told her she couldn't wear any of that war paint you women are so fond of, so she defied me and started putting it on before she went to bed."

"She's exercising her rights as a person."

"By spurning my word? I swear that girl drives me to the edge of insanity. What's gotten into her the past couple of years? She used to be an all-right kid. Now it seems I can't say a word without setting her off."

"She's a teenager."

"What's that supposed to mean?" he barked.

"Don't you remember what you felt like at fourteen? How terribly important it was to dress and act like everyone around you?"

"No," Russ stated flatly. His features tensed. He didn't want to discuss his sister with Taylor. She didn't know any more than he did about raising kids. The problem with Mandy was that she was getting too big for her own britches.

Standing, Taylor reached for her bowl and glass. "I'll clear the table."

"Leave it for Mandy," Russ insisted.

Taylor ignored him, which was getting to be a habit with the women in this house. Russ had yet to fully understand what it was about womenfolk that made them want to challenge the fact a man was the master of his own home.

"Why?" Taylor demanded, startling him out of his reprieve. Even more astonishing was the fact she looked downright angry.

"Why what?"

"Why would you want to leave the dishes for Mandy?"

"Because that's woman's work," he explained.

"You're possibly the worst male chauvinist I've ever encountered," she said, carting what remained of the plates to the sink. "The way I feel about it, those who cook shouldn't have to wash dishes."

"It'll be a cold day in hell before you'll ever see me washing dishes, lady." He found the thought downright comical. He hadn't taken kindly to being called a chauvinist, but instead of arguing with her, he'd been gallant enough to drop the matter. They were having enough trouble being civil to each other without him throwing gasoline on the fire.

Taylor hurried to the sink, filling it with hot water. "Since the task belongs to a woman, I'll do the dishes."

"The hell you will. No guest of mine is washing dirty dishes."

"Fine then," she said, motioning toward the sink filled with hot sudsy water. "Everything's ready for you."

Although he was struggling against it, Russ was getting thoroughly irritated. He was standing almost directly in front of her. Not more than two inches separated them.

Taylor stared up at him and must have recognized his mood, because he watched as she swallowed tightly. It wasn't consternation he saw in her eyes, but something that stabbed through him as sharply as a pitchfork. Longing and need. The same emotions he'd been battling from the moment he'd laid eyes on her.

He recognized something else. She didn't want to experience it any more than Russ wanted to feel the things he had been feeling for her. From the moment they'd sat next to each other in the truck, he'd never been more profoundly aware of a woman in his life. The air had been thick with tension and seemed to throb like a living thing between them all evening.

Russ felt it.

Taylor felt it.

Both seemed determined to ignore it.

Bracing her hands against the edge of the sink, she anxiously moistened her lips. Russ's dark, brooding eyes fell to her mouth. Her sweet, honeyed mouth. The sight of her tongue and the tiny movement mesmerized him. Her eyes reluctantly met his, and the look they shared was as powerful as a caress. It demanded every ounce of willpower Russ possessed not to groan. His treacherous body responded immediately, and he tore his gaze away from her and lowered it until it all but collided with her breasts. He swallowed a gasp as he watched her nipples pearl. An intense heat began to warm him. He scrambled for something to say or do that would break this all too dangerous mood.

"I...think I should be going," she whispered.

"You called me a chauvinist."

"I...apologize." Her pride was apparently crumbling at her feet. The fight had clearly gone out of her.

He pulled his gaze back to her mouth, experiencing a small sense of triumph at the power of his will. His eyes held her prisoner. "Where'd you ever get a name like Taylor?"

"It was my mother's . . . maiden name."

Once more her voice came out sounding whispery and soft. Too soft. Too whispery for comfort.

"My mother's from Atlanta, and it was an old Southern tradition to give the first daughter her mother's maiden name." By the time she finished, her voice was little more than a thin thread of sound.

Neither of them spoke for the longest moment of Russ's life. Taking in a deep, shaky breath, he was about to remind her that he was ready to drive her home. Instead, Russ found himself leaning toward her.

"I'm sorry I ran out of the kitchen like that," Mandy announced, coming back into the room.

Russ's shoulders sagged with frustration. He frowned at his younger sister, irritated. The girl couldn't have chosen a worse time to make her entrance. For her part, Taylor looked as if she were ready to leap across the room and hug Mandy for interrupting them.

"I was just about to take Taylor back to town," Russ announced gruffly.

"Do you have to leave so soon?" Mandy asked. "It's barely even dark."

"It will be any time, and I still have a lot to do before school starts. Thank you so much for having me . . . both of you. You're a wonderful cook . . . I really appreciate this."

"You'll come again, won't you?" Mandy asked.

"If you'd like."

"Oh, we would, wouldn't we, Russ?" Mandy asked.

He made a response that could have been taken either way.

Mandy walked to the door and down the porch steps with them. Her arms hugged her waist against the evening chill. "You're driving the Lincoln, aren't you?"

Once more Russ gave a noncommittal reply. His truck was in the shop, having the transmission worked on, and he'd been forced to take the older one into town that morning. That Mandy would suggest he'd opt to take Taylor home in that dilapidated old thing was something of an insult. The look he gave her suggested as much.

"I was just asking," she said with a smile innocent enough to convince a judge.

Taylor and Mandy chatted while Russ went around to the garage and pulled out the luxury sedan. The two women hugged, and Taylor climbed inside the car and ran her fingertips over the leather upholstery before snapping the seat belt into place.

"You ready?" he asked more brusquely than he intended.

"Yes."

They drove a few minutes in uncomfortable silence. "How large a spread do you have here?" she asked.

"A thousand acres and about that many head of cattle."

"A thousand acres," Taylor echoed.

The awe and surprise in her voice filled him with pride. He could have gone on to tell her that the Lazy P was anything but lazy. His spread was one of the largest in the southern half of the state. He could also mention that he operated one of the most progressive ranches in the entire country, but he didn't want to make it sound as if he was bragging.

They chatted amicably about nothing important until they arrived in town. Russ turned off the side street to old man Halloran's house without even having to ask where Taylor was living. If she was surprised he knew, she didn't say.

When he pulled into her driveway, he cut the engine and looped his arm over the back of her seat. Part of him wanted to ask her to invite him inside for coffee, but he already knew it wasn't coffee that interested him. Another part of him demanded he stay the hell away from this schoolteacher. Every part of her luscious, ripe body spelled trouble.

"Thank you again," she said softly, staring down at her purse, which was tightly clenched in her lap.

"No problem."

She raised her eyes to his, and despite all his good intentions, Russ's hungry gaze fixed on her lips. His body tightened in the effort to curtail a sudden, ravenous need. He became aware that he was going to kiss her about the same time he realized he'd die if he didn't. He reached for her, half expecting her to protest. Instead she whimpered and wrapped her arms around him, offering him her mouth. The sense of triumph and jubilation that Russ experienced was stronger than any aphrodisiac. He wrapped her in his arms and dragged her softness against him, savoring the pure womanly feel of her.

His kiss was wild, and he thrust his tongue into her mouth. Dear God, he'd been right; she did taste like honey. She was incredibly sweet, so damn sweet that he wanted more and more of her. His callused hands framed the satin-smooth skin of her face as he slanted his mouth over hers, famished beyond reason. He kissed her again and again and again, sliding his mouth back and forth over hers in a slow, drugged exercise.

Her throaty plea was what reluctantly brought him back to reason. For an instant Russ worried that he'd frightened her, until he heard his name fall from her lips in a low, frantic whisper. It was then that he realized she was enjoying their kisses as much as he.

"Do you want me to stop?" he asked, his voice little more than a husky murmur. He spread damp kisses down her neck and up the underside of her chin until he reached her mouth once more. Drawing her lower lip between his teeth, he sucked gently.

"Please . . . stop," she pleaded, but at the same time her hands ruffled his hair, holding him against her. She arched her back, and the feel of her breasts against his torso intensified the already throbbing ache in his loins.

Taylor lowered her hands to his shoulders and dragged herself away, leaving only an inch or so distance between them. Her shoulders heaved as she struggled for control.

"I can't believe that happened," she whispered.

"Do you want an apology?"

"No," she answered starkly. Then, after a moment, she added, "I wanted it as much as you did. God knows why. We're about as opposite as any two people can get."

"Maybe so, but I think we just discovered one way we're compatible, and it beats the hell out of everything else."

"Oh, please, don't even say that," she moaned, and pushed him away. She braced her shoulders against the back of the seat and ran a hand down her face as if to wipe away all evidence of their kissing. "What just happened was a fluke. I don't know why we kissed. . . . I think it might be best if we pretend it never happened."

Russ went still, his thoughts muddled and unclear as a December fog. What she'd said was right. He had no business being this attracted to her. No business even kissing her. She was from the city and didn't have a clue about the complexities of his life. She was the new school-teacher, and not a woman the community would approve of him dallying with.

That they were attracted to each other was a given. Why seemed to be a question neither of them could answer. One thing Russ knew: Taylor was right. It was best to forget this entire episode had ever happened.

For the next week Taylor did an admirable job of pushing the memory of Russ Palmer from her mind. It helped somewhat that she didn't have any contact with either member of the Palmer family.

Taylor didn't question what had come over her to allow Russ to kiss her like that. She refused to ponder what had taken place and instead had resolutely pushed the memory from her mind, contributing it to a bad case of repressed hormones. That was the only thing the kiss could have been, and analyzing it to death would accomplish nothing.

School started, and Taylor threw herself into the task with gusto, more convinced than ever that she was born to be a teacher. She was an immediate hit with her third and fourth grade students.

On Wednesday afternoon at about four, an hour after her class had been dismissed, Taylor was sitting at her desk, cutting out letters for her bulletin board, when there was a polite knock at her door. Suspecting it was one of the grade-schoolers, she glanced up to discover Mandy standing there, her books pressed against her breast as though she expected to fend off Nordic invaders.

"Mandy, hello," Taylor said, genuinely pleased to see the teenager. "Take a seat." She waved the scissors at the chair next to her desk.

"I'm not bothering you, am I? Russ said I wasn't to trouble you after school if you were real busy. He thinks I'll be a pest."

"You can come and trouble me anytime you want," Taylor said, as she continued to cut out the blunt letters from the bright sheets of colored paper.

Plopping herself down on the chair, Mandy crossed her legs and smiled cheerfully. "Notice anything different about me?"

Taylor nodded. "I dare say, isn't that war paint you're wearing?"

Russ's sister giggled shyly. "I came to thank you. I don't know what it was you said to my brother about me being old enough to buy my own clothes, but it worked. The next morning he said he'd thought about it overnight and decided that if I was old enough to cook dinner and wear a little makeup, then I was mature enough to buy my own clothes without him tagging along, giving his approval."

Taylor wasn't entirely convinced that Russ's change of heart had anything to do with her, but nevertheless, she was pleased Mandy thought so. "That's great."

"I heard from Cassie Jackson that you're a really good teacher."

Cassie was a fourth-grader in Taylor's class. She smiled at the compliment.

"Word has it half the boys in your class are in love with you already," Mandy told her. "I told Russ that, and I think he's a little jealous because he frowned and reached for the paper and read it for ten minutes before he noticed it was one left over from last week."

The last person Taylor wanted to discuss was Russ Palmer. "I don't suppose you'd like to help me cut out these letters, would you?" she asked, more to change the subject than because she needed any assistance.

"Sure, I'd love to." Mandy was eager to lend her a hand, and within a half hour the two had assembled a bright brown, yellow and orange autumn leaf bulletin board.

Once they'd finished, Taylor stepped back, looped her arm around her young friend's shoulder and nodded, pleased with the finished project. "We do good work."

Mandy nodded. "We do, don't we?"

Noting the time, Taylor felt guilty for having taken up so much of the girl's afternoon. "It's almost five. Do you need me to give you a ride home?"

"That's all right. Russ said he'd pick me up. He's coming into town for grain and I'm supposed to meet him at Burn's Feed Store. It's only about a block from here."

Mandy left soon afterward. Taylor gathered up the assignments she needed to grade and her purse and headed toward the school parking lot. Her blue Cabriolet was the only car left in the small lot. She was halfway there when a loud pickup barreled into the lot behind her. Just from the sick sounds the truck was making, Taylor knew it had to belong to Russ.

He rolled to a stop, his elbow draped out the side window. "Have you seen Mandy?"

She nodded, her eyes avoiding his. "You just missed her. She's walking over to the feed store."

"Thanks." His gears ground as he switched them, and he looked over his shoulder, about to back out, when he paused. "Is that your car there?"

"Yes." He made the question into a comment, as if to say this fun car was exactly the type of vehicle he suspected a city girl would drive. Normally Taylor walked to and from school. It was less than a mile and she liked the exercise, but it had been raining that morning, so she'd opted to bring her car.

"Did you know your back tire is flat?"

Taylor's eyes flew to her Cabriolet, and sure enough the rear tire on the driver's side was completely flat. "Oh, great," she moaned. She was tired and hungry and in no mood to face a hassle.

"I'll change it for you," Russ volunteered, vaulting from his truck like a knight in shining armor.

It was kind of him, and Taylor was about to tell him so when he ruined it.

"You independent women," he said with a loud chuckle. "You claim you can take care of yourselves and are too damn proud to admit you need a man. But every now and again we come in handy. Now admit it, Taylor. You couldn't possibly deal with this without me." He was walking around toward her trunk, as haughty as could be. It was as if he'd been waiting weeks to find something that would put her in her place.

"Hold it," Taylor cried, stretching out her arm. "I don't need you to change my tire. I can take care of this whole thing myself."

Russ gave her a patronizing look and then chose to antagonize her even more. This time he laughed. "Now that's something I'd like to see." He leaned against her fender and righteously crossed his arms over his broad chest. "Feel free," he said, gesturing toward the flat.

"Don't look so smug, Palmer. I said I could take care of this myself and I meant it."

"You wouldn't know one end of the jack from the other."

Taylor wasn't going to argue with him about that. "Would you care to make a small wager on my ability to deal with this problem?"

Russ snickered, looking more pompous every minute. "It would be like taking candy from a baby. The problem with you women's libbers is that you're too damn stubborn to admit when a man is right."

"And I say I can deal with a flat tire any day of the week."

"And I say you can't. You haven't got the strength to turn the tire iron. Fact is, lady, you couldn't get to first base without a man here to help you."

"Oh, come off it. It's about time you men were willing to admit women aren't the weaker sex."

"Sure," Russ said, doing a poor job of disguising his amusement.

"All right," Taylor said slowly. She deliberately walked past him, paused and then turned to give him a sultry smile. She narrowed her eyes and took a good deal of delight in tossing the gauntlet at his feet. "Perhaps you don't care to place a small wager on my ability. Having to admit you're wrong would probably be more than a big he-man like you could handle."

His dark eyes flared briefly. "I didn't want to do this, but unfortunately you've asked for it. What do you want to bet?"

Now that he'd agreed, Taylor wasn't sure. "If I win..."

"I'll be willing to do something I think is woman's work?" he suggested.

"Such as?"

Russ took a moment to think it over. "I'll cook dinner for you next Saturday night."

"Who'll do the dishes?"

Russ hesitated. "I will. You thought I'd have trouble agreeing to that, didn't you? But then I don't have a thing to worry about."

"Dream on, Palmer. If I were you, I'd be sweating blood."

He snickered, seeming to derive a good deal of pleasure from their exchange. "Now let's consider what you'll owe me when you realize how sadly mistaken you are."

"All right," she said, "I'd be willing to do something you consider completely masculine."

"I'd rather have you grill me a steak."

"No way. That wouldn't be a fair exchange. How about if I...do whatever it is you do around the ranch for a day?" Taylor felt perfectly safe making the proposal, just as safe as he'd felt offering to cook her dinner.

"That wouldn't work. You're a woman."

"I'd be willing to try."

Russ shrugged. "If you insist."

"I do," Taylor agreed.

Still smugly leaning against the side of her car, Russ gestured toward the trunk. "All right, Ms. Goodwrench, go to it."

Taylor opened her front door, placed her papers and purse inside and got out the key to her trunk.

"You might want to roll up your sleeves," Russ suggested. "It'd be a shame to ruin that pretty blouse with a bad grease stain. It's silk, isn't it?"

Taylor paused and glared at him defiantly.

Russ chuckled and raised both arms as though she'd just placed him under arrest. "Sorry. I won't say anything more."

Opening the trunk, Taylor systematically searched through the back until she found what she was looking for.

"A tire iron is about this size," he said, holding up hands apart by a couple of feet, mocking her.

Finding the spray can, Taylor walked around to the flat tire and squatted down in front of it. "I like my steak medium rare and barbecued over a hot charcoal grill. My baked potato should have sour cream and chives and the broccoli should be fresh with a touch of hollandaise sauce drizzled over the top.'' Having given him those instructions, she removed the cap from the tire and proceeded to fill up her deflated tire with the spray can.

''What's that?'' Russ demanded, his hands placed challengingly on his hips.

''You did say this Saturday, didn't you?'' she taunted.

His gaze narrowed when she handed over the spray can for him to examine. ''Fix-it Flat Tire?'' he said, reading the label.

''That's exactly what it is,'' Taylor informed him primly. ''Whatever this marvelous invention is, it fills up the tire enough so I can drive it to a service station and have the attendant deal with it.''

''Now wait a minute,'' Russ cried. ''That's cheating.''

''I never said I'd change the tire,'' Taylor reminded him. ''I told you I could deal with this situation myself. And I have.''

''But it's a man who'll be changing that tire.''

''It could be a woman. In Seattle several women work for service stations.''

''In Seattle, maybe, but not in Cougar Point.''

''Come on, Russ, admit it. I outsmarted you.''

He glared at her, and despite his irritation, or perhaps because of it, Taylor laughed. She scooted inside her car, started the engine and headed out of the parking lot. Halfway out, she detoured and made a sharp turn, returning to Russ who was standing just outside his pickup.

''What do you want now?'' he demanded.

''Before I forget, I like blue cheese dressing on my salad.'' With that she zipped out of the lot. She was still smiling when she happened to glance in her rearview mirror just in time to see Russ slam his black Stetson onto the asphalt.

Chapter Three

No doubt the psychologists had a word for the attraction Taylor felt for this cowman, she decided early Saturday evening. Why else would a woman, who was determined to avoid a certain man, go out of her way to goad him into a wager in which she was sure to win? Taylor couldn't fathom it herself. Maybe it was some perverse method of inflicting self-punishment. Perhaps her disastrous relationship with Mark had lowered her to this level. Taylor didn't know anymore.

She'd like to place all the blame on Russ. If he hadn't made her so furious with his hype about a woman needing a man, she probably would have been able to stand aside and smile sweetly while he changed her tire. But he'd had to ruin everything by making a flat tire an issue between the sexes.

At least Mandy would be there to run interference.

* * *

"What do you mean you're going over to Chris's?" Russ demanded of his sister.

"I told you about it Thursday, remember?"

Russ frowned. Hell, no, he didn't remember. He needed Mandy to help him with this stupid dinner wager he'd made with Taylor. Damn it all, but the schoolmarm had tricked him. By all rights she should be cooking and fussing over him, not the other way around. He'd have been happy to take her to dinner in town and be done with it, but he knew better than to even suggest it. She'd insisted that he cook dinner himself.

"What's so important at Chris's that you have to do it now?" he demanded brusquely.

"We're practicing, remember? Drill team tryouts are next week, and I've got to make it. I've just got to."

The girl made it sound like a matter of life or death. "Couldn't the two of you practice some other time?"

"No," Mandy pleaded. "I want to see Taylor, but I can't. Not tonight."

Grumbling under his breath, Russ opened the refrigerator and gazed inside, wondering where the hell he should start. Make the salad first? Cook the broccoli? Earlier in the day he'd bought everything he was going to need, including a packet of dry hollandaise sauce.

"I'm sorry, Russ," Mandy said, sounding as if she meant it. "I'd offer to help..."

His spirits lifted. "You will? Great. Just don't let Taylor know. If she found out, she'd have me branded and strung from the highest tree for allowing another woman to slice lettuce for me."

"I can't help you, Russ. That would be cheating."

"All I want you to do is give me a few pointers, for God's sake."

"It wouldn't be right." She paused and lowered her voice to a soft whisper. "Don't slice the lettuce, and I shouldn't even be telling you that."

"What do you do with salad if you don't chop it?" Russ asked with a weary frown. He was worse off than he realized. He followed Mandy into the living room where she gathered her homemade pom-poms. "What am I supposed to do with the lettuce?"

"I can't answer that," she said, looking apologetic.

"You can't tell me how to make a salad?" he roared. The grip on his temper was wearing precariously thin. "Why the hell not?"

"It'd be unfair. You're supposed to prepare this meal entirely on your own. If I gave you any help, you'd be breaking your agreement with Taylor." A car horn blared from the backyard, and Mandy reached for her jacket. "That's Chris's mom now. I've got to go. I'll see you later, and good luck with dinner."

She was out the door before Russ could protest.

Russ wandered around the kitchen for the next five minutes, debating what to do first. Grilling the steaks wouldn't be a problem. Anyone with half a brain knew how to cook a decent T-bone. The baked potato wasn't any concern, either. It was everything else. He took the head of lettuce and a variety of other vegetables from the refrigerator and set them on the countertop. Without giving it much thought, he reached for an apron and tied it around his waist. God help him if any of the hands walked in the door.

Taylor was impressed with the effort Russ had made when she arrived at the Lazy P. He opened the door for her and jerked the apron from his waist.

"I hope you're happy," he said, looking anything but.

"I'm more than pleased. Thanks for asking," she returned with equal seriousness, but inwardly she was struggling not to laugh outright. This entire scene was almost too good to be true. Next to her own father, Russ was the worst chauvinist she'd ever met. The sight of him working in a kitchen, wearing a woman's apron, was too good to miss.

"Something smells good," she said.

"I'll tell you right now it isn't the hollandaise sauce. That stuff tastes like sh—" He stopped himself just in time. "You can figure it out."

"I can," she said. Smiling softly, she strolled across the kitchen and set a bottle of wine on the counter. "A small token of my appreciation," she said as means of explanation.

His reply was masked as he furiously whipped the sauce simmering on the front burner. "Maybe it'll taste better once it's boiled," Russ muttered, concentrating on the task at hand.

The table was set. Well sort of. The silverware was piled in the center between the two place settings. The water glasses were filled.

"The broccoli's already done," Russ grumbled as he turned off the burner. "It looks all right from what I can tell." He sprinkled a dash of salt and pepper over the top with a flair a French chef would envy.

"I'll open the wine, if you like."

"Sure," Russ said absently. He opened the oven door, and Taylor felt the blast of intense heat clear from the other side of the room.

"What's in there?"

"The baked potatoes," he said, slamming the door closed. "How long does it take to cook these things, anyway? They've been in there fifteen minutes and they're still hard as rocks.''

''Normally they cook in about an hour.''

''An hour?'' he echoed, and his shoulders sagged. ''Damn it, the sauce!'' he cried. Grabbing a dish towel, he jerked the saucepan from the burner. Once more he stirred it as if he were afraid it would turn to concrete. ''I hope it didn't burn.''

''I'm sure it'll be just fine. Where's Mandy?''

''Gone,'' he grumbled. He stuck his finger into the sauce and licked it, then nodded, apparently surprised. ''She's over at Chris's practicing for drill team. And before you ask, she didn't help me any.''

''Mandy's not here?'' Taylor echoed. A sense of uneasiness gripped her hard between the shoulder blades. After what had happened the first time she was alone with Russ, she had darn good reason for being apprehensive.

She was overreacting, she told herself. It wasn't as if she was going to spontaneously fall into Russ's arms because his sister wasn't there to act as a chaperon. They were both mature adults, and furthermore, they'd agreed to forget they'd let matters get out of hand. The fact they'd kissed was as much an embarrassment to Russ as it was to her. She certainly wasn't going to bring up the fact. Russ didn't look inclined to discuss the subject, either.

''Don't think I had anything to do with Mandy being gone, either.''

''I didn't,'' she said with a shrug of indifference, appearing as if the fact hadn't so much as crossed her mind. It hadn't, at least not before Russ mentioned it.

He was scowling at her as if he expected her to give him an argument.

''Can I do anything to help?'' she asked in an effort to cover up her nervousness.

"No thanks. This meal is completely under control," he boasted, sounding self-confident and pridefully stubborn. "I'm a man of my word, and when I said I was going to cook you the best damn steak you've ever eaten, I meant it."

"I'm looking forward to it." Wordlessly she opened a series of drawers until she located the corkscrew and proceeded to agilely remove the cork from the wine.

"I realize it's traditional to serve red wine with beef, but I prefer white. This is an excellent chardonnay."

"Whatever you brought is fine," he mumbled as he opened the refrigerator and took out a huge green salad.

It looked as if there was enough lettuce in it to feed a Third World country, but Taylor refused to antagonize him by commenting on the fact.

"I want you to know I didn't slice the lettuce," he said proudly as he set the wooden bowl in the center of the table, scooting aside the silverware.

"Oh, good," Taylor replied, hoping she sounded appropriately impressed. The second cupboard she inspected contained crystal wineglasses. Standing on tiptoe, she brought down two. They were both thick with dust, so she washed and rinsed the pair before filling them with the wine.

"I wanted to bring dessert, but there isn't a deli in Cougar Point," she said conversationally as she handed Russ his wineglass.

He paused and turned away from the burner to confront her. He was scowling when he asked, "You were going to buy dessert at a deli?"

"It's the best place I know to get New York cheesecake."

Russ muttered something she couldn't understand before returning to the stove. He turned down the burners and reached for his wine. "Since it's going to take the potatoes a little longer than I realized, we might as well sit down."

"Sure," Taylor agreed readily, following him into the living room. The furniture consisted of large and bulky pieces that looked as if they'd been lifted from an old-time western series from television.

A row of silver-framed photographs lined the fireplace, and, interested, Taylor walked over to examine them. A picture of Russ, probably from his high school graduation, caught her attention immediately. He'd been a handsome cuss even then. Boyishly good-looking, but nevertheless, his appeal was potent enough to cause many a young woman to spend more than one sleepless night.

"That's my dad and Betty," he said, pointing out the second large portrait. "It was taken shortly after they were married." The resemblance between father and son was certainly striking, Taylor noted. They both possessed the same brooding, dark eyes, and their full mouths were identical. Her gaze returned to Russ's high school picture, and she found herself zeroing in on his youthful features. Even in his youth there had been a male wildness about him that challenged a woman to try to tame him. No man had provoked, defied or taunted her the way Russ had, and she barely knew the man. By all rights she should be as far removed from him as possible, yet she was in his home, studying his picture and analyzing his secrets. Taylor discovered she was tempted by Russ. More tempted than she hated having to admit.

The realization produced a sense of panic so strong that she immediately turned away from the fireplace and sat in the thick overstuffed chair. She was as far removed from Russ as she could get and still remain in the same room.

"You were telling me before that you've got several hundred head of cattle," Taylor said, making conversation while her fingers nervously moved against the padded arm of the chair.

"I've sold most of the herd off. I'm wintering five hundred head, but by summer the numbers will be much higher."

"I see." She really didn't understand what he meant, but she didn't know enough to ask intelligent questions. Thankfully Russ seemed to understand her dilemma and explained of his own accord.

"The men are rounding up the cattle now. We keep them in a feed ground."

"A feed ground?"

"It's a fenced pasture with no irrigation ditches."

"Why? I mean, don't they need water?"

"Of course, but the heavy snows start in December, and sometimes earlier. When the ground's covered, the cattle can't see the ditches, and if a steer falls into one, he often can't get out, and I've lost a valuable animal."

"If the snow's that high, how do you get the feed to them?"

"Sometimes by sleigh."

Taylor warmed at the thought of riding through a field blanketed with snow. She could almost hear the bells jingling and Christmas music playing while she snuggled under a thick blanket, holding tight to Russ in an effort to keep warm.

Shaking her head to dispel the romantic fantasy, Taylor swallowed tightly, furious with the path her daydreams had taken. Her pulse quickened, and she took a sip of wine, hoping to set her thoughts in order before they became so tangled that she lost all reason. "That sounds like fun."

"It's demanding physical labor," Russ told her gruffly.

His tone surprised her, and she raised her eyes to meet his.

Dark brown melted into soft blue.

He may be saying one thing, but Taylor would bet her first paycheck that he was battling the same fiery attraction she'd struggled with from the moment he'd first kissed her. His eyes continued to stare at her in that restless, penetrating way that unnerved her.

He seemed impatient to get away from her, and unexpectedly vaulted to his feet. "I better check on dinner."

Once he was out of the room, Taylor pinched her eyes closed and sagged against the back of the bulky cushion. This evening had seemed safe enough until she had learned Mandy was gone. The air was thick with static electricity that sparked and crackled behind even the most bland conversation.

Taylor heard Russ move back into the room, and assuming that everything was ready, she rushed to her feet. "Let me help," she said.

Russ caught her by the shoulders, and her eyes met his. "The potatoes aren't even half done."

Her hair fell back and slipped over her shoulder and down her spine. Mark had liked the thick dark strands styled and short, and in a small act of defiance, she'd allowed it to grow longer than at any other time in her life. With her head tilted back as it was now, her hair fell to the middle of her spine.

"You have beautiful hair," he said, and seemed unable to take his eyes from it. He slid his hand from her shoulder to the curly dark mass, and with splayed fingers ran his fingertips through its length. The action, so slow and deliberate, was also highly exciting. Against every dictate of her will, Taylor's heart quickened.

Soon his other hand joined the first as he continued to let his fingers glide through her hair, as if acquainting his sense of touch to the silky softness. Taylor felt as if she were falling into a trance. His hands, buried deep in her hair, felt more sensual than anything she'd ever experienced. Her eyes drifted shut, and when she felt herself being tugged toward him, she offered no resistance. His mouth met hers in a gentle brushing of lips. Their breaths merged as they each released a broken sigh.

"Tell me to stop," Russ ordered. "Tell me to take my hands away from you."

Taylor knew she should, but emotions that had been hiding just below the surface swamped her. She meant to push him away, extract them both from this temptation, but the instant her hands made contact with the hard, muscular feel of him, they lost their purpose.

"Russ..."

His answering kiss was anything but gentle, as if he wanted to punish her for making him want her so much. His hands tangled with the wavy bulk of dark hair as he angled her head to one side and slanted his demanding mouth over hers. His tongue breached the barrier of her lips and plundered deep, leaving her engulfed with confusion.

Every part of her was responding to him. Her breasts had never felt fuller or more ripe, and against her better judgment, she found herself moving against him.

His hands found her hips, and he pressed her against his swollen front. She didn't mean to move, but once she started she couldn't stop. His fingers bit hard into her hipbones, forcing her to be still against him.

Their kisses were tempestuous. Their heads twisted back and forth, their mouths rubbing hard, while their tongues mated and made love to each other. Soon they were both panting and breathless.

The kiss ended as abruptly as it had started when Russ tore his mouth from hers. His eyes remained closed. "I haven't stopped thinking about you all week," he confessed, not sounding very pleased by it. "I didn't want to, but God help me, you're there every night when I close my eyes. I can't get rid of the taste of you. Why you?" he demanded harshly. "Why do I have to feel these things for a city girl? You don't belong here and you never will."

Taylor's head fell forward for a moment while she mulled over his words. He was right. She was as out of place in this cattle town as a trout in a swimming pool. She snapped up her head while she had the courage to confront him. Anger was her friend. It took away the guilt she was feeling for being so willing to fall into his arms.

"You think I'm pleased about this?" she cried. "Trust me, a cowpoke is the last person in the world I want to get involved with. A woman in your life is there for convenience' sake, to cook your meals and pleasure you in bed. I knew exactly what you were the minute we met and I could never align my thinking with yours."

"Fine then, don't," he barked.

"I don't have any intention of getting involved with you."

"Listen, lady, I'm not all that thrilled with you, either. You and your women's lib friends have caused nothing but problems. Go back to the big city where you belong, because in these parts the men are men and the women are women. We don't much take to all that unisex talk."

Taylor was becoming more outraged by the minute. It was abundantly clear that Russ had no conception of what it meant to be a woman in the nineties. He might as well be living on another planet.

"Let's eat," Russ snarled.

Taylor had half a mind to gather her things and leave then. She would have if she'd thought she could get away with it. But Russ had cooked this dinner on a wager, and Taylor strongly suspected he'd make damn sure she ate every last bite of it. Knowing what she did about Russ, Taylor wouldn't put it past him to feed it to her himself if she backed out of it now.

How Taylor managed to down a single bite was something of a minor miracle. The salad was good. The broccoli was excellent, the sauce marginal, the baked potato raw, but the steak succulent and exactly the way she liked it—medium-rare.

Silence stretched between them like a tightrope, and neither seemed inclined to cross it or try to bridge the gap. A good ten minutes passed before Russ spoke.

"I shouldn't have said that about you not belonging here," he murmured, stabbing his fork into the lettuce with enough energy to spear leather.

"Why not?" she asked, swallowing the flash of pain his words spawned. "It's true and we both know it. I *am* a city girl."

"From everything I hear, you're one hell of a teacher," he admitted grudgingly. "The kids are crazy about you and I don't blame them."

She lifted her eyes to his, uncertain if she should believe him, registering surprise and pleasure.

"Word has it you're enthusiastic and energetic and everyone who's met you says nothing but good. I don't want you thinking folks don't appreciate what you're doing because I ran off at the mouth like that."

Her voice dropped to a raspy whisper. "I didn't mean what I said either, about not wanting to have anything to do with you because you're a cowpoke."

Their eyes met, and they each fought a battle with a smile. Knowing she was about to lose, Taylor lowered her gaze to her dinner plate. "I will admit to being surprised at how well you managed dinner."

Russ chuckled softly. "It wasn't that difficult."

"Does that mean you'd be willing to tackle it again sometime?"

"No way. Once in a man's lifetime is more than enough. I may have lost the wager, but I still consider cooking woman's work."

"I thought for a moment that our wager would change your mind. Besides, at this point, why do anything to spoil your reputation as a world-class chauvinist?"

Russ chuckled again, and the sound wasn't that extraordinary, but it gladdened Taylor's heart. Whatever it was about this cowboy that intrigued her tugged at her heart. He wasn't like any other man she'd ever dated. His opinions diametrically opposed her own on just about every subject she would care to mention. Yet every time he touched her, she all but melted in his arms. There wasn't any logic to this attraction they shared. Nor reason.

Russ helped himself to seconds on the salad and replenished their wineglasses. "Now that you know what Cougar Point thinks about you, how are you adjusting to us?"

"It's been more of a change than I anticipated," she said, holding on to the wineglass with both hands. She rotated the stem between her palms while she mulled over her thoughts. "It's the lack of conveniences that I notice the most." He arched his brows in question. "Let me give you an example. I came home from work the other night, exhausted. All I wanted to do was sit down, put my feet up and hibernate until morning. The problem was, I was starving. My first impulse was to order a pepperoni pizza, and when I realized I couldn't, I wanted to weep with frustration.''

''The bowling alley serves a decent pizza.''

''But they don't deliver.''

''No,'' Russ agreed, frowning, ''they don't.''

Feeling a twinge of homesickness, Taylor downed the last of her wine and stood. ''I'll help you with the dishes,'' she said, feeling sad and weary as she glanced at Russ. Even in the friendliest conversations their differences were impossible to ignore.

''I'll do them,'' he responded, standing himself.

''And risk dishpan hands?'' she challenged. ''I wouldn't hear of it.'' She started the water and squirted a dash of liquid soap into the rushing liquid. Monster bubbles quickly formed, and she lowered the water pressure.

She was clearing off the table when Russ suggested, ''How about a cup of coffee?''

''Please,'' she said, smiling over at him.

He busied himself with that while Taylor loaded the dishwasher.

''Here,'' he said from behind her, ''you might want this.''

She turned around to discover Russ holding the very apron he'd been so quick to remove when she'd first arrived. Her hands were covered with soapsuds. She glanced at them and then to Russ.

''I'll put it on for you,'' he said.

She smiled her appreciation and raised her arms for him to loop the long strands around her trim waist and knot it behind her back.

Russ moved to within two steps of her and hesitated. Slowly his eyes moved to her. Thirsty eyes. Hungry eyes. They delved into hers and then slowly lowered until they centered on her lips.

Unable to resist, Taylor swayed toward him. God help her, but once more she found herself trapped, a willing victim to his spell.

Their gazes held for a long moment before Russ roughly pushed the apron at her. "It might be best if you do it."

With trembling hands, Taylor shook the suds into the sink and deftly tied the apron behind her. "I wish Mandy were here," she mumbled, shocked by how close they'd come a second time to walking into each other's arms. Apparently they enjoyed the lure of the forbidden. Maybe it was a sense of the mystical that was so appealing. Whatever the attraction, it was explosive, and they'd been dancing around a keg of lit gunpowder all evening.

"I think I'll call her and tell her to come home," Russ grumbled, but he didn't reach for the phone.

Once the dishwasher was loaded, Taylor vigorously scrubbed the first pan, venting her frustration on it.

"Are you going to the dance?" Russ asked her next, grabbing a dish towel and slapping it over his shoulder.

His harsh words came at her like sharp knives. "I . . . don't think so."

"Why not? It'll give you a chance to meet all the young bucks in town and you can flirt to your heart's delight."

"I'm far beyond the flirting stage," she returned coolly.

He shrugged, appearing to give the matter little concern. "You could have fooled me. Fact is, you've been doing an admirable job of trifling with me from the moment we met."

Taylor's hand stilled. "I beg your pardon?"

"Take those jeans your wearing."

"What's wrong with these jeans?"

"They're too tight. Stretched across your fanny like that, they give a man ideas."

Closing her eyes, Taylor counted to ten slowly. The effort to control her temper was a vain one, however, and when she turned to face him, her eyes were snapping.

"How dare you suggest anything so ridiculous? You nearly kissed me a moment ago and now you're blaming me because you can't control your libido. Obviously it's all my fault."

He grunted and looked away.

"My jeans are too tight!" she echoed, not bothering to disguise her outrage. "What about my sweater? Is that too revealing?" She bunched her breasts together and cast a meaningful look in their direction. "Did you notice how far the V goes down? Why, a mere glimpse of cleavage ought to be enough to drive a man to drink. Maybe I should have you censor my perfume, as well. It's a wonder the good people of Cougar Point would allow such a brazen hussy near their children. And one tainted with a big-city attitude, no less."

"Taylor—"

"Don't you dare say another word to me," she cried, and jerked off the apron as if she found it offensive. Tears clouded her eyes as she hurriedly located her purse. "Good night, Mr. Palmer. I won't say it's been a pleasure."

"Taylor, damn it, listen to me."

She raced down the stairs to her car, barely able to see through the tears that brimmed in her eyes. The whole world took on a watery, blurred image, but Taylor was in too much of a hurry to care. This man said the most ridiculous things she'd ever heard. Only a fool would have anything more to do with him. Taylor had been a fool once.

Never, never again.

Russ sat in the living room, calling himself every foul name he could think to use, and the list was a long one. He heard the back door open and knew it would be Mandy. He reached for a newspaper and pretended to be reading.

"Hi!" She waltzed into the room with flair. "How'd dinner go?"

"Great," he mumbled, not taking his eyes off the front page.

"Has Taylor left already?"

"Yeah."

"Oh, shucks, I wanted to talk to her. Do you want to see the routine Chris and I made up?"

Russ's interest in his sister's drill team efforts was less than nil. Nevertheless, he grinned and nodded. "Sure."

"Okay, but remember it's not quite the same without the music." She held the pom-poms to her waist, arms akimbo, then let loose with a high kick and shot her arms toward the ceiling. She danced left, she leaped right, her arms and legs working with an instinctive grace that astonished Russ. This was Mandy? Fourteen-year-old Mandy? Why, she was really quite good at this.

She finished down on one knee, her pom-poms raised high above her head. Her smiling eyes met his, seeking his approval. "What do you think?"

"There isn't a single doubt in my mind that my sister is going to make the high school drill team."

"Oh, Russ," she shouted, "do you really think so?" She vaulted to her feet and threw her arms around his neck, squeezing hard. "Just for that I'll finish the dishes for you."

"Thanks," Russ murmured absently. He didn't want to think about dinner or anything else that had to do with this disastrous evening. To do so would only bring Taylor to mind, and she was the one person he was determined to forget. He'd suffered enough. All week she'd been eating at his conscience. He'd even dreamed of her. Hell, he hadn't felt this way about any woman since he was sixteen years old.

Then he had to go and say those things. The reason was even more ridiculous. He'd been jealous. The thought of her attending the Grange dance and having all the men in town dancing with her was more than he could bear thinking about. Other men putting their arms around her. Someone else laughing with her.

If anyone was going to dance with Taylor Manning, it would be him. Not Harry Donovan. Not Les Benjamin. Not Cody Franklin.

Him.

"Russ?"

He turned and found his sister staring at him. "What?"

"You've been pacing for the past five minutes. Is something wrong?"

"Hell, no," he growled, then quickly changed his mind. "Hell, yes." He marched across the kitchen and reached for his hat, bluntly setting it on his head.

"Where are you going?" Mandy demanded, following him.

"To town," he muttered. "I owe Taylor an apology."

Mandy giggled, seeming to find that bit of information amusing. "You going to ask her to the dance?"

"I might," he said, his strides long and purposeful.

"All right!" his sister cheered from behind him.

Chapter Four

"Taylor!" Russ shouted, pounding hard on the front door with his fists. Sweet heaven, but this woman was stubborn. "I know you're in there. Answer the damn door, will you?"

"I can't," a soft, feminine voice purred from the other side. "I'm wearing something much too revealing." The kittenlike purr quickly became an angry shout. "Army boots and fatigues!"

"I need to talk to you," Russ insisted.

"Go away."

Forcefully exhaling, Russ pressed his palms against the wood grain of the door. "Please," he added persuasively, knowing few women could resist him when he used that imploring tone.

"If you don't leave, I'm calling the police."

"The deputy's name is Cody Franklin, and we went through twelve years of school together."

"That doesn't mean he won't arrest you."

"On what charge? Wanting to apologize to my lady?"

The door flew open with such force that Russ was surprised it stayed on the hinges. Taylor's index finger connected with his chest with enough strength to force him to stumble back a step.

"I am not your lady! Understand?" Ice-blue eyes sliced straight through him.

Russ's grin was so big, his face ached. "I figured that comment would get a reaction out of you. I just didn't think it would be quite this zealous. Did anyone ever tell you you've got one hell of a temper?"

"No," she said, clearly disliking being tricked. She crossed her arms in a protective band around her waist and glared at him with enough venom to poison an elephant. "There's only one other man in this world who can make me as angry as you and I'm related to him."

"Which means you can't avoid him, but you can me."

Taylor rolled her eyes skyward. "The cowboy's a born genius."

Russ removed his hat and rotated the rim between his fingers. "I came to apologize for what I said earlier. I don't know what came over me," he hesitated, realizing that wasn't entirely true. "All right, I have a good guess. I was jealous."

"Jealous," she exploded. "Of what?"

This wasn't easy. Swallowing his pride and confronting her was one thing, but admitting the things he'd been feeling seemed downright petty in afterthought. An uncomfortable sensation tightened his chest. "I was thinking about other men dancing with you and it bothered the hell out of me," he admitted in a low murmur, none too proud of it.

"That makes about as much sense as my jeans being too tight. I already told you I wasn't going to the dance."

"Yes, you are," he countered swiftly. "I decided you're going with me."

To his consternation, Taylor threw back her head and laughed. "In your dreams, Palmer."

His first reaction was hot anger. There were any number of women in town who would leap at an invitation to attend the Grange dance with him. He could name four off the top of his head without thinking twice. It didn't set right to have the one woman he really wanted to take mock his invitation. He could feel the red burning in his ears, but he swallowed the protest, figuring he owed Taylor one. However, they were even now.

"Some women may appreciate those caveman tactics of yours," she informed him, smiling much too broadly to suit his already wounded pride. "But I'm not one of them."

"What do you want me to do? Get down on one knee and beg? Because if that's the case, you've got one hell of a long wait!" He slammed his hat back on his head with enough force to put a crick in his neck.

Some of the amusement and indignation left her eyes.

Russ tried once more, forcing his voice to a much softer tone. "There isn't anyone in Cougar Point I'd rather have attend the dance with me more than you." Their eyes held for a few seconds longer before Russ added, "Will you go with me, Taylor?" In case she hadn't noticed, he felt obliged to inform her, "I asked real polite like."

It was clear she was waging a battle with herself. Maybe she needed some inducement, Russ decided. He settled his hands on her shoulders and brought her against him. She remained as stiff as a branding iron, refusing to relax the way he wanted. He could kiss her; that might help her with her decision. Dear Lord, he loved the taste of her. Every time his mouth settled over hers it was like drinking rainwater, sweet and fresh from the heavens. He settled his chin on the crown of her head and felt some of the fight go out of her. A smile twitched at the edges of his mouth. He knew she'd come around once she had time to think about it.

"Taylor?" he whispered, lifting her chin so he could look into her eyes. What he saw puzzled him. Russ expected to find sweet submission, perhaps even a hint of desire. Instead he discovered bewilderment and distress.

When she spoke, her voice was little more than a husky murmur. "I...it'd be best if you asked someone else, Russ."

"You're going to the Grange dance, aren't you?" Mary Beth Morgan asked, popping into Taylor's room after class on Wednesday afternoon.

Taylor shook her head and bounced a stack of papers against the top of her desk. "I don't think so."

"But, Taylor," the fifth/sixth grade teacher protested, walking into the room, "everyone in town will be there."

"So I heard." Taylor stood and placed the papers inside her folder to take home and grade that evening.

"Why wouldn't you want to go?"

Taylor hedged, wondering how she could explain. "First, I don't have anything appropriate to wear, and second," she hesitated and lifted one shoulder in a half shrug, "I'm not sure I know how to square dance."

Mary Beth smiled and shook her head. "You don't have a thing to worry about. You could show up at the Grange in a burlap bag and you'd have more offers to dance than you'll know what to do with. And as for the square dancing part, put that out of your head. This isn't a square dance.''

''I'll think about it,'' Taylor promised.

''You better do more than that,'' Mary Beth suggested. ''I personally know of three young men who'll be mighty disappointed if you aren't at that dance.''

''I suppose I could sew up a dress,'' Taylor said, her spirits lifting. She knew the minute she arrived that Russ would believe she was there just for him, but the thought of staying home while everyone else in town was having fun was fast losing its appeal.

''Listen, Taylor, there aren't all that many social functions in Cougar Point. Take my advice and enjoy yourself while you can because there probably won't be anything more happening until Christmas.''

''Christmas?''

''Right,'' Mary Beth said with a solid shake of her head. ''Now I'll tell you what I'll do. My hubby and I will pick you up at seven.''

''I know where the Grange Hall is,'' Taylor said, brightening. ''You don't need to give me a ride.''

Mary Beth laughed. ''I figured you did. I just want to see if it's Russ Palmer, Cody Franklin or Harry Donovan who takes you home.''

True to her word, Mary Beth and Charles Morgan were by to pick up Taylor promptly at seven on Saturday night.

''Oh, my heavens, we're in for a fun evening,'' Mary Beth said as she walked a full circle around Taylor. She pressed her hands over her mouth and slowly shook her head. ''That dress is absolutely gorgeous.''

''Do you really think so?'' Taylor had been up until midnight two evenings straight, sewing. She'd chosen a pattern for a western-style dress with a tight-fitting lace-up bodice and snug waist. The skirt flared out gently at her hips and fell to midcalf. An eyelet-ruffled petticoat of white dropped three inches below the lavender dress. Brown boots complemented the outfit.

"We're in for a really good time tonight." Mary Beth chuckled as she looped her arm through Taylor's and led the way out the door.

The music could be heard coming from the Grange Hall even before they parked the car. Bright lights poured out from the large brick structure set on the highway on the outskirts of town. The parking lot was filled with trucks and four-wheel-drive vehicles. Without meaning to, Taylor found herself looking for Russ's truck, then quickly chastised herself.

She was hardly in the door when Mandy flew to her side. The teenager's youthful face was glowing with a warm smile.

"I knew you'd come. Russ said you wouldn't be here, but I knew otherwise. Oh, Taylor," she whispered wide-eyed when Taylor removed her coat. "Where did you ever find a dress that pretty?"

Taylor whirled around once to give her young friend the full effect. "You like it, do you? Well, I told you before there were advantages in knowing your way around a sewing machine."

"You made your dress?"

"Don't look so shocked."

"Could I ever sew anything that complicated?"

"With practice."

"If I took all the money I've been saving for a new saddle and bought a sewing machine, would you teach me to sew? I know it's not polite to ask, but I'm not taking home economics until next trimester, and I don't want to wait that long to learn. Not when I can make clothes that pretty.''

''I'd be happy to teach you.''

''Howdy, Taylor.'' A young man with soft ash-blond hair stepped in front of her, his hands tucked into the small front pockets of his jeans.

''Hello,'' she returned, not recognizing him, but he apparently knew her.

''I was wondering if I could have the next dance?''

''Ah...'' Taylor didn't know what to say. She hadn't so much as hung up her coat yet, and she would have liked to find her way around and talk to a few people before heading toward the dance floor.

''For crying out loud,'' Mandy muttered. ''Give Taylor a minute, will you, Harry? She just got here.''

Harry's cheeks flushed with instant color. ''If I don't ask her now,'' he protested, ''someone else will and I won't get a chance the rest of the evening.'' He blushed some more. ''Can I have this dance, Miss Manning?''

''Ah...sure,'' Taylor said, not knowing what else she could do. Mandy took her coat for her, and Harry led her to the dance floor, smiling broadly as if he were pulling off a major coup.

Once they reached the dance floor, Harry slipped his arm around her waist and gently guided her through a simple two-step. They hadn't been on the floor more than a few minutes when the music ended. Reluctantly Harry let his arm drop.

''I don't suppose you'd consider dancing the next one with me, would you?'' he asked hopefully.

Taylor hesitated. The room was growing all the more crowded, and she had yet to talk to anyone.

''I believe the next dance is mine,'' a deep masculine voice spoke from behind her. Taylor didn't need a house detective to recognize it was Russ. She stiffened instinctively before turning around to confront Mandy's brother.

Bold, dark eyes meshed with Caribbean blue.

Russ stood directly in front of her in a rich gray western-tailored suit with a suede yoke, his gaze challenging hers. His look alone was enough to steal a denial straight from the tip of her tongue. His was lean and serious, his eyes moving over her like a warm caress. Tiny glints of mischief sparked in the dark depths.

The music started once more, and as Harry moved away, Russ slipped his arms around her. There wasn't an ounce of protest left in Taylor as he pressed his hand to the small of her back. A muted sensation spread down the entire length of her legs. She closed her eyes and pretended to be engrossed in the music when it was Russ who held her senses captive.

Several moments passed before he spoke. His mouth was close to her ear. "I knew you'd come."

Taylor's eyes shot open, and she jerked herself away from him, putting several inches between their bodies. "I'll have you know right now that my being here has absolutely nothing to do with you, and furthermore—"

He pressed a finger over her lips, stopping her in midsentence.

Slowly Taylor raised her eyes to his. Deeply etched lines from long hours in the afternoon sun crinkled around the edges of his warm eyes.

"Thank you for coming," he whispered, and his warm breath tinged her cheek. Then he removed his finger.

"It wasn't for you," she felt obliged to inform him, but the indignation in her voice was gone. "Mary Beth Morgan . . . invited me."

Russ's mouth quirked an infinitesimal fraction. "Remind me to personally thank her."

His grip tightened, and although Taylor was determined to keep a safe, respectable distance from this man, she found herself relaxing in his embrace. He slid his hand up and down the length of her back, sending a hungry pain shooting through her stomach. She eased closer, reveling in the strength she sensed in the rugged, hard contours of his male body. She didn't mean to, she didn't even want to, but when he tucked her hand between them and pressed his jaw against the side of her head, she found herself waging a losing battle, and she closed her eyes and relaxed. He smelled of rum and spice, and she breathed in deeply, inhaling the scent of him.

When the song ended, it was Taylor who swallowed a sigh of regret. Dancing was a lost art form in the city. The last time she'd danced with a man, one who placed his arms around her and held her as if she were made of delicate porcelain, had been her date for her Junior-Senior Prom. She'd almost forgotten how good it was to feel so cherished.

Russ refused to release her; if anything, he pulled her closer. "Let's get out of here...just for a few minutes."

Taylor groaned inwardly. She couldn't believe how tempted she actually was to agree. "I...can't...I just got here. People will talk."

"Let them."

"Russ, no." Using her hands for leverage, she pushed herself free of him. He didn't offer any resistance, but the effort it had cost her to move away left her weak. And furious. How dare he assume she'd race into the parking lot with him—and for what? She'd bet cold cash he wasn't planning on discussing cattle breeding techniques with her.

"I'm not going anywhere with you, Russ Palmer."

"My, my, aren't we a bit testy."

"I . . . just want it understood that I'm not going anywhere near that parking lot with you."

"Whatever you say." But a smile tugged at his insolently sensual mouth.

The music started up again, and they stood facing each other in the middle of the dance floor with couples crowding in around them. Russ didn't draw her into his arms, nor did she make a move toward him.

Tiny glints of amusement flickered in his eyes. There was no resisting him, and soon Taylor found herself responding to his smile. He slipped his hands around her waist, drawing her back into the circle of his arms. They made a pretense of dancing, but they were doing little more than staring at each other and shuffling their feet.

No woman in her right mind would deliberately get involved with an avowed chauvinist like Russ Palmer, yet here she was a thoroughly modern woman so attracted to him that she ached all the way to the soles of her feet.

The music came to an end, and his arms relaxed. A careless, handsome grin slashed his mouth. "Enjoy yourself," he whispered. "Dance with whomever you like, but remember this. It's me who's taking you home tonight. No one else. Me."

An immediate protest rose in Taylor's throat, but before she could utter a single word, Russ bent forward and set his mouth over hers. Her fists knotted against his gray suit jacket while his lips ruthlessly plundered hers. Taylor could hear the curious voices murmuring around them, and she gave a small cry of protest.

Russ ended the kiss, smiled down on her and then whispered, "Remember."

With that he walked off the floor.

Taylor felt like a first-class fool, standing by herself in the middle of the dance floor with several couples staring at her. The hushed whispers started, and she smiled blandly in everyone's direction and all but ran from the dance floor.

Taylor was so mortified that she headed directly for the ladies' room and stayed there a full five minutes, trying to compose herself. If there had been a sofa, she would have sat down and wept. Wept because she'd been so tempted to let Russ take her outside. Wept because she felt so right in his arms. Wept because she hadn't learned a thing from her disastrous affair with Mark Brooks.

Once Taylor reappeared, she didn't lack for attention. She waltzed with Cody Franklin, chatted over punch with Les Benjamin, another rancher, and even managed a couple more two-steps with Harry Donovan. She smiled. She laughed. She pretended to be having the time of her life, but underneath everything was a brewing frustration she couldn't escape. Every now and again she'd catch a glimpse of Russ dancing with someone else. Usually someone young and pretty. Someone far more suited to him than she would ever be. Yet, each time, she felt a stab of jealousy unlike anything she'd ever experienced.

By the time the evening started to wind down, Taylor decided the best way to thwart Russ was to simply accept someone else's offer to give her a lift home.

Only no one asked.

Of the dozen or so men she danced with not a single, solitary one asked to take her home. Charles and Mary Beth Morgan had already left by the time Taylor realized she had no option except to find Russ.

He was waiting for her outside, standing at the bottom of the stairs when she walked out of the Grange Hall, looking as arrogant and pleased as could be.

"I want to know what you said to everyone," she demanded, marching down the stairs. It was more than a tad suspicious that she would be left at the dance without a ride home.

Russ's eyes fairly skipped with devilment. "Me? What makes you think I said anything?"

"Because I know you, and I want one thing clear right now. You can take me home, but nothing else. Understand?"

"You insult me, madam!"

"Good. Now where's Mandy?" Taylor demanded.

"She's spending the night with Chris," Russ explained, but dropped his voice to a lower pitch. "However, rest assured, you're perfectly safe with me."

"I'd be safer in a pit of rattlesnakes," she informed him, carefully measuring her words for effect. "Do you have any idea how humiliating it was to have you kiss me on that dance floor and then leave?" Her words were issued in a low hiss.

"I promise I'll never do it again," he vowed, and led her across the parking lot where he held open the truck door for her.

This was a newer model than the one she'd ridden in earlier. She paused and glanced inside and was amazed to discover seat belts! However, it stood a good three feet off the ground, and there wasn't any way she was going to be able to climb inside without assistance.

"Here," Russ offered, "I'll help you up." His hands closed around her waist and he lifted her effortlessly off the ground as if she weighed no more than a few pounds.

Once she was inside and Russ had joined her, she asked him, "Where do you drive this thing? Over Mount Fuji?"

Russ chuckled and started the engine. "You'd be surprised the places this truck has been."

"I'll bet," Taylor grumbled.

She didn't say another word during the short drive to her rented house. Russ didn't, either.

He pulled into her driveway, cut the engine and was out of the cab before she could object. Opening her door, Russ helped her down. But when her feet were firmly planted on the ground, he didn't release her.

His eyes held hers, and a rich current of awareness flowed between them. "You were the most beautiful woman there tonight."

"I'm surprised you even noticed." The minute the words escaped, Taylor regretted having spoken. In one short sentence she'd let slip what she'd been doing all evening.

Watching him.

She'd counted the number of women he'd danced with and, worse, envied them for the time spent in his arms.

Russ didn't answer her. Not with words, anyway. Instead he firmly pulled her into his arms and kissed her. His mouth was hard, his kiss thorough. When he lifted his head, their panting breaths echoed each other.

"Invite me inside," he whispered, his voice so husky it sounded raw.

Taylor felt powerless to do anything but what he asked. Her hands were shaking when she drew the keys from her purse. Russ took them from her and unlocked the door, pushing it open for her to precede him.

Taylor walked through the living room and to the kitchen, turning on the lights. "I'll... make some coffee."

"No," Russ said, stopping her. His arms anchored her against the wall. "I don't want any coffee and neither do you."

Taylor gazed into his face and recognized his hunger, knowing it was a reflection of her own. Closing her eyes, she sagged against the wall, feeling weak and needy.

"Trust me," Russ whispered. "I know what you're thinking. We're both crazy. I should stay as far away from you as humanly possible. You don't want to feel these things for me any more than I do for you. We argue. We fight. But, lady, when we kiss, everything else pales by comparison."

"What we're experiencing is a physical attraction," she whispered as her fingers sank deep into his thick, dark hair.

"Pure physical attraction," he echoed, just before his mouth came crashing down on hers. Their tongues mated, and low, animal-like sounds came from deep within his throat as his mouth twisted and turned over hers.

Braced as she was against the wall, she could feel every hard, rugged inch of him. He felt so hard. So good.

Restlessly she moved against him as her hands clenched fistfuls of his hair. His tongue slid along hers, slipping deeper and deeper into her mouth as their kiss grew wilder. More carnal. More savage.

"Russ," she panted, lifting her head away from him. "I . . . I think we should stop now."

"In a minute." Gripping her by the waist, he dragged her against him and groaned when her softness nestled against the hard evidence of his desire.

He was so hard. She was so soft.

Woman to man.

Cowboy to Lady.

They fitted so perfectly together, and were so hungry for each other.

Drawing in deep and uneven breaths, Russ buried his face in the curve of her neck. It took him several seconds to regain control of himself.

It took several minutes for Taylor to regain control of herself.

Russ lifted his head and smoothed the hair from the side of her face. "I've changed my mind," he said, and plowed his fingers through his hair with punishing force. "I will take that coffee, after all."

Grateful for something to occupy herself with, Taylor moved to the counter where she kept her automatic coffee machine. While waiting for the steaming brew to drip through, she brought down the mugs and placed them on a tray. She was so absorbed in her task that when she turned around she nearly collided with Russ.

He took the tray out of her hands and carried it into the living room. "I think it's time we cleared the air," he said, setting their mugs down on the oak coffee table.

"How's that?" Taylor asked, sinking into the edge of the sofa cushion.

"Above all else we've got to be honest with each other."

"Right."

Taylor sipped from her mug, the scalding coffee too hot to savor, or appreciate.

"Are you wearing a bra?" he asked with a mischievous twinkle in his eye.

"What?" She leaped forward, setting her cup back on the tray to avoid spilling it down her front. The hot coffee sloshed over the edges of the mug.

Taylor's mouth gaped as she glared at him with shock and outrage. "You demand honesty and then ask me if I'm wearing a bra?" Unable to stand still she started pacing, so furious that she was tempted to throw him out of her home.

"All right, I'm sorry. Forget I asked that. I was holding you and it felt as if you weren't and the question just slipped out. You're right... that was a stupid question."

He lowered his gaze, and Taylor noted that his ears were red. As red as Harry Donovan's had been when he'd asked her to dance. Russ Palmer embarrassed? The very thought was inconceivable.

Stepping around the low-lying table, Taylor sat back down and reached for her coffee. "As a matter of fact, no."

"Oh, God..." Russ closed his eyes as though in pain. "You shouldn't have told me."

"This bodice is so snug I didn't think anyone would notice." Taylor couldn't actually believe they were having this discussion.

"I'm sure no one else did. But when we were kissing just now, I felt you against me and I could have sworn you weren't." He took a gulp of coffee, then stood abruptly. "Maybe it'd be best if I left now."

"I thought you wanted to talk. Other than responding to personal questions like the last one, I think you're right about us being honest with each other."

Now it was Russ's turn to do the pacing. He stood and stalked across her living room carpet as if he fully intended to wear a pattern in the thick nap.

"Russ?"

He rammed his fingers through his hair and turned abruptly to face her. "If you want honesty, I'll give it to you, Taylor, but I'll guarantee you aren't going to like what I have to say."

She wasn't sure she was up to this. But, on the other hand, she didn't want him to leave, either. "Just say what you want, and we'll deal with it."

"All right," he said sharply. "Right now I want you so damn much I'm having one hell of a problem thinking straight. I want to hold your breasts in my hands and I want to taste them, and that's only the beginning." He raked his hand down his face. "Does that shock you?"

"No," she cried softly, and centered her attention on her coffee.

"Well, damn it, it should. You should throw me out of this house for even talking to you like this."

"Maybe I should." Holding the mug so tightly in her hands that it burned her palms, Taylor gathered her courage. "I objected when you called me your lady, but it wasn't the lady part that offended me. I am a lady. And I'll always be a lady."

Russ frowned. "I know that, Taylor. No one can look at you and not realize the kind of woman you are."

"I have no intention of falling into bed with you, Russ. I wish I understood why we're so physically attracted to each other, but I don't. As far as I can see, we're playing with fire. Unfortunately, if we continue like this, one of us is going to end up getting burned."

Briefly Russ closed his eyes and nodded. "You're right, of course." He inhaled deeply. "Does this mean you want me to leave?"

"No," she said, smiling at her own lack of willpower. "But I think you should, anyway."

Chapter Five

M andy, I'm not going near that horse.''

"Taylor, please. I want to do something to thank you for all the sewing lessons you've given me."

As far as Taylor was concerned, the chestnut gelding looked as huge as the Trojan horse approaching Troy. He didn't look all that friendly, either. Her palms were sweating, and her throat felt dry from arguing with the persistent teen.

"Shadow is as gentle as they come," Mandy assured her, stroking the white markings on the horse's face. "You don't have a thing to worry about."

"That's what they said to Custer," Taylor muttered under her breath. This whole episode had started out so innocently. Taylor had spent an hour after school helping Mandy cut out the pattern for a vest. Then, because Russ was busy with an errand in Miles City, Taylor had dropped her off at the ranch. One of the men had been exercising a horse, and Taylor had innocently inquired about the stock. Before she knew how it had happened, Mandy was insisting on teaching her to ride, claiming she couldn't accept sewing lessons from Taylor without giving her something in return.

"Once you climb into the saddle, you'll feel a whole lot better about it," Mandy assured her.

"I'm not much of a horse person," Taylor insisted.

"That doesn't matter. Shadow's real gentle. I promise you."

"Another time perhaps," Taylor said, stalling.

"But today's perfect for riding."

Before Taylor could answer, she saw Russ's truck come speeding down the driveway, leaving a thick plume of dust in its wake. Taylor hadn't seen Russ since the night of the Grange dance, and she hated the way her pulse raced.

Russ pulled to a stop and leaped out of the truck, intent on his task, but he paused when he noted Taylor's Cabriolet parked near the barn. Setting his hat farther back on his head, he altered his direction and stalked toward them.

"Hello, Taylor," he said, dipping his head slightly.

"Russ."

"Maybe you can talk some reason into her." Mandy gestured toward Taylor, looking wistful. "I think she should learn to ride. Here she is giving me all these sewing lessons, and I want to repay her."

"You've already had me over for dinner," Taylor reminded the girl. "Really, horses just aren't my thing. The last time I sat on a horse's back was on a carousel when I was ten years old."

"If Taylor's afraid . . ."

"What makes you think that?" Taylor demanded of Russ. "I'm not frightened of horses. It's just that I'm unfamiliar with them. I don't think now is the time for me to gain anything more than a nodding acquaintance with Shadow here, but I most certainly am not afraid.''

"Then prove it," Russ challenged. He patted Shadow on the rump. The gelding returned the greeting with a nicker and a friendly swish of his thick tail.

"I promise you. You'll enjoy it," Mandy pressed.

Grumbling under her breath, Taylor took the reins from Mandy's hands. "Why do I have the sinking suspicion I'm going to regret this?"

"You won't," Mandy vowed.

"This kid is much too free with her promises," Taylor informed Russ. Lifting her left foot and placing it inside the stirrup, Taylor reached for the saddle horn and heaved herself upward.

"You might need some help," Mandy advised. "Russ, help her."

"She seems to be doing a fine job without me."

Taylor had hoisted her weight halfway up when she started to lose her strength and then her grip. Russ was behind her immediately, clutching her waist. "All right, Annie Oakley, I'll give you a hand."

Swinging her leg over the back of the chestnut, Taylor held on to the saddle horn as if it were a life preserver and she were lost at sea in a storm.

"See?" Mandy cried triumphantly. "There isn't anything to it. Didn't I tell you?"

Russ adjusted the stirrups for her. "You look a little green around the gills. Are you all right?"

"It's just a little higher up here than I imagined. Can I get down now?"

Mandy started to giggle. "But you haven't gone anyplace yet."

"Isn't *this* enough to prove I'm not afraid? You didn't say anything about actually moving him."

"Josh, bring me Magic," Russ instructed the hand who had saddled Shadow earlier. Within a couple of minutes a large black gelding was led from the barn. Russ followed and slapped the saddle over the horse's back.

"You go ahead and take Taylor out and I'll start dinner," Mandy suggested. "By the time you two get back, everything will be ready."

"Ah . . . I'm not so sure now would be the best time for me to ride," Taylor said, struggling to hide the panic in her voice. "There are papers that need to be corrected and a couple of loads of wash to be done . . . and other things."

"It's Friday," Mandy announced over her shoulder as she strolled toward the house. "You can do all that tomorrow."

"Of course," Taylor muttered. "I should have thought of that."

"Don't look so terrified. This is going to be a good experience for you," Russ told her, looking far more pleased than she liked.

He mounted the black gelding, gave instructions to the hands to unload the pickup and then turned to Taylor. "I'll take it nice and easy. You haven't got a thing to worry about."

"If that's the case, why do I feel like a frog swimming around in a kettle on top of the stove?"

Russ's returning chuckle warmed her heart. She'd missed him this week. She'd had to search her soul to even admit that. With Mandy stopping in three days after school, Taylor had been well-informed about Russ's activities. He'd done the ordering on Tuesday and was grumpy most of the night, and Mandy didn't have a clue why. Thursday he was riding the range, looking for strays, and Friday he'd traveled into Miles City for supplies. Taylor had never openly pried about Russ, but she was always pleased when Mandy slipped her small pieces of information about him.

Russ, riding Magic, led the way, and once they were past the barn, he pointed out a trail toward rolling hills of fresh, green grass. "We'll head this way."

"Do you mind if we go a bit slower?" she protested. She felt as if she were sitting on top of a pogo stick. Her head was bobbing up and down, and it was a small miracle that she'd managed to stay on the beast at all.

"If we went any slower, the horses would have time to chew grass between steps."

"Is there anything wrong with that?" she cried. "By the way, if it isn't too much to ask, exactly where are you taking me?"

Russ wiggled his thick eyebrows suggestively. "Now she asks."

"And what's that supposed to mean?"

"Nothing." But his dark eyes were twinkling with devilment. Taylor had seen that look before, once too often.

Her insides felt like a bowlful of Jell-O when Taylor pulled back on the reins several minutes later. She was mildly surprised when Shadow slowed to a stop. "Russ Palmer, I don't trust you. Tell me this minute exactly where we're headed."

Russ lazed back in the saddle, nonchalantly settling one leg around the saddle horn and knotting his hands behind his head. He was as at ease in a saddle as he was in his own living room. "No place in particular. Do you want to stop and rest a minute? There's a grassy knoll about a quarter mile from here."

Taylor hated to admit how sore her posterior was feeling. And they hadn't gone very far. If she squinted, she could just make out the backside of the red barn far off in the distance.

"All right, we can stop and rest," she agreed. "But no funny business."

Theatrically Russ removed his hat and pressed it over his heart. His dark eyes took on a roguish, imploring look. "You injure me, madam."

Rather than argue with him, Taylor said nothing.

"Mandy says you're helping her sew a vest," Russ mentioned conversationally. He slowed Magic and then swung himself to the ground with a gracefulness Taylor could only envy. It had taken all the strength she possessed just to raise her weight to the saddle. If Russ hadn't given her a boost, she would have been caught for eternity with one foot in the stirrup and the other madly waving in midair.

"Need any help?"

"I'm sure I can do it myself," she announced, not the least bit confident. Surely lowering herself to the ground would be much less of a strain than mounting the horse had been. Besides, if Russ lent her a hand, he'd use it as an excuse to kiss her. Not that she'd mind terribly much, but for once she'd enjoy having a relaxed conversation with the man without them falling into each other's arms like love-starved teenagers.

Taylor was pleased with how easy dismounting turned out to be. Her legs felt a little shaky, but once her feet were squarely on the ground and she'd walked around a bit, she decided this horseback riding business wasn't nearly as difficult as she'd assumed.

"I don't expect many more warm days like this one," Russ said. He tilted his hat back on his head and stared into the distance. Several head of cattle were grazing on a hill opposite them.

Taylor joined him, and he slipped an arm around her waist as familiarly as if he'd been doing so for years.

"It's a good thing you're doing for Mandy."

"What is?"

"Teaching her to sew. Encouraging her. She comes home high as a kite after she's been with you, chattering a mile a minute." A boyish grin slashed his sensual mouth. "For that matter, I come home happy, too."

Taylor lowered her gaze to the ground. "I think her making the drill team is what boosted her spirits more than anything. She could have walked on water the day she learned she'd been chosen."

"Only three freshmen made the squad," Russ said, grinning proudly.

Linking her hands behind her back, Taylor strolled over to a large tree, probably a sycamore, but she couldn't be sure. Pressing her back against it, she raised one knee and rested her booted foot at the trunk. "I've enjoyed working with Mandy this week. She reminds me of my sister, Christy, when she was fourteen. Unfortunately I was sixteen at the time and considered Christy a major pest."

"Mandy told me you came from a large family."

"By today's standards, I guess you could say that. I have three older brothers, Paul, Jason and Rich. Paul's the only one married, and believe me, the rest of us are eternally grateful because he quickly gifted my parents with twin sons. Now that Mom and Dad have grandchildren, the rest of us are off the hook, at least for a while."

"You're close to your family, aren't you?"

Taylor nodded. "I can't believe how much I miss them. They must be feeling the same way because I've gotten tons of mail."

Russ lowered himself to the grass, stretching his long legs out in front of him and crossing his ankles. "Mandy said something about your father reminding you of me."

"Is nothing sacred anymore?" she teased. If his sister had been dropping tidbits of information regarding him, she'd also done a bang-up job of keeping Russ informed of their conversations. "My dad's a born chauvinist. I don't think he's sure it was a good thing that women were granted the right to vote."

Russ didn't laugh the way most people would. "I don't mind if women vote. It's holding public office that concerns me."

Taylor came away from the tree so fast, she nearly stumbled. Her mouth worked for several seconds before any words came out. "I can't believe you just said that. Why the hell shouldn't a woman hold public office?"

"My, my, you're always so touchy."

"Who can blame me when you say something so ludicrous?"

"Think about it, Taylor. A woman is the very heart of a home and a family. What kind of wife and mother would she be if she was deeply involved in politics when her family needed her."

"I'm not actually hearing this," she muttered.

"Don't you think a woman's place is with her children?"

"What about a father's place?"

"The husband's got to work in order to support the family."

Taylor covered her face with both hands. Arguing with him would do little good. She'd tried often enough with her father, but to no avail. The two men were equally hard-nosed, opinionated and difficult.

Not knowing what possessed her, she leaped forward, jerked Russ's hat from his head and took off running.

"Taylor?" Russ vaulted to his feet in one smooth movement and chased after her. "What are you doing with my hat? Sweet heaven, woman, what's gotten into you?"

Walking backward, keeping a safe distance from him, Taylor hid the Stetson behind her back. "You're narrow-minded and the second worst chauvinist I've ever known."

"You stole my hat because of that?"

"Yes. It was the only way I could think to make you suffer."

Russ advanced toward her, taking small, even steps. "Give me back the hat, Taylor."

"Forget it." For a good portion of her life, Taylor had been playing keep-away with her brothers. She may not be as big as Russ and not nearly as agile, but she was as quick as greased lightning and as nimble as a mountain goat.

"Taylor, give me the hat," he demanded. His gaze narrowed as he advanced toward her in measured steps, holding out his hand.

"No way. Women don't have any business holding public office? I can't let something that outrageous pass without making you pay."

Laughter flashed from his eyes like a neon light as he lunged for her. Taylor let out a playful shriek and darted sharply to the left. Russ missed her by a good yard.

Russ turned and was prepared to make another diving move toward her when Taylor took the black cowboy hat and tossed it with all her might straight into the sky. "Catch it if you can!" she shouted, bobbing past him. She was in such a rush that she stumbled and would have crashed face first onto the lush grass if Russ hadn't captured her around the waist and brought her roughly against him. The full force of her weight caught him off balance, and twisting so that he received the brunt of the impact, they collided with the soft ground.

Within the space of a heartbeat, Russ had reversed their positions, pinning her hands to the ground above her head. Taylor looked up into the dark warmth of his eyes and smiled. Her breasts were heaving with churning excitement.

"Who's making who pay?" Russ demanded, his eyes filled with devilment. He pressed his mouth to her neck, running the tip of his tongue over the smooth skin of her throat and up the underside of her chin. The ribbon of sensation wove its way down her spine, and she moaned softly and buckled. "No..."

"You're going to be doing a lot more begging before I'm through with you," Russ promised. He kissed her then, his lips teasing and taunting hers with soft nibbles, promising but never quite delivering. Again and again his tongue darted in and out of her mouth with small, ruthless movements that sent shock waves vibrating throughout her slender body.

Arching her back, she struggled and was immediately released. With her hands free, she buried her fingers in his hair, raised her head and fused her mouth to his. She could feel herself dissolving, melting against him. He was so incredibly hot. His heat licked at her senses, stoking the flames, hotter and hotter.

Russ kissed her mouth, her eyes, her throat. Taylor felt as if she were on fire, her whole body aflame with a feral need. His hand found her breast, and Taylor sighed as a fresh wave of fiery sensations engulfed her.

"Oh, Russ," she pleaded, not entirely sure what she was asking of him. The pure physical need to join their bodies was strong and compelling, but there had to be so much more before she could freely give herself to him. A merging of their hearts. Commitment. Love.

She had no time to voice her concerns. Russ kissed her, and a swift, acute sensation of hot, urgent desire rose up in her, blocking out everything but her awareness of Russ and her growing need.

Taylor's head was spinning, and the only sounds she made were soft incoherent noises that implored him to continue and in the same heartbeat pleaded with him to stop.

Russ groaned as he spread open her blouse. His chest heaved as he buried his face in the gentle slope of her neck. His body was pressed over hers with a fierce, undiluted passion. His mouth devoured hers, and while he kissed her, his fingers were busy with the fastening to her bra. When he'd completed the task, he gently peeled it open, exposing her lush breasts to the cool air.

A rush of warmth invaded her when he fitted his hand over a plump breast.

"I knew you'd feel this good. I knew...I knew." He began to stroke the nipple with the side of his thumb. "Like silk," he moaned. "Like velvet. I've got to taste you." He lowered his head, and his tongue glided smoothly, moistly, over her nipple, then gently encircled the nubbin in moist, hot forays before pulling it more completely into his mouth and sucking.

Taylor tossed her head to one side and bit into her lower lip as Russ searched and found the snap of her jeans and pulled down the zipper. He placed his hand firmly on the smooth skin of her abdomen, but went no lower.

He began to kiss her breasts in earnest, sliding his mouth from one to the other, sucking and nibbling on her as though she were a delectable feast and he were greatly in need of her nourishment.

Taylor's hands frantically tangled with his dark hair as she raised her hips and rhythmically moved against him.

The juncture between her legs became a welcome cradle for him, and she slipped her leg over his calf, unsatisfied and demanding a more intimate contact.

"Taylor," he groaned anew. A low guttural sound came from deep within his throat. Slowly, as if it demanded every ounce of strength he possessed, he lifted his head and fused his mouth with hers once more. Taylor welcomed him as her lips closed around his tongue.

Swiftly, when she least expected it, Russ gripped her hard around the waist and rolled, taking her with him, their positions reversed so that she was poised above him.

Taylor gave a small gasp of surprise at the sudden movement. Then his hands were in her hair, pulling the long strands free of the confining pins. With his mouth slanted over hers, he let his fingers glide through the silky softness. His breathing was labored and hard as he dragged his mouth from hers.

"Don't move. Dear God, whatever you do, don't move." His voice was husky and deep, and his hands imprisoned her hips. "Taylor, no," he cried.

His sharp words brought Taylor out of her drugged state. She blinked and dragged in several breaths of cool air. The terrible tightness in her body started to ease, but the hot, heavy feeling lingered. Her lips felt swollen from his kisses, and her hair fell in a mass of winding curls over her shoulders, reaching all the way to the ground, wreathing Russ's face. It took several exaggerated seconds for reason to return, and with it came the startling realization that she had become a wanton in his arms.

"Either we stop now or we finish." His breathing was raspy as he slid his hands from her hips to her shoulders. "The choice is yours."

Taylor squeezed her eyes shut. A tightness gripped her throat as she slowly shook her head. She didn't need to think twice; the decision had been made for her the moment she'd met Russ. He was as much a part of the barren, harsh landscape as the sycamore trees. She was as misplaced in this unforgiving territory as a hothouse flower. But beyond that, Russ was a chauvinist. After the years of battling with her father, Taylor had no intention of falling in love with a man who shared the same outdated attitudes toward women.

She gave a forced shake of her head.

Russ exhaled sharply. "That's what I thought." His breath left him in a defeated gush like air rushing from a balloon. His hands stroked the hair from her face. "Did I hurt you?"

She shook her head again, wishing she could bury her face in her hands and never look at him again. She certainly hadn't intended for matters to go this far. One moment she was teasing him, playfully tossing his hat into the air, and in the next, her body was pleading for completion with his own.

"Are you sure you're all right?"

"Of course." But that was far from the truth. Taking the cue, she lifted herself from him and sat on the grass. With trembling fingers, she refastened her bra, but when it came to the delicate buttons of her blouse, she found she was useless. Gently Russ brushed her hand away and completed the task for her. Her hair was another matter. Locating the scattered pins would have been impossible, so she ran her fingers through it and left it hanging free.

"I'm sure Mandy will be wondering about us," she said, doing her best to keep her voice from trembling as badly as her hands had.

"You don't need to worry. She won't send out a search party."

To Taylor's way of thinking, it might have been better if Mandy had.

It seemed everyone was looking at Taylor when she rode back into the yard. The ranch hands' curiosity about her was probably due to her precarious perch atop Shadow more than anything. As soon as she was able to stop the gelding, she tossed the reins over his head and ingloriously slipped off the saddle. Her feet landed with a jarring thud when she connected with the ground.

Mandy was coming out of the house, waving. "Gee, what took you guys so long?" she called, walking toward them. "I've had dinner ready for ages."

"We stopped and rested a bit," Russ explained, sharing a secret smile with Taylor, who was confident the instant color in her cheeks spelled out exactly what they'd been doing.

"I thought you guys were going to be back right away, so I just fixed soup and sandwiches for dinner. That's all right, isn't it?"

"Actually, I should be getting back to town," Taylor said, eager to make her escape. Only when she was alone would she be able to properly analyze what had happened with Russ. Of one thing she was sure: there wouldn't be a repeat of this. Flirting with fire was one thing, but walking across a bed of hot coals was something else again.

All her good intentions to take the time to properly heal her broken heart were like dust particles caught in the wind, blowing every which way. She had no business getting involved with Russ.

"Oh, please, don't go yet." Mandy's young face fell at Taylor's announcement.

"I really must," Taylor insisted. Spending any more of this day with Russ would have been agonizing. Every time she looked at him, her pulse accelerated and her breasts grew heavy.

Taylor hadn't been in her rental house more than five minutes when she had the urge to talk to her mother. But it was her father who answered on the third ring.

"Hi, Dad."

"Taylor, sweetheart, how are you?" No matter what his mood he always sounded gruff.

"Fine." How pleased he sounded to be hearing from her.

The pause that followed was infinitesimal. "What's wrong?"

Taylor smiled to herself. She had never been very good about keeping something from her parents. "What makes you ask?"

"You don't call home that often."

"Dad," she whispered, closing her eyes. "Is Mom around? I'm in the mood for a mother-daughter chat."

"Your mother's shopping. Just pretend I'm her and talk."

"I can't do that." She loved him dearly, but they were constantly arguing. Of all the Manning children, Taylor was the one who didn't think twice about standing toe to toe with her father in any given argument. Her bravery had won her the esteem of her siblings.

"Why can't you talk to me? I'm your father, aren't I? You're the one who's always throwing the equality of the sexes in my face. So talk."

"But, Dad, this is different."

"Hogwash. I haven't been married to your mother for the past thirty-five years without knowing how she thinks. Tell me what you want and I'll respond just as if I were your mother." He sounded concerned and a little gruff.

"It's nothing really, but, well..." She hesitated, and decided to jump in with both feet. "What would you say if I told you I met a cowboy I think I might be falling in love with? The thing is, I'm not entirely sure I could even get along with this man. From the moment we first met he set my teeth on edge."

"I take it things have changed?"

"Not really," she mumbled, knowing she wasn't making the least bit of sense. "He still says things that make me so mad that I could scream, but then at other times he does something that's so sweet and sincere I want to cry." A soft catch shook her voice. "I realize the whole thing probably goes back to Mark, and you're going to say I'm on the rebound, and you'd probably be right. Russ and I are as incompatible as any two people could get. I can't even believe I'm so attracted to him." She pulled in a deep breath once she'd finished. Silence greeted her on the other end. "Dad? Are you still there?"

"I'm here," he grumbled.

"Well, say something."

"You want me to say something?" he repeated, but he didn't even sound like himself. He paused and cleared his throat. "In this case I think you might be right. The best thing to do is talk this over with your mother. She knows about these things."

Taylor laughed softly into the phone and shook her head. For the first time in recent history she'd won an argument with her father.

On Tuesday afternoon Taylor stopped off at the grocery store on her way home and mailed her electric bill payment at the pharmacy. She loved going into Cougar Point's lone drugstore. Not only could she have a prescription filled, but she could buy just about anything else she needed. A tiny branch of the post office operated there, as well, along with a liquor store. In Seattle one-stop shopping generally referred to a large mall, but in Cougar Point it meant stopping off at the pharmacy.

Humming to herself, Taylor carried her groceries home, noticing that the leaves on the trees were starting to change. As she turned off Main Street and onto Oak, she saw Mandy sitting on her front porch.

"Mandy?" she questioned softly. The teenager's eyes were puffy and red from crying. "Sweetheart, what's wrong?"

Russ's sister leaped to her feet and wiped the moisture from her eyes. Her chin was tilted at a proud, indignant angle. "I'm leaving."

"Leaving?" Taylor wasn't sure she understood.

"Running away," she explained in a tight, pain-filled voice. "But before I go I thought I should tell someone so Russ won't send Cody Franklin out looking for me."

Chapter Six

Come inside," Taylor urged the teenager. "I think we should talk about this."

Mandy hedged, keeping her eyes downcast. "I don't really have the time."

"It'll take just a few minutes. I promise." Withdrawing the key from her purse, Taylor opened the door to her home, walked inside and deposited her groceries on the kitchen counter.

Mandy followed, looking anxious to be on her way.

Scooting out a chair, Taylor indicated the teenager should sit down, at least for a few moments, and talk things out. Grabbing them each a can of cold soda as inducement, she pulled out the chair opposite Russ's sister.

"It's Russ," Mandy said in a choked whisper. "He's making me quit the drill team."

Taylor struggled to hide her dismay. "Is it your grades?"

"No. I've always been high honor roll. We were assigned our uniforms this afternoon and I tried mine on and Russ happened to come into the house. He saw me and got all bent out of shape, saying that the skirts were too short. I tried to tell him that the skirts have been the same length for the past hundred years, and that just made him all the madder."

"I don't think your brother appreciates sarcasm."

"You're telling me. He insisted that I drop the hem on the skirt five inches. I know I should have been more subtle, but I couldn't help it. I laughed and then told him that was ridiculous."

"I don't imagine that pleased him any."

"No," Mandy said, lowering her gaze. She held on to the can with stiff fingers, but as far as Taylor could see she hadn't taken a single drink. It was as if she needed something to grip. "Then he said that this wasn't an issue we were going to discuss. He was ordering me, as my legal guardian, to lower the hem of the skirt, and he didn't want any arguments."

"Naturally you refused."

"Naturally. What else could I do?" Mandy charged. "I'd look totally asinine with a drill team skirt that hit my legs at midcalf. I'd be the laughing stock of everyone in the entire school district, and all because my bullheaded brother won't listen to reason."

"Is that when he issued the ultimatum?"

"H-how'd you know?"

"I know Russ, or at least I know someone a whole lot like him. The way I figure it, he suggested that either you lower the hem or you quit the drill team, and with that he stalked out of the house."

Mandy blinked, then took a deep swallow of the soda. "That's exactly what happened."

"You've gotten into plenty of arguments with your brother before without deciding to run away. Why now?"

Mandy's green eyes clouded with tears as she lifted one shoulder in a halfhearted shrug. "Because."

"That doesn't tell me much." Taylor stood and reached for a box of tissue, setting it in the center of the table.

"He doesn't want me around."

"I'm sure that isn't true," Taylor said softly. "We were talking about you making the drill team just the other day, and Russ's eyes shone with such pride. He loves you, Mandy. I'm sure of it."

"I'm not. At least not anymore. He's so stubborn."

"Opinionated?"

"That, too, and . . ." She hesitated, searching for another word.

"Difficult?"

Mandy slowly raised her eyes to Taylor. "I didn't realize you knew Russ so well."

"I told you before that my father and I had trouble getting along when I was your age, didn't I?"

Mandy nodded and jerked a tissue from the box, as though admitting that she needed one was a sign of weakness and a character defect.

"Sometimes I swear my father and your brother were cut from the same bolt of fabric. It would be easier to change the course of the Columbia River than to get them to alter their opinions." Bringing her feet up to the edge of the chair, Taylor looped her arms around her bent knees. "My dad didn't think us girls should have a college education. To his way of thinking, educating the boys was far more important. They were going to assume the role as heads of the family, while Christy and I would end up housewives."

"But you went to college."

"Indeed I did, but I paid for every cent of it myself. It took me eight years to complete my education. I worked summers in Alaska when I could, in addition to nights and weekends during the school year. Once I was a senior, I was able to get on as a dorm mother, and that took care of my room and board."

"But, Taylor, that's not fair!"

"In my father's eyes it was. To his credit, if Christy and I had been the only two, I'm sure he would have gladly paid for our education, but Dad was financially strapped paying for the boys."

"Yeah, but your brothers will probably end up getting married, too."

Mandy's logic closely aligned Taylor's own. "Yes, but they won't be having babies, and it's unlikely that they'll have to delay whatever career they choose in order to raise a family."

"Women are entitled to a career if they want one."

"I realize that. But it wasn't only a college education that my father and I disagreed over. It was everything. It started with the usual things, like clothes and makeup and friends, but later we found ourselves at odds over just about everything else. When I was eighteen and could vote, he decided he'd choose the candidates worthy of my consideration. On election day he handed me a slip of paper listing the candidates he'd picked."

"You're kidding."

"No, unfortunately I'm not."

"W-what about boyfriends? Did your dad find reasons to dislike them all?"

"No. Just one." Now it was Taylor's turn to lower her gaze. From the moment her father had met Mark, he hadn't liked the up-and-coming financial planner. When Taylor had questioned him about his instant dislike, Eric

Manning had given her the most nonsensical reply. Her father had claimed Mark was too smooth. Too smooth! He'd made Mark sound like a used car salesman. Her father had refused to look past the friendly smile and the easy laugh to the talented man beneath. Mark had tried hard to win him over; Taylor gave him credit for that. The more effort he'd put forth, the more she'd loved him. Taylor and her father had argued bitterly over Mark.

Then one day, in a matter of minutes, she'd learned everything her father had guessed about Mark was true. She'd gone to him and broken down into bitter tears. For the first time in years he hadn't said I told you so. Instead, he'd held her in his arms and gently patted her head while she'd wept. She'd heard later from her brothers that their father had wanted to confront Mark and tell him what a bastard he was. It had taken some fast talking on their parts to convince him it was best to leave matters be.

"You've had arguments with Russ before," Taylor said, tearing herself away from the memories of a painful past best forgotten.

Mandy reached for another tissue, noisily blew her nose and nodded. "Lots of times, especially lately. He's always finding things to gripe at me about."

"But why run away now?"

"I have my reasons."

Her words were so low that Taylor had to strain to hear. "But where will you go?"

"I have an aunt in New Jersey.... I'm not exactly sure where. She was my mother's half sister, and she sent me a birthday present once before my mom died. I think she might let me live with her."

It would do little good for Taylor to point out the numerous holes in Mandy's plan. "Don't you think it would be a good idea to contact her first?"

"I . . . was hoping to surprise her."

"You mean show up on her doorstep so she can't say no?"

"Something like that," Mandy admitted with a delicate nod.

The phone rang, and standing, Taylor walked across the kitchen to answer it. Apparently Mandy thought this was a good time to use the bathroom and left.

"Hello."

"Taylor, this is Russ. I don't suppose you've heard from Mandy, have you?" He sounded impatient and troubled. "I'm at my wit's end with that girl. I've practically called everyone in town. Hell, I've got enough to do without playing hide-and-seek with her."

"She's here."

"We had another one of our fights and—" He stopped abruptly. "She's there? In town? With you?"

"That's what I just got finished saying."

"How'd she get there?"

"From the looks of it, she either walked or hitch-hiked."

"Into town? Dear God . . ." He groaned. "Listen, keep her there. I'll be at your place in ten minutes. You can warn her right now, she may be on restriction for the rest of her natural life."

"Russ, there seems to be a lack of communication here that needs to be settled."

"You're damn right there is. She can't go running to you every time she needs someone to champion her cause. And while I'm on the subject, I refuse to listen to your arguments regarding this skirt issue. I'm not going to have any sister of mine exposing her thighs like some can-can dancer."

"Mandy didn't come to me to champion her cause," Taylor returned, having trouble holding back her own quick temper. "She came to tell me she was running away."

Russ's response was a short, harsh laugh. "We'll just see about that," he said, and slammed down the receiver.

Stifling a groan of her own, Taylor hung up, then took several seconds to compose herself.

"I should be leaving," Mandy said when she returned to the kitchen.

"What about clothes?"

"I packed a bag and hid it in the bushes outside. I wasn't going to tell you I was running away at first. I only came to thank you for being my friend. I...I think Russ is sweet on you and I hope that you two...well, you know." The teenager smiled bravely, but tears rolled down the sides of her face and she smeared them across her cheeks with the back of her hand.

"Money?" Taylor tried next, thinking fast. She had to find a way to stall Russ's sister until he arrived, although in his present frame of mind, she wasn't completely sure he would help matters any.

"I have enough."

"How much is enough?"

"A couple of hundred dollars. I was saving it for a new saddle, but after I saw the dress you made for the dance I was going to buy a sewing machine. Now I'll need it to get to New Jersey."

"But, Mandy, that wouldn't even pay for a bus ticket."

"I'll...think of something."

"I've got some cash," Taylor said, reaching for her purse. "It's really a shame you're leaving. I was asked to be a chaperon when the drill team goes to Reno next month. I was looking forward to seeing you perform."

"You were?" Mandy brightened somewhat. "It's going to be so much fun. We've been practicing early every morning for this competition, and by next month we should really be good. The larger high schools almost always win, but all the girls who go have such a good time." Some of the excitement left her, and her young shoulders sagged. She forced a small smile. "At least in Reno you'll be able to use your American Express."

"And order pizza. I would kill for a good pepperoni pizza on any given Friday night."

"The bowling alley makes a decent one. You should try it sometime."

"I suppose I will," Taylor said, rummaging through her wallet. "Are you sure you won't change your mind? Mandy, sweetheart, it's a cold, cruel world out there. If you like, you can call your aunt from here and feel her out before you leave Cougar Point."

"I guess maybe I should," Mandy murmured, not looking the least bit certain about anything. She hesitated, then turned huge appealing eyes to Taylor. "I was wondering...do you think that maybe I could live with you? No, don't answer that," she said quickly. Regretfully. "Russ would never allow it, and, well, it wouldn't work. Just forget I asked."

"I'd love it if you did, but, honey, that isn't any solution."

Mandy tucked her chin against her collarbone. "I'll be just a minute."

"Mandy." Taylor stopped her. She couldn't continue this pretense. "That was Russ on the phone a few minutes ago. He's on his way to talk to you."

The pale green eyes widened with offense. "You told him I was here? How could you, Taylor? I thought you were my friend. I trusted you...."

"I am your friend. I care about you and can't let you ruin your life because you've had a spat with your brother."

"It's more than that."

"I know. Trust me, I know," Taylor said gently, resisting the urge to pull Mandy into her arms. "What I'd like to suggest is that when your brother arrives you stay in the kitchen, and I'll keep him in the living room and try to talk some sense into him."

"He won't listen," Mandy cried, and her voice fluctuated between two octaves in her distress. Tears ran unrestrained down her cheeks, and she knotted her fists at her sides. "It would be best if I just left."

The sound of Russ's truck screeching to a stop outside the house was a welcome relief, at least to Taylor. "Give me ten minutes alone with him," she pleaded.

"All right," Mandy reluctantly agreed. "But that's all the time I've got to wait." She made it sound as if she had a plane to catch and time was of the essence.

Taylor was at the front door before Russ could even knock. What she saw didn't give her any cause to hope this matter could easily be put to rest. It was apparent from the way he walked that he was madder than a nest of hornets. His face was red and his steps were quick and abrupt as he let himself into the house. Taylor practically had to throw herself in front of the kitchen door to keep him in the living room.

"Where is she?"

"Before you talk to Mandy, you and I need to discuss something."

"Not now," he said, looking past her. "I've never raised a hand to that girl, but by God she's tempting fate. Running away? That's a good laugh. And just where does she intend to go?"

"Russ, would you kindly stop shouting and listen to me." Taylor used her best schoolteacher voice and placed her hands threateningly on her hips as if to suggest one more cross word and she'd have him report to the principal.

"I have somewhere to go, so you needn't worry," Mandy yelled from the kitchen.

"Sit down," Taylor said, pointing at her sofa. "We've got a problem here that isn't going to be settled by you hollering threats at your sister."

"They're a lot more than threats," Russ barked. He continued pacing the floor, occasionally removing his hat long enough to angrily plow his fingers through his hair.

"Mandy didn't come to me about the length of the drill team uniform—"

"It's a damn good thing because I'm not changing my mind. No sister of mine is going to parade around a field, waving her bare thighs around for all damnation to examine." One choice look informed Taylor that he didn't appreciate her interference in what he considered strictly a family affair.

"I'm leaving," Mandy shouted from the other room.

"Over my dead body," Russ retaliated. "I'll drag you back to the ranch if I have to pull you by the hair."

"Then I'll run away tomorrow. You can't force me to live with you."

"She's right, you know," Taylor whispered.

Russ shot her a look hot enough to boil water.

"Listen to what she's really saying," Taylor pleaded.

"What she needs is someone to take her across their knee."

"I'd like to see you try," Mandy spat. "You think you're so big and strong, but I'm here to tell you right now, you'll never lay a hand on me and walk normally again."

Furious, Russ advanced a step toward the other room. Taylor's hand on his arm stopped him. He looked down on her and blinked as if he'd almost forgotten that she was there. "This is between me and my sister," he growled.

"Listen to her," Taylor repeated, more forcefully this time. "Hear the doubt and pain in her voice. She doesn't want to leave any more than you want her to go."

Russ frowned. "Then why...?"

"Because she's convinced you don't love her and you don't want her living with you anymore."

Russ removed his hat and slapped it against the coffee table. "Of all the foolish notions..." Suddenly he seemed lost for words. "That's the most ridiculous thing I've ever heard."

"Mandy," Taylor called, "come out here and sit down." She gestured toward Russ, motioning for him to do likewise. "The only way I can see that will do any good is for the two of you to clear the air. You need to talk face-to-face instead of hurling insults from one room to the other."

Mandy, looking small and broken, hesitantly moved into the living room. She sank slowly into the chair and picked up a women's magazine sitting on the arm, absently flipping through the pages.

Russ sat on the other side of the room, looking nonchalant and laid-back. He propped his ankle over one knee and spread his arms across the back of the davenport as if they were discussing the abrupt change in the weather instead of the fate of his sister and his relationship with her.

"Mandy, why do you want to move in with your aunt?" Taylor asked, after taking a moment to compose her thoughts.

"Because my pigheaded brother is so unreasonable."

"You've gotten along with him up until now."

"No, I haven't." Her voice grew smaller and smaller. "Besides, I'm just in the way."

"Russ," Taylor said, twisting around to confront him, "is Mandy in the way?"

"Hell, no, I need her."

"Sure, to cook your meals and wash your clothes. You can hire someone to do that. I bet Mary Lu Randall would do it for free. She's been sweet on you forever."

"You're the only family I've got," Russ countered gruffly.

"I'm nothing but a problem," Mandy returned, and using the heels of her hands, rubbed the tears from her eyes. "You think I don't notice, but I do. There isn't a single thing you like about me anymore. You're always complaining. If it isn't my hair, it's my clothes or I'm wearing too much makeup or spending too much time on the phone."

Russ dropped his leg and leaned forward, pressing his forearms on the tops of his thighs. He studied Mandy and started to frown. "I'm just trying to do the best job I know how to make sure you grow into a responsible adult."

Mandy looked away. Unable to stand still any longer, Taylor crossed the room, sat on the arm of the chair and looped her own over Mandy's thin shoulders.

"I love you, Amanda," Russ said starkly. "Maybe sometimes I don't show it the way I should, but I do. You're as much a part of my life as the Lazy P. I need you, and not to do the cooking and the laundry, either."

Mandy sniffled in an effort not to cry, and Taylor reached inside her pocket for a fresh tissue, handing it to her. Mandy took it in both hands and blew gently.

"I...didn't realize this drill team thing was so important to you. I suppose Taylor's going to tell me I should've been more sensitive." Russ paused and rubbed a hand down his face. ''When I saw you all dressed up like that, it made me realize how grown-up you're getting, and I guess I didn't want to have to face the fact you're soon going to be a beautiful young woman. It frightens me a little. Before long, the boys are going to be swarming around the ranch like hungry ants.''

''I-if you really want me to quit the drill team, I will,'' Mandy offered in a raspy, thin voice.

''No, you can stay on the team. If every other parent in town is willing to let their daughter prance around a playing field with her thighs exposed, then I'll just have to get used to the idea.'' Russ stood and crossed the room, standing in front of his sister. ''Friends?''

Mandy nodded, and fresh tears streaked her face. She stood and walked straight into Russ's arms, hugging him tight around the middle. ''I didn't really want to live with Aunt Joyce in New Jersey.''

''It's a good thing because the last I heard she retired someplace in Mexico.''

''She did? How come you never told me?''

''Maybe because I was afraid you'd think it was an exotic, fun place to be and decide you'd rather live with her than me. I meant what I said about loving you, Mandy. You're going to have to be more patient with me, I guess, but I promise I'll try harder.''

''I . . . will, too.''

Russ slowly shut his eyes as he hugged his sister close.

Taylor felt her own eyes cloud with tears. She hadn't expected Russ to be so open about his feelings for his sister. When he'd first arrived, she'd been convinced everything was going to go from bad to worse. Russ was so proud and so furious, but once he'd stopped to listen to his sister and heard her fears, he'd set the anger aside and revealed a deep, vulnerable part of himself Taylor had never seen.

"Say, how about if I treat my two best girls to dinner?" Russ said unexpectedly.

"Yeah," Mandy echoed. "Pizza?"

"Anything you want," he said, smiling down on his sister. He raised his eyes to Taylor, and they softened perceptibly.

"I . . . can't," she said, declining the invitation. "This should be a time for the two of you to talk things out. I'd only be in the way."

"No, you wouldn't. We'd never have been able to do it without you," Mandy insisted. "I really want you to come."

"Another time," Taylor promised. "You two go and have a good time."

Russ squeezed Mandy's shoulders. "I don't know about you, but I'm famished. If Taylor wants to turn down an offer for the best pizza in town, then there's only one thing we can do—let her suffer."

"It's your loss," Mandy reminded Taylor on their way out the door.

"Yes, I know," she said, holding on to the catch for the screen door. Mandy bounded down the front steps and ran around the side of the house, where she'd apparently hidden her bag of clothes.

While Russ was waiting for his sister to reappear, he turned to Taylor and mouthed the words, "Thank you." Then he touched his fingertips to his lips and held his hand out to her. She pantomimed the kiss and pressed her open palm against the screen door.

The following evening Taylor sat with her feet propped up at the kitchen table, stirring a bowl of soup. "You're in deep yogurt here,'' she muttered to no one in particular. ''If you don't watch it, you're going to fall in love with a cowboy. You're halfway there already. Admit it.''

She grumbled and vigorously stirred her thick chicken noodle soup until it sloshed over the rim of the bowl. Setting the spoon aside, Taylor braced her elbows on the table and buried her face in her hands.

The whole purpose in coming to Montana was to avoid relationships. She hadn't been in town a week when she'd met Russ. And from there everything had quickly gone downhill. From the first time he'd kissed her she'd known she was headed for trouble. But had that stopped her? Oh, no. Not even the cool voice of reason had given her pause. Instead she was walking straight into his arms, knowing full well that nothing could ever come of their relationship. She wouldn't have an affair with him. Marriage was out of the question; Russ would agree with her there. So exactly where was their relationship headed?

Nowhere.

''Nowhere,'' she repeated out loud. ''Save yourself some heartache,'' she advised herself, then sat back and wondered if she was wise enough to follow her own advice, immediately doubting that she was. The voice in her heart echoed so much louder than anything her brain was telling her. She'd been a fool once. Hadn't she learned anything? Apparently not!

The phone caught her by surprise, and she lazily dropped her legs and stood to answer it, fearing it was Russ and not knowing what she would say if it was.

It was.

''Hi,'' she said, forcing some enthusiasm into her voice. The man had no idea of the turmoil he was causing her.

''I'm calling to thank you for what you did for Mandy and me yesterday.''

"It wasn't anything," she said lightly, dismissing his appreciation. Her hand tightened around the telephone receiver as she leaned against the kitchen wall, needing its support. She hated the way her pulse reacted to the sound of his voice. If he had a voice like other men, it wouldn't affect her so strongly. His was deep and sexy as hell. A bedroom voice.

"You were right about me not hearing the doubt and fear in Mandy's voice," he went on to say. "I don't know what I did to make her think I don't want her around any longer, but she couldn't be more wrong."

"You were wonderful with her." Taylor meant that. She hadn't expected him to be half as understanding, or nearly as sensitive to his sister's needs. Perhaps it would be easier to walk away from him if she could continue to view him as a difficult male, but he'd shown her another side of his personality, one so strongly appealing that she found her heart softening toward him more each minute.

"I felt bad because I'd overreacted to the whole issue of her drill team uniform," Russ explained. "I'd come into the house, and finding Mandy dressed in that outfit caught me by surprise. My nerves were on edge, anyway. We'd just found a dead calf, and when I saw Mandy, I took my frustration and anger out on her. She didn't deserve that."

"Taking her out to dinner was a nice touch."

"I wish you had come along. We both owe you."

"Nonsense. That was your time with Mandy."

Taylor could sense Russ's smile from the other end of the line. "I will admit that we did have fun. I'd forgotten what a kick my sister can be. She's a sweet kid, but she's growing up too fast." He paused. "Listen, I didn't call you up to talk about Mandy. Well, not entirely. How about dinner Friday night?"

Taylor closed her eyes. The lure of the invitation was as strong as the pull of the tide. Squaring her shoulders, Taylor shook her head.

"Taylor?" Russ repeated the invitation with her name.

"I don't think it's a good idea for us to continue seeing each other," she said flatly. The words could have been an aerobic workout. She felt incredibly weak after having said them.

Chapter Seven

"What the hell do you mean?" Russ demanded. He didn't know what kind of game Taylor was playing, but he wasn't about to become a willing participant. If there was a problem, he wanted it out in the open.

"Just what I said," she returned, sounding shaky and unsure. "I don't think it would be a good idea for us to continue seeing each other."

"Why not?" He tried to keep his voice even, but damn it, Taylor was getting on his nerves, not that this was anything new. She had been troubling him from the moment they'd met. He could have dealt with a pesky heat rash more effectively than he'd dealt with this city girl.

Russ had never known a woman quite like Taylor Manning. She could make him madder than anyone he'd ever known, but when he kissed her, the earth moved, angels sang, and whatever else people said when this type of thing occurred. Russ didn't know what it was. No one had ever affected him the way Taylor did.

He'd tried staying away from her. Tried exercising a little more self-control, but five minutes with her and all his good intentions went the way of all flesh. He wanted her in his bed, all soft and mussed with her hair spread out over his pillow. He thought about that a lot, far more than he should. Not for the first time, the image brought with it the stirrings of arousal. How could this schoolteacher— and worse, one from a big city—inspire such hunger in him? It made no sense.

He'd run into his cocktail waitress friend when he'd been in Miles City the week before. Those minutes had been uncomfortable ones for him. April had expected him to come home with her for what she called "a little afternoon delight." Instead, Russ couldn't get away from her fast enough. Not that he wasn't hungry for a woman. He'd been ready to explode long before he met Taylor, but deep down he'd known no woman would ease the ache in his loins. No woman, that is, except Taylor.

That afternoon Russ had seen April for what she was, jaded and cold, and he wanted nothing to do with her. He'd quickly escaped and hurried back to the Lazy P, only to discover Taylor there with his sister. Good Lord, he'd wanted her that day. There was no use lying to himself when it was the plain truth. He'd have gladly made love to her right there in the sunshine and on the grass if she'd have agreed. Even now, days later, when he closed his eyes, he could still smell the fragrance of her cologne. Her mouth had parted beneath his, hot and quick, eager for his kisses. Every touch had hurled his senses into chaos. Her breasts had been perfect. Ripe and full, and dear heaven, one taste of them had been enough to drive him to the outer reaches of sanity.

"I . . . don't want there to be any misunderstandings between us," Taylor, said slicing into his thoughts.

Reluctantly Russ pulled himself from his musings. "I don't, either. If you won't have dinner with me, I want to know why. That's not such an unreasonable request, is it?"

"I . . . think the reasons should be obvious."

"Tell me, anyway."

Russ felt her hesitation, and when she spoke again, her voice sounded deep and a little raspy as if it were difficult to share her thoughts. "Our personality differences should be more than adequate excuse for us to use caution."

She sounded exactly like the schoolteacher she was, he thought. "That hasn't stopped us before. Why should it now?"

"Damn it, Russ Palmer," she cried. "You aren't going to make this easy, are you?"

"All I want is the truth."

The sound of her sigh sang over the wire. "I can't give you anything less than the truth, can I?"

"No," he coaxed softly. "I'm willing to admit we're different. Good God, anyone looking at us would be able to see that. Our outlook on a good many subjects tends to line up opposite each other, but frankly, I'm willing to work around that. I like you, Taylor, better than anyone."

"I know," she whispered, sounding dismal, as if the knowledge caused her distress instead of celebration.

That didn't sit well with Russ, but he wasn't going to make an issue over it. "There are plenty of girls in Cougar Point who'd be mighty pleased if I called to invite them to dinner," he added, thinking that might set her back some, help her realize she had plenty of competition.

"Ask them out then," she returned tartly.

"I don't want to. The only woman who interests me is you."

"That's the problem," she mumbled, and it sounded like she was close to tears.

The thought of Taylor crying did something funny to Russ's stomach. The protective urges ran deep and powerful when it came to the schoolmarm. "Taylor, maybe I should drive into town and we can talk this out face-to-face."

"No," she returned abruptly, almost as if she were afraid. "That would only make this more difficult." She paused, and Russ had to restrain the yearning to set the phone aside gently and go to her.

"Is all this about what happened the other day?" he pried softly. "I know our lovemaking went further than it should have, but that wasn't intentional. If you want an apology..."

"No, that's not it. Oh, Russ, don't you see?"

Frankly he didn't. "Tell me."

"I like you too damn much. We both know where this is going to lead—one of these fine days we're going to end up in love and in bed together."

Personally that didn't sound all that tragic to Russ. He'd been dreaming about exactly that for weeks. "So?"

"So?" she shouted, and her high voice vibrated through the phone lines with enough velocity to shatter crystal. "I'm not interested in a permanent relationship with you. You're a wonderful man—and you'll make some woman a terrific husband, but not me."

He let a moment of tense silence pass before he commented. "If you'll recall, the invitation was for dinner. All I was asking for was us to enjoy a simple meal together. I'm not looking for a lifetime commitment."

"You're doing your best to make this difficult, and I'm finding that all too typical. I refuse to have an affair with you, and that's exactly where our relationship is headed. People are already talking, especially after the Grange dance. And then we went horseback riding and... before I know how it happened you're going to be telling me how to vote and insisting a woman's place is in the home." She paused only long enough to inhale a quick breath. "I'm sorry... I really am, but I don't think it's a good idea for us to have anything to do with each other. Please understand."

Before Russ could say another word, the line was disconnected. He held the receiver in his hand for several moments in disbelief. His first response was anger. He didn't know what the hell Taylor was mumbling about. He found her words about voting and a woman's place in society utterly nonsensical, but he'd never been one to understand women.

He had every right to be upset with her; no one had ever hung up on him before. Instead he felt a tingling satisfaction. Slowly, hardly aware it was happening, Russ felt a smile creep over his face.

Mandy happened to stroll past him just then. "Hey, what's so funny?"

"Taylor," he said, grinning hard. "She likes me."

Russ was riding the range, looking for strays when he saw his lifelong friend come barreling toward him in a battered pickup. Removing his hat, Russ wiped his forearm across his brow and exhaled sharply. He'd been in the saddle since morning, and he was wearier than he could remember being in a good long while. He hadn't been sleeping well the past couple of nights; Taylor had been on his mind, and he still hadn't figured out what to do about her. If anything. He'd delayed confronting her, thinking it was best to give her time. But he was growing anxious. In the past couple of days Russ had faced a few truths about the two of them.

"Cody, it's good to see you," Russ greeted, climbing down from Magic. "Problems?"

"None to speak of," Cody said, opening the cab door and stepping out.

"You didn't come looking for me to discuss the weather."

Cody wasn't wearing his sheriff's deputy's uniform, which was unusual. Instead, he'd donned jeans and a thick sweater. He was about the same height as Russ, but he kept his dark hair trimmed short.

"It's been real nice the past week or so, hasn't it?" Cody said, glancing toward the blue, cloudless sky. He tucked his fingertips into the hip pocket of his Levi's and walked to the front of the truck. Leaning his back against the grille, he raised one foot and rested it on the bumper.

For early October the weather had been unseasonably warm. They'd experienced several Indian summer days, and while Russ appreciated the respite before winter hit, he knew better than to take anything about Montana weather for granted.

"It isn't like you to beat around the bush."

Cody smiled and nodded, looking slightly chagrined. "I came to talk to you about the new schoolteacher."

"What about her?" Russ asked, tensing. He stepped over to the truck and pressed his foot against the bumper, meeting Cody's eyes.

The deputy glanced away, but not before Russ noted the troubled look in his hat-shadowed features.

"We've been friends a good many years, and the last thing I want is for a woman to come between us now."

"I take it you want to ask Taylor out?"

Cody nodded. "But only if you have no objection. She's right pretty, and word has it that the two of you aren't seeing each other anymore."

"Who told you that?" Russ demanded, fighting to repress the surge of instant jealousy that tightened around his chest like thick ropes. He'd resisted the temptation to rush into town and talk some sense into Taylor, thinking she'd have second thoughts before now. Apparently that wasn't the case. If the truth be known, Russ had been doing some heavy thinking about their situation. They were both mature adults and they weren't going to leap into something that would be wrong for them both. Okay, so they were strongly attracted to each other, that much was a given. Anyone with a lick of sense would realize not seeing each other wasn't going to change a damn thing.

It came as something of a shock for Russ to admit he was falling in love with Taylor. There wasn't any use in fighting it—hell, he didn't even want to. Nor was he going to pretend he didn't care about her. Her hooks were in him, and they were buried deep.

"Mary Beth Morgan said something to me this morning," Cody continued. "Apparently Taylor confided in her. Mary Beth claimed Taylor and she were having coffee in the faculty lounge and she inquired about the two of you. Evidently Taylor told her you'd decided not to see each other again."

"Taylor came right out and said that?"

"I don't know her exact words. Damn it all, I'm repeating what someone else repeated to me. How close it is to the truth, I wouldn't know. That's why I'm here."

The mental image of Cody holding Taylor in his arms brought a sudden flash of rage so strong that for a moment Russ couldn't breathe. Twisting around, he returned to Magic, reached for the reins and leaped onto the gelding's back.

"Russ?" Cody asked, frowning.

"Go ahead and ask her out."

Taylor couldn't remember Friday nights being so lonely before moving to Cougar Point. It seemed she'd always had something to do, someplace to go. But that wasn't the case any longer. Her entertainment options were limited at best. The town sported one old-time theater. One screen. One movie. The feature film for the week was one Taylor had seen six months earlier in Seattle. By now it was probably available on video in most parts of the country.

There had been an offer for dinner from Cody Franklin, which had been a pleasant surprise, but she'd turned him down. In retrospect she wished she hadn't been so quick to refuse him. He was pleasant enough. They'd met before at the dance, and she'd found him reserved, and perhaps a little remote.

If she was looking for some way to kill time, she could always sew, but Taylor simply wasn't in the mood. After a long week in the classroom, she was more interested in doing something relaxing.

There were always books, and with such limited options, she reached for one. Locating a promising romance, she cuddled up in the chair and wrapped an afghan around her legs. She hadn't finished the first chapter before her eyes started to drift closed. Struggling to keep her lids open, she concentrated on the text. After the third yawn, she gave up the effort, set the open book over the arm of the chair and decided to rest for a few minutes.

The next thing she knew someone was at her front door, pounding hard.

Taylor tossed aside the afghan and stumbled across the floor, disoriented and confused. "W-who is it?" she asked. The door didn't have a peephole; most folks in town didn't even bother to lock their front door.

"Russ Palmer," came the gruff reply.

Taylor quickly twisted the lock and opened the door. "What are you doing here?" she insisted. It took every ounce of willpower she possessed not to throw her arms around him; she was so grateful to see him.

Now that Russ was standing in the middle of her living room, he didn't look all that pleased about being there.

The wall clock started to chime, and Taylor absently counted ten strikes. It was ten! She'd been "resting" for nearly two hours. Good grief, she'd been reduced to falling asleep at eight o'clock on a Friday night.

"Russ?" she prodded. He didn't look right; in fact, he was frowning as if he wasn't exactly sure where he was. "Is something wrong?"

"No." He gave her a silly, lopsided grin. "Everything's wonderful. More than wonderful. You're wonderful. I'm wonderful. The whole world's wonderful."

"Russ?" She squinted up at him. "You've been drinking?"

He pointed his index finger toward the ceiling. "Only a little."

She steered him toward the sofa and sat him down. "How much is a little?"

"A couple of beers with the guys." His brows drew together as he considered his words. "Or was that two guys and a lot of beers? I don't remember anymore."

"That's what I thought," she mumbled. From the looks of him he'd downed more than two beers! "I'll make you some coffee."

"Don't go," he said, reaching out and gripping her around the waist. "I'm not drunk, just a little tipsy. I had this sudden urge to visit my lady, and now that I'm here, I want to hold you."

Although she resisted him, he effortlessly brought her into his lap. Her hands were on his shoulders. "I thought we agreed this sort of thing had to stop," she whispered, struggling against the warm, loving feel of his hands on her.

His mouth found the open V of her shirt, and he kissed her there, gliding his tongue over her warm skin, creating sensations that were even warmer.

"We weren't going to see each other anymore, remember?" she tried again. Her nails dug into the hard muscles of his shoulders as she exhaled slowly.

"I've been doing some thinking about that," Russ said between nibbling kisses that slid along the delicate line of her jaw. "In fact, I haven't thought of anything else all week."

"Russ, please stop," she whimpered. His hands were on her breasts, gently kneading them, sending jagged waves of longing through her.

To her surprise, he did as she asked. Her hands were in his hair, and she reluctantly withdrew them. "You shouldn't be driving."

"I know. I left the truck at Billy's and walked over here. Only I didn't realize where I was headed until I arrived on your doorstep."

Billy's was one of the town's three taverns. The most popular from what Taylor had heard. During the summer months, they brought in a band every third Friday, and gossip had it every adult in town showed up.

"You shouldn't have come," she whispered. Then why was she so glad he had? Taylor didn't want to analyze the answer to that, afraid of what she'd discover.

"You're positively right," Russ concurred. "I have no business being here. Go ahead and kick me out. I wouldn't blame you if you did. The fact is, you probably should."

"If you promise to behave yourself, I'll put on a pot of coffee." She squirmed off his lap and moved into the kitchen. She'd just poured cold water into the automatic drip machine when Russ stole up behind her. He slipped his muscle-hard arms around her waist and buried his head in the curve of her neck.

"Russ . . . you promised."

"No, I didn't."

"Then . . . perhaps you should leave."

Reluctantly he dropped his arms, walked over to the chair, twisted it around and straddled it. He was grinning, obviously pleased about something. "Cody told me."

Taylor busied herself bringing down two mugs and setting them on the counter. Apparently nothing was kept secret in this town. By all rights, Taylor should have accepted his dinner invitation. She certainly wished she had now.

"You turned him down. Why?" His dark eyes held her with unwavering curiosity, demanding a reply.

"I . . . don't think that's any of your business."

He shrugged, his look marked with indifference. "I'd like to think it was my business."

"You don't own me." She pressed her hands into the counter behind her.

He grinned. "Not from lack of trying." He held out his arms to her, beseeching her to walk over to him. "We've got a good thing going between us, and I can't understand why you want to throw it away." His eyes continued to hold hers prisoner. The smile had drained out of him. "The first time I met you, I recognized trouble. That didn't stop me, and it didn't stop you, either, did it?"

She lowered her gaze rather than answer the obvious. When she raised her head, she discovered Russ standing directly in front of her. Brazenly he cupped both her breasts in his palms, weighing them as though they were more precious than gold. Using his thumbs, he stroked their fullness until her nipples were throbbing. A familiar heat quickened her pulse with each gentle caress. She should have knocked his hands away, should have demanded he leave her home, but she did neither of those things.

"Did it?" Russ repeated. He gripped her around the waist, and with one swift movement set her on top of the counter.

She stared at him, wondering at his mood. "Russ?"

He slanted his mouth over hers, kissing her long and hard, and when he'd finished, she was panting. "Did it?" he asked a third time. His mouth found her earlobe and sucked gently.

By now Taylor had forgotten the question. Her eyes were closed, and she was gnawing on her lower lip. Russ made quick work of her blouse and her bra, laying them open. A sharp jolt of pleasure shot through her when he fastened his lips around one taut nipple and sucked gently, greedily. Taylor's grip tightened on the counter as he continued to torment her.

"Russ, you're drunk." From somewhere she found the strength to stop him, although it was the most difficult task of her life. On her own part, not Russ's. She wanted him so much, but her whole body seemed to defy her.

Ever so slowly he raised his head. His grin was sultry and teasing. "I'm not that drunk."

"You shouldn't have come here."

"Yes, I know." His hands were in her hair. He couldn't seem to leave it up. Every time they were together, he tangled his fingers through it. Gently he removed the combs, then arranged it over her shoulder, gliding its length over his callused fingertips. Then his hands framed her face and he kissed her once more.

Unable to resist him, she parted her lips in welcome, and they clung to each other. His tongue invaded her mouth, sought and found hers, and when she submitted to him, unreservedly, he gave a small sound of triumph. Taylor moaned; she couldn't help it. Russ's kisses made love to her in the gentlest, sweetest ways.

When he finally dragged his mouth from hers, he smiled at her. "Go ahead and give me that coffee, and then you can drive me home."

Without question, Taylor did as he asked. They drank their coffee in silence, and its sobering effects hit her like hard, cold pieces of hail. After all her intentions to stay away from him, she'd been almost giddy with happiness when he'd arrived. It hadn't mattered that he'd been drinking. It hadn't mattered that he took liberties with her body. All that had concerned her was seeing him again. Taylor had never thought of herself as a weak person, but that was how Russ made her feel. Spineless and indecisive.

Russ fell asleep on the drive out to the ranch. The back porch light was on when she pulled into the yard, and wondering what to do, Taylor parked the car and hurried around to the passenger side.

"Russ," she said, shaking him by the shoulders. "Wake up."

His eyes opened slowly, and when he recognized her, he grinned sheepishly, his gaze warm and loving. "Taylor."

"You're home."

His arms circled her waist. "Yes, I know."

Taylor managed to break free. "Come on, let's go inside, and for heaven's sake, could you be a little less noisy? I don't want anyone to know I brought you here."

"Why not?" He tilted his head as if the question were a weighty one and the answer demanded serious concentration.

"There's enough talk about us as it is. The last thing I need is for someone to report seeing my car parked at your house late on Friday night."

"Don't worry. No one can see the house from the road."

"Just get inside, would you?" She was fast losing her patience with him. The coffee was supposed to have sobered him up, but if anything it had had the opposite effect. His actions were more deliberate and unhurried than before.

The back door was unlocked, and Russ slammed it closed with his foot. The sound shot through the kitchen like a blast from a shotgun, startling Taylor.

"Shh," Russ said loudly, pressing his finger over his lips. "You'll wake Mandy."

Taylor wished the teenager would wake up and come to help her. Russ was becoming increasingly difficult to handle.

"You need to go to bed," she said, and prepared to leave.

"I'll never make it there without help." His smile was roguish and naughty, and he staggered a few steps as though that was proof enough. "I need you, Taylor. There's no telling what might happen to me if I'm left to my own devices."

"I'm willing to chance that."

"I'm not." With his arm around her waist, he led her toward the stairs. He stumbled forward, bringing Taylor with him. She had no choice but to follow. She didn't know if it was an act or not, but he really did seem to need her assistance.

They were two steps up the stairway when Russ sagged against the wall and sighed heavily. "Have I ever told you I think you're beautiful?"

"I believe the word was wonderful," she muttered, using her shoulder to urge him forward.

"You're both. A man could drown in eyes that color of blue and not even care."

"Russ," she said in a heated whisper, "let's get you upstairs."

"In bed?" He arched his thick brows suggestively.

"Just get upstairs. Please."

"You're so eager for my body, you can hardly wait, can you?" he asked, and then chuckled softly, seeming to find himself exceptionally amusing. He leaned forward enough to kiss the side of her neck. "I'll try to make it worth your while."

Taylor was breathless by the time they reached the top of the stairway. "Which room is yours?" she asked.

Russ turned around in a full circle before raising his arm and directing her to the bedroom at the end of the hall. "There," he said enthusiastically, pointing straight ahead as if he'd discovered uncharted land.

With her arm wrapped firmly around his middle, Taylor led the way. The hall was dark, lit only by the fading light of the harvest moon. She opened the door, and together the two of them staggered forward, landing on the mattress with a force that drove the oxygen from her lungs.

Russ released a deep sigh and rolled onto his back, positioning Taylor above him. His unrelenting dark eyes stared up at her.

"I . . . should be going."

"Not yet," he whispered. "Kiss me good-night first."

"Russ, no." She tried to move, but his hands, hard at her hips, held her prisoner.

"All I'm asking for is one tiny kiss. Just enough so that when I wake up in the morning I'll remember that you were here and be glad."

She rolled her eyes toward the ceiling. "The only thing you're going to have in the morning is a world-class headache."

"If you won't kiss me, then you leave me with no option but to kiss you." Once more his fingers were busy with her blouse, and the material seemed to part in his hands without him doing anything more than touching her. A protest lodged in her throat, but remained unspoken as his palms cupped her breasts. He released a soft sigh of pleasure.

So did Taylor.

He began to kiss her lips, nibbling tiny kisses that promised so much more than they delivered. Then he changed tactics, drugging her with long, prolonged kisses that drove away all grounds for complaint.

For some unknown reason he stopped. Suddenly. He threw back his head and dragged several deep breaths through his lungs. Then, as though he still needed to keep touching her, he caressed her breasts, working his thumbs until her nipples puckered and pulsed.

"Does this prove anything?" he asked her, as if the question were of utter importance.

"That . . . that I should have left you to your own devices. You didn't need my help."

"I did. I do. I always will." Lifting his head, he sucked languidly at her left breast, creating an entirely new range of pulsing sensations within her. Her fingers tangled with his hair, holding him to her, and at the same time wanting to push him away. Whatever magic he was performing, she craved. It was what she'd feared from the first. What she'd wanted from the beginning.

Until this moment, Taylor had always thought it impossible for one woman to experience both misery and ecstasy at the same time.

"In case you haven't figured it out yet," Russ informed her, "you belong in my bed, and that's exactly where you're going to end up."

With what remained of her shredded dignity, Taylor pushed herself free from his hold. She bolted off the bed and paced the room as she fumbled with the buttons of her blouse. While they opened of their own accord for Russ, they gave her nothing but problems.

By the time she finished, Russ was sitting up, leaning against the bunched pillows, looking smug and arrogant. "Good Lord, you're beautiful."

It was all Taylor could do not to throw her hands in the air and rant at him. "This doesn't change a damn thing," she insisted.

His answering grin was filled with cocky reassurance. "Wanna bet?"

Chapter Eight

Hi, Taylor,'' Mandy said as she stepped into Taylor's classroom early the following week.

"Howdy."

Mandy grinned, her entire face lighting up with the smile. "You're beginning to sound like a country girl."

That gave Taylor cause to sit back and take notice. "I am?"

Mandy nodded. "Russ told me just the other day he was going to make a country girl out of you yet." Mandy sheepishly walked over to the front row of desks and sat on the edge of one.

At the mention of Russ, Taylor quickly started fiddling with the pencils on her desk.

"Do...you remember the day when we talked and I was thinking about running away?" Mandy asked, and her young voice lowered a little.

"Of course," Taylor assured her.

"I asked you what your father thought about the boys you dated, and you told me that he'd generally approved of your boyfriends." The teenager pressed her school books close to her chest, and Taylor noted how tense the younger girl's hands were. "There was...a reason I asked about that. You see, there's this boy in school—he's a junior and his name is Eddie and...well, he's really nice and my family knows his family and we've known each other almost all our lives and..."

"You like Eddie?"

Mandy's responding nod was fervent. "A whole, whole lot, and I think he likes me, too. We've only talked in the halls a couple of times, but this morning when I was putting my books in my locker, he walked up and we started talking...not about anything in particular, at least not at first, then all of a sudden he asked me if I wanted to go to the movies with him Saturday night."

"I see." Taylor did understand her young friend's dilemma. All too well. Mandy was only fourteen, and Russ would surely consider a high school freshman too young to date. In fact, Taylor agreed with him, but she'd also been fourteen once herself and attracted to a boy who liked her. He'd been older, too, and had asked her to a party, which her father had adamantly opposed her attending. The memory of the argument that had followed remained painfully vivid in her mind.

"I really, really want to go to the movies with Eddie, but I'm afraid Russ will get upset with me for even asking. Not right off. I mean, he's been trying hard to listen to my point of view, but dating is something that's never come up before and...well, I have a feeling we aren't going to be able to talk about me having a boyfriend without...problems." She hesitated and sighed heavily. "What should I do, Taylor?"

Taylor adamantly wished she had an easy answer. "I really don't know."

"Will you talk to him for me?"

"Absolutely not."

"Oh, please, you don't know how much this would mean to me. Don't you remember what it's like to be fourteen and have a boy like you?"

That was the problem; Taylor did remember. "When I was your age a sixteen-year-old boy invited me to a party. My father made it sound as if he wanted to drag me into an opium den. More than anything else in the world, I wanted to attend that party."

"Did you?"

Taylor sadly shook her head. "I was too young to date."

Mandy's shoulders sagged with defeat. "It's only a movie, and I don't understand why it should be such a terrible thing if Eddie and I were to go to a show together."

Crossing her arms, Taylor started to pace the width of her classroom, her thoughts spinning. "What about a compromise?"

"H-how do you mean?"

"What if Russ were to drop you off at the theater, you paid your own way in and you just happened to sit next to Eddie? I don't think that would pose much of a problem, do you?"

Mandy looked more perplexed than relieved. "He could buy me popcorn, though, don't you think?"

"Sure. It wouldn't be like a real date, but you'd still be at the movies with Eddie."

Mandy's hold on her schoolbooks relaxed somewhat. "Do you think Russ would go for it?"

"He's a reasonable man." Taylor couldn't believe she was actually saying this, but in some instances it was true, and he was trying hard with his sister. "I think he'd at least take it into consideration."

Mandy nodded, but her lips remained tightly pinched. "Will you talk to him about it?"

"Me?" Taylor returned spiritedly. "You've got to be joking!"

"I'm not. Russ listens to you. You may not think he does, but I know better. It's because of you that I'm able to wear makeup and buy my own clothes. Russ and I are trying real hard to get along, but I'm afraid this thing with Eddie will ruin everything. Oh, Taylor, please. I'll do anything you want. Cook your meals, do your laundry... all year, anything. Please."

"Russ will listen to you."

"Maybe," Mandy agreed reluctantly, "but this is too important to mess up. I told Eddie I'd have to talk it over with my brother, and he said I should let him know tomorrow. I'm afraid if I put him off that he'll ask some other girl, and I think I'd die if he did."

Against her better judgment, Taylor felt herself weakening. She hadn't seen Russ since Friday night when she'd dropped him off at the house, taken him up the stairs and put him to bed. That whole escapade was best forgotten as far as Taylor was concerned.

"Please," Mandy coaxed once more.

"All right," Taylor muttered. When she'd been growing up, she was able to go to her mother and have her smooth matters over with her father. Mandy didn't have anyone to run interference for her. Taylor didn't mind so much as she worried that Russ would use this opportunity to press her with a few arguments of his own, ones that had nothing to do with his sister.

Russ had been having a bad day from the moment he'd woken up that morning. The minute he'd stepped out of the house he'd encountered one problem after another, the latest being a calf standing two feet deep in mud and mire. After an hour of fruitless effort, Russ had lost his patience and accepted the fact he was going to need help. He'd contacted his hands by walkie-talkie and was waiting for one or more of them to arrive to lend assistance.

Every calf was valuable, but this one, trapped and growing weaker, had been marked for his breeding herd. Like most of the ranchers in Cougar Point, Russ kept two herds. One for breeding purposes, which he used to produce bulls that he often sold for a handsome profit. Bull calves that didn't meet his expectations were turned into steers and raised for beef.

His second herd was strictly grade cattle, sold off at the end of the season. This particular calf had been the product of his highest quality bull and his best cow. Russ had great expectations for him, and he sure as hell didn't want him lost to a mud hole.

Russ checked the sun and wondered how much longer he'd be left to wait. He'd sent his two best hands out to mend fences, a tedious but not thankless task.

There was still a good deal of work left to complete before winter set in, and he didn't have a lot of time to waste. Miles of fence to inspect and mend was no small chore. If the fences weren't secure, Russ would soon be left to deal with the elk that come down out of the mountains in winter. If elk could get through his fence, they'd eat up his oats and hay. No rancher could afford to feed elk, and a good fence was the best protection he had.

If Russ had to choose his favorite time of year, it would be autumn. The sun was still warm, but the morning frost warned of encroaching winter. When he drove his cattle into the feed ground, it was like a homecoming, a harvesting of his year's efforts.

The calf mewled, reminding Russ of his predicament.

"I know, fellow," Russ muttered. "I tried everything I could think to do for you. I'm afraid you're stuck here until one of the other men swings by and lends me a hand."

No sooner had the words escaped his mouth when he noted a truck slowly heading in his direction. He frowned, wondering who'd be coming out this way, knowing all his men were on horseback. Maybe there had been trouble at the house.

After the day he'd been having, Russ didn't look forward to dealing with any more problems than those he already had. As the blue truck neared, Russ realized it was Taylor at the wheel.

He walked out of the mud and stood with his hands braced against his hips, waiting for her. He hadn't seen her since the night she'd driven him home. If the truth be known, he wasn't proud of the way he'd finagled her into his bedroom. Yes, he'd had too much to drink, but he hadn't been nearly as drunk as he'd led her to believe.

"Hello," Taylor said as she awkwardly climbed out of the cab. She was dressed in jeans, but they were several inches too short and a tad too small. The sweater looked suspiciously like one of Mandy's.

Russ removed his gloves. "What brings you out here?" He didn't mean to sound unfriendly, but he was frustrated, tired and hungry, a lethal combination where he was concerned. The fact was, he was damn glad to see her. He always was.

She didn't answer him right away, but instead focused her attention on the calf, which mewled pitifully at this latest arrival. "Mandy suggested I drive out so I could talk to you," she muttered, then pointed toward the mud hole. "That calf's stuck."

"No kidding."

"There's no need to be sarcastic with me," she announced primly, hands on her narrow hips. The material of the jeans was stretched taut across her hips and pulled tight at the juncture between her legs, diverting his attention.

"Aren't you going to do something?" she demanded.

Undressing her slipped into his mind.... Russ brought his musings to an abrupt halt. "Do something about what?" he asked.

"That cow. She needs help."

"She's a he, and I'm well aware of the fact."

"Then *help him*," Taylor ordered, gesturing toward the calf as though she suspected that Russ hadn't actually seen the poor thing and was bent on ignoring the problem.

"I've just spent the past hour helping him."

"Well, you certainly didn't do a very good job of it."

"Do you think you can do any better?" he barked.

She looked startled for a moment, then added, "I bet I could."

"Here we go again," he muttered, and removed his hat long enough to slap it against his thigh and remove the dust. "Because you're a woman, an independent, competent one, you're convinced you can handle this problem, while I, a chauvinist and a drunk, am incapable of assessing the situation."

"I...I didn't exactly say that."

"But it's what you implied."

"All right," she said tightly, "I'll admit I can't see why you aren't helping that poor, pathetic animal."

"I guess I just needed you. Go to it, lady."

"All right, I will," she said, looking downright indignant. Cautiously she approached the edge of the mud hole. She planted her boots just outside the dark slime and leaned forward slightly. In a low, evenly pitched voice she started carrying on a soothing, one-sided conversation with the calf as if she could reason him out of his plight.

"You're going to have to do a whole lot more than talk to him," Russ couldn't resist telling her. He walked over to the truck, crossed his arms and leaned against the side. Already he could feel his sour mood lifting. Just watching Taylor deal with this would be more entertainment than he'd enjoyed in a good long while.

"I'm just taking a few minutes or so to reassure him," Taylor returned between clenched teeth. "The poor thing's frightened half out of his wits."

"Sweet-talkin' him is bound to help."

"I'm sure it will," she said, giving him a surly look.

"It works wonders with me, too," Russ felt honor bound to tell her, although he couldn't keep the humor out of his voice. "It works real well. However, it's been my belief that actions speak louder than words. When you're finished, would you care to demonstrate your concern for me?"

"Absolutely not."

Russ chuckled softly. "That's what I thought."

Taylor cast him an infuriated glance before walking around the edges of the mud-caked hole. The calf continued to mewl, not that Russ could blame him. The fellow had gotten himself into one fine quandary.

"It appears he's completely trapped," Taylor announced in formal tones.

It had taken Russ all of three seconds to come to that conclusion himself.

"Can't you put a rope around his head and pull him out?" She looked around and started motioning toward Russ's gelding. "You could loop one end around the calf and the other around the saddle horn and have Magic walk backward. I saw it done that way in a movie once. Trigger, at least I think it was Trigger, saved Roy Rogers from certain death in quicksand doing exactly that."

"It won't work."

Taylor gave her shoulders an indignant shrug. "Why won't it? If it worked for Roy Rogers, it should work for anybody."

"With a rope around his neck, he'd probably strangle before we budged him more than a few inches."

"Oh." She gnawed on her lower lip. "I hadn't thought of that."

Russ hated to admit how much he was enjoying this. She'd outsmarted him once before with that flat tire business, but sweet Taylor was walking on his turf now, and Russ was in control. "I don't suppose you'd care to make a wager on this?"

"No more bets."

"What's the matter? Are you afraid you'll lose?"

Taylor firmly shook her head. "I'm not getting caught in that trap a second time."

"How about if you get the calf out I'll come willingly to your bed. If by some gross error in judgment on your part you fail, then you'll come willingly to my bed."

"Does everything boil down to *that* with you?"

"*That*, my sweet lady, is exactly what we both want."

"You're impossible."

"If you'd be honest with yourself, you'd admit I'm right."

Her hair was tied up in a tight chignon at her nape, and her mouth was pinched so tightly together that her lips were pale and white. "You're disgusting."

"That isn't what you said the other night," Russ reminded her.

"If you don't mind, I'd prefer it if we don't talk about Friday night."

"As you wish," he said, then yawned lazily.

Taylor stroked her chin, reassessing the situation with his bull calf. "Couldn't we prod him out?"

"We? It was my understanding that you could do this all on your own."

"All right," she flared, "if you won't help me, then I'll do it myself." She took two tentative steps into the thick molasseslike mud and wrinkled her nose as she warily approached the distressed calf. "For being this great rancher, you certainly seem to be taking this business rather casually," she accused him, glancing over her shoulder. Her arms were stretched out at her sides as though she were walking across a tightrope.

Russ shrugged. "Why should I be concerned when you're doing such a bang-up job?"

Taylor took another two small steps. Her face was scrunched up as if she found being this close to this much mud utterly disgusting.

"You're doing just great," Russ called out to her. "In another week or so you'll have reached the calf."

"I never realized how sarcastic you were before now," she muttered.

"Just trying to be of service. Are you sure you're not willing to stake something on the outcome of this?"

"I'm more than sure," she called. "I'm positive."

"That's a shame."

She glared at him once more. "It seems you've forgotten that this calf happens to belong to you. The only reason I'm doing anything is because I find your attitude extremely callous."

"Extremely," Russ echoed, and unable to restrain a chuckle, he laughed outright. He managed to disguise it behind a cough, but the irate look she shot him told him he hadn't done a good job of it.

The sound of pounding hooves caught his attention, and Russ turned to find two of his men galloping toward him. Apparently they'd finished the fence-mending he'd assigned them earlier.

"Who's coming?" Taylor demanded. She twisted around to glance over her shoulder and somehow lost her balance. Her arms flung every which way as a look of sheer terror came over her. "Russ..."

Russ leaped forward, but it was too late. He heard her shriek just as she vaulted, hands first into the thick slime. For a shocked second he did nothing. Then, God save him, he couldn't help it, he started laughing. He laughed so hard, his stomach hurt and he gripped it with both arms.

A long list of unladylike words blistered the afternoon air when Russ waded into the mud and helped her. Taylor was sitting upright in the muck, her knees raised holding out her hands while the gunk slowly oozed between her fingers. At least the upper portion of her body had been spared.

"Get away from me you...you..." She apparently couldn't think of anything nasty enough to call him. "This is all your fault." Taking a fistful of black mud, she hurled it at him with all her strength, using such a force that she nearly toppled with the effort.

The mud flew past Russ, missing him by several feet. "Here, let me help you," he said, wiping the tears of mirth from the corners of his eyes.

"Stop laughing," she shouted. "Stop right this moment. Do you understand me?"

Russ couldn't. He swore he'd never seen anything funnier in his life. He honestly tried to do as she asked, but he simply couldn't. His belly shook with the effort to repress the rolling waves of amusement.

Taylor was so furious that despite several attempts she couldn't pull herself upright. Finally, unable to stand by and do nothing, Russ moved behind her and, gripping her by the underarms, heaved her upward.

The second they were out of the mud, Taylor whirled around and confronted him. She was talking so fast and so furiously that he couldn't make out more than a few words. From those he recognized, he figured he was better off not knowing what she was saying.

Russ's two hands, Slim and Roy, arrived, and when Russ caught their eyes, he noted that they were doing an admirable job of containing their own amusement. Unfortunately Russ wasn't nearly as diplomatic.

"You two can handle this?" he said, nodding toward the calf.

"No problem," Slim said.

"Taylor didn't think she'd have a problem, either," Russ said, and started laughing all over again.

Both Slim and Roy were chuckling despite their best efforts not to. They climbed down off their horses and leaned against the side of the truck and turned away so that Taylor couldn't see them. It wasn't until then that Russ noted that Taylor was missing. He turned around and discovered her walking like a militant protester in the direction of the house, which by his best estimate was a good three miles north. Her backside was caked with mud, and her arms were swinging at her sides with enough force to churn a windmill.

"Looks like you got woman problems," Roy said, glancing toward Taylor.

"Looks that way to me, too," Slim said, reaching for his kerchief and wiping his eyes. "I'd be thinking about what Abe Lincoln said if I were you."

"And what's that?" Russ wanted to know.

"Hell hath no fury like a woman scorned."

"That wasn't Abe Lincoln," Roy muttered. "That was Johnny Carson."

Whoever said it obviously knew women a whole lot better than Russ did. The way he figured it, if he ever wanted Taylor to ever speak to him again, he was going to have to do some fast talking.

Taylor had never been more furious in her life. The mud was the most disgusting thing she'd ever seen, and to have it against her clothes and skin was more horrible than she even wanted to contemplate. She was cold and wet, and all Russ had done was laugh.

He had laughed as if she were some sideshow sent to amuse him with her antics. To add to her humiliation she couldn't find the key to the stupid truck. She'd thought she'd left it in the ignition. One thing she did know: she wasn't going to stand around and listen to those men make fun of her.

The least Russ could have done was tell her he was sorry! But he hadn't done that. Oh, no! He'd stepped back and roared so loud she swore she'd hear the echo on her dying day.

The sound of the pickup racing toward her did little to quell her fury. She didn't so much as turn and look at him when Russ slowed the truck to a crawl beside her.

"Do you want a ride?"

"No." She continued, upping her pace, arms flying like propeller blades at her sides. Already she was winded, but she'd keel over and die before she'd let Russ know that.

"As best I can figure, we're about three miles from the ranch house."

She whirled around and planted her hands on her hips. "What makes you think I'm going to stop there?"

He shrugged. "Would it help if I said I was sorry and meant it?"

"No." Her voice cracked on the lone syllable, and her shoulders started to shake while she worked to suppress the tears. Her effort was for naught, and rivulets ran down her face, so hot they felt like acid against her skin. Forgetting about the thick mud caked on her hands, she tried to wipe the tears aside and in the process nearly blinded herself. The sobs came in earnest then, and her whole body shook with them.

She heard Russ leap out of the pickup, and before she could protest, he was wiping the grit from her face, using a handkerchief. She only hoped it was clean, and once she realized how preposterous that thought was, she cried harder.

"I think I hate you," she sobbed, and her shoulders bobbed with the vehemence with which she spoke. "I hate Montana. I hate everything about this horrible place. I want to go home."

Russ's arms came around her, but before she could push him away, he'd lifted her into his arms and carried her to the pickup.

"I . . . can't sit in there," she wailed. "I'll ruin the upholstery."

Russ proceeded to inform her how little he cared about the interior of his truck. He set her inside the cab, with her feet hanging out the door, then reached into the back and pulled a blanket from the bed and placed that around her shoulders.

"You're cold."

"I'm not cold. I'm perfectly all—" She would have finished what she was going to say, but her teeth had started to chatter.

Gently Russ brushed the hair from her face, his fingers lingering at her temple. "I am sorry."

"Just be quiet. I'm in no mood for an apology."

Russ lifted her legs and twisted them around, then closed the door. The blast of heat coming from the heater felt like a wind straight from paradise, and tucking the blanket more securely around her, Taylor hunched forward. She didn't want to think where this tattered old blanket had been.

Russ raced around the front of the truck and climbed in beside her. "Hold on," he instructed. "I'll have you to the house in two minutes flat."

If Taylor had thought the ride from town the day they'd met had been rough, it was a Sunday School picnic in comparison to the crazy way Russ drove across the pasture.

Mandy must have heard them coming, because she was standing on the back porch steps when Russ pulled into the yard and screeched to a halt. He turned off the engine and vaulted out of the cab.

Taylor couldn't seem to get her body to move. Russ opened the door and reached for her, effortlessly lifting her into his arms.

"What happened?" Mandy cried, racing toward them.

"Taylor fell into the mud. She's about to freeze to death."

"I...I most certainly am not going to freeze," she countered. "All I need is a warm bath and my own clothes."

"Right on both accounts," Russ said, racing up the back stairs with her in his arms. He paused at the landing and sucked in a deep breath. "How much do you weigh, anyway?"

"Oh," Taylor cried, squirming in his arms, struggling for him to release her.

All her efforts were to no avail as Mandy held open the door and Russ carried her through the kitchen and down a narrow hallway to the bathroom.

"How'd it happen?" Mandy demanded, running after them.

Russ's eyes met Taylor's. Smiling dark brown fusing with furious ice-blue. "You don't want to know the answer to that," Taylor informed the teenager.

"I'll tell you later," Russ mumbled out of the corner of his mouth. When they reached the bathroom, Mandy opened the door wider so that Russ could haul Taylor inside.

"Boil some water and get down the whiskey bottle from the top cupboard," he instructed.

Mandy nodded and was gone like a shot.

"Put me down," Taylor insisted between clenched teeth. If it wasn't for this egotistical, pigheaded, perverse man, she wouldn't be in this mess.

Russ surprised her by doing as she asked. Gently he set her feet on the tile floor, then leaned over the tub to adjust the knobs, starting the flow of warm water.

For the first time Taylor had the opportunity to survey the damage. She looked down at her legs and gasped at the thick, black coating that covered her calves and thighs. A look in the mirror was her second mistake.

Her lower lip started to tremble, and she sniffled in an effort to hold back the tears.

"You're going to be just fine in a few minutes," Russ said softly in an apparent effort to comfort her.

"I'm not all right," Taylor wailed, catching her reflection in the mirror once more. "I look like the Creature from the Black Lagoon."

Chapter Nine

"Taylor," Russ shouted from the other side of the bathroom door, "close the shower curtain. I'm coming in."

Resting her head against the back of the tub until the soothing warm water covered her shoulders, Taylor turned a disinterested glance toward the door. She felt sleepy and lethargic. "Go away," she called out lazily, and then proceeded to yawn loudly, covering her mouth with the back of her hand.

"If you don't want to close the curtain, it's fine with me. Actually, I'd be grateful if you didn't."

The doorknob started to turn and, muttering profusely at the intrusion, Taylor reached for the plastic curtain and jerked it closed.

"Damn," Russ said from the other side, not bothering to hide his disappointment. "I was hoping you'd be more stubborn than this."

"Why are you here?" she demanded.

"I live here, remember?"

"I mean in this bathroom! You have no business walking in on me like this." Actually Taylor should have been out of the bathtub long ago, but the water was incredibly warm and wonderfully relaxing, and it felt so good to sit and soak.

"I'm taking your clothes out so Mandy can stick them in the washing machine," he said, and his voice faded as he traipsed down the hall.

All too soon he was back. "Stick out your arm."

"Why?"

"You'll find out."

Taylor exhaled sharply, her hold on her temper precarious at best. "May I remind you that I'm stark naked behind this curtain."

"Lady, trust me, I know that. It's playing hell with my imagination. Now stick out your arm before I'm forced to pull back this shower curtain."

Grinding her teeth, Taylor did as he asked, knowing full well he'd follow through with his threat given the least bit of provocation. Almost immediately a hot mug was pressed into her palm. She brought it behind the curtain and was immediately struck by the scent of whiskey and honey mixed with hot water. "What's this for?"

"It'll help warm you."

"I wasn't really that chilled." Actually she'd been far too angry to experience anything more than nominal discomfort.

"If you want the truth," Russ said in low, seductive tones, "I was hoping the drink would help take the edge off your anger."

"It's going to take a whole lot more than a hot toddy to do that."

"That's what I thought," he muttered. "I've left a couple of Mandy's things here for you to change into when you've finished. There's no hurry, so take all the time you want."

"Are you leaving now?" she asked, impatient to have him gone.

"Yes, but I'll be waiting for you."

"I knew you would be," she grumbled.

Taylor soaked a good ten minutes more until the water started to turn cool, then she reluctantly pulled the plug and climbed out of the bathtub.

A thick pale blue flannel robe that zipped up the front was draped over the edge of the sink, along with a pair of fuzzy pink slippers. After Taylor had finished drying, she slipped into those, conscious she wore nothing underneath.

Russ was sitting at the kitchen table, waiting for her. "Where's Mandy?" she asked, doing her best to sound casual and composed, as if she often walked around a man's home in nothing more than a flimsy robe.

"She's on the phone, talking to Travis Wells's boy."

This must be the famous Eddie who had caused Taylor so much grief. Not knowing exactly what she should say or do, she walked over to the counter and filled her empty mug with coffee. She'd just replaced the pot when Russ's hands settled over her shoulders. He turned her around, and his eyes held her prisoner.

"I shouldn't have laughed." His voice was husky, his look regretful.

She lifted one shoulder in a delicate shrug. "I don't think you could have helped it—laughing was a natural reaction. I must have looked ridiculous."

"Do you forgive me?"

She nodded. Actually she hadn't been completely guilt-less in this fiasco. "You weren't to blame, either. I did it to myself with my stubborn pride. You're the rancher here, not me. I was a fool to think I could free that poor calf when you couldn't. I brought the whole thing on myself, but you were handy and I lashed out at you."

Russ lifted her chin with his index finger. "Did you mean what you said about hating Montana?"

Taylor didn't remember saying anything about the state, although she'd muttered plenty about Russ and his stupid cows and everything else she could think of to link with the rancher's life.

"Not any more than I meant what I said about every-thing else."

"Good." Russ apparently took that as a positive an-swer. He raised his finger from the underside of her jaw and slowly traced it over her cheek to her lips. His touch was unhurried and tender as if he longed to ease every moment of distress he'd caused her, intentionally or oth-erwise. His eyes didn't waver from hers, and when he leaned forward to kiss her, there wasn't a single question in Taylor's mind that this was exactly what she'd wanted.

His mouth settled over hers, and she sighed softly in hopeless welcome. His tongue prodded gently at the seam of her lips, and when she opened herself to him, he wrapped his arms more fully around her and pulled her closer. His kisses, as always, were devastatingly sensual. Taylor felt so mellow, so warm. Desire nipped at her senses, and she started to move against him, reveling in the feel of his solid strength against her softness. A sublime ache clawed at her, an ache that had been disquieting her from the time they'd first touched all those weeks ago.

"I could get drunk on you," Russ murmured in awe.

"It's the whiskey, remember?" she whispered back.

He shook his head, denying that this incredible sensation they shared could be in any way linked to the hot drink he'd given her earlier. His hands were in her hair, his lips at her throat, and the delicious, delirious feelings flooded her from all the places he was kissing and touching her.

Sliding her hands over the open V of his shirt, she wound her arms around his strong neck. He braced her against the counter and gently rotated his hips against her feminine mound, creating a whole new kaleidoscope of delectable sensations. Taylor let her head fall back as his mouth continued kissing and tasting her neck. He was pressed so close that she could feel the snap of his jeans. He was power. Masculine strength. Heat. She sensed in him a strength she had never known in any man. A hunger and need. One only she could fill.

His hands slipped over her buttocks, and he lifted her higher. His sighs grew deeper and more intense when he forced his mouth over hers with an urgency that from anyone else would have frightened her. The hunger she'd sensed in him seconds earlier flared like a raging fire as he slipped his tongue into her mouth. Taylor whimpered and strained against him.

Then, when she least expected or wanted it, Russ stilled his body and his hands and roughly dragged his mouth from hers. Not more than a second had passed when . . .

"Oops...oh, sorry," Mandy said as she walked into the kitchen. "I bet you guys want me to come back later. Right? Hey, no problem." She started backing out of the kitchen, her hands raised.

Russ's arms closed protectively around Taylor, but she broke free and forced a smile, although she wasn't certain she succeeded, and deftly turned toward the teenager. "There's no reason for you to leave."

"Yes, there is," Russ countered. "Taylor and I need to talk."

"No, we don't," she countered sharply. "We've finished . . . talking."

Russ tossed her a challenging glance that suggested otherwise, and Taylor, who never blushed, did so profusely.

"We haven't even started *talking*," Russ whispered for her ears alone. Taylor wasn't going to argue with him, at least not then in front of his sister.

Mandy cast her gaze to the linoleum floor and traced the octagonal pattern with the toe of her tennis shoe. "You've already talked to Russ?" she asked, darting a questioning look at Taylor. The teenager's soft green eyes implored her.

"Not yet," Taylor returned pointedly.

"Disappear for a while, Mandy," Russ urged, turning back to Taylor.

"No," Taylor returned forcefully. The minute the teenager was out of the room, the same thing would happen that always did whenever they were alone together. One kiss and they would each burst spontaneously into a passion hot enough to sear Taylor's senses for days afterward.

"No?" Mandy echoed, clearly confused.

"I haven't talked to Russ yet, but I will now."

The fourteen-year-old brightened and nodded eagerly. She pointed toward the living room. "I'll just wait in there."

"What's going on here?" Russ demanded once Mandy was out of the room.

"Nothing."

"And pigs fly."

"Sit down," she coaxed, offering him a shy smile. She took down a second mug and filled it with coffee, then carried it to the round oak table where Russ was waiting for her. His arm slipped around her waist, and she braced her hands against his shoulders.

"You're supposed to talk to me?"

She nodded.

"This has to do with Mandy?"

Once more Taylor nodded.

Russ frowned. "That was the reason you drove out to see me earlier, wasn't it?"

"Yes," she answered honestly. He kept his arms securely tucked around her waist, but he didn't look any too pleased. Taylor felt the least she could do was explain. "Mandy came to talk to me after school, and she asked me to approach you about . . . I agreed, but reluctantly."

"She isn't comfortable coming to me herself," Russ muttered, looking offended. "I've been trying as hard as I can to listen to her. I can't be any fairer than I'm already being. What the hell does she want now? To live in an apartment in town on her own?"

"Don't be silly," Taylor answered, riffling her fingers through his hair, seeking some way to reassure him. "Mandy knows you're trying to be patient with her, and she's trying, too. Only this was something special, something she felt awkward talking to you about, so she came to me. Don't be offended, Russ. That wasn't her intention and it isn't mine."

He nodded, but his frown remained. From the first, Taylor hadn't been sure she was doing the right thing by approaching Russ on Mandy's behalf. She'd only wanted to help, but regretted her part in this now. Look where it had led her! Two feet deep in mud and gook.

Positioning herself on his lap, she rested her arms over his shoulders, her wrists dangling. "You're right," she said, and kissed him long and leisurely by way of an apology.

His eyes remained closed when she'd finished, his breathing labored.

"Mandy," Taylor called, and was amazed how noticeably her voice trembled.

The teenager raced into the kitchen so fast that she nearly skidded across the polished floor. "Well?" she asked expectantly. "What did he say?"

"I haven't said anything yet," Russ growled. "I want to know what's going on here. First of all, Taylor drives out on the range to talk to me, and from what I can tell she's wearing your clothes."

"I couldn't very well send her out there in the dress she was wearing from school. I'm certainly glad I did insist she put on something of mine, otherwise look what would have happened!" Mandy declared, as if that explained the situation entirely.

"What's that got to do with this?"

"You were supposed to be back early today, remember," Mandy reminded him pointedly. "You said something about driving over to Bill Shepherd's this afternoon—"

"Oh, damn," Russ muttered, "I forgot."

"Don't worry. He phoned while you were out with Taylor, and I said that you'd probably run into some trouble. He's going to call you back later tonight."

Russ nodded abruptly. "Go on."

"Well, anyway, I thought it might even be better if Taylor talked to you when I wasn't around, so I suggested that she take the truck and—"

"How'd you know where I was?" Russ asked his sister, clearly confused.

"I heard you say something to Slim this morning about checking the south fence lines. I just headed Taylor in that direction. I knew she'd find you sooner or later."

Russ's gaze shot to Taylor. "She found me all right. Now tell me what it was you were going to talk to me about." The tone of Russ's voice suggested he was fast losing patience.

"Mandy, I'm holding him down, so you do the talking," Taylor said, smiling at Russ.

"You ask him, Taylor. Oh, please . . ." the teenager implored.

"Nope, you're on your own, kiddo."

"Will the two of you kindly stop playing games and tell me what the hell's going on here?"

"Okay," Mandy said, elevating her shoulders as she released a giant breath. She paused, pushed up the sleeves of her sweater and discharged an additional sigh, this one wobbly. "You know Travis Wells, don't you?" She didn't give Russ time to respond. "His son Eddie goes to school with me."

"Eddie's older than you."

"He's just sixteen," Mandy returned quickly. "Actually he's only twenty-two months and five days older than I am. If he'd been born in October and I'd been born in August we might even have been in the same class together, so there's really not that big a difference in our ages." She paused as though waiting for Russ to comment, or agree.

"All right," he said after an uncomfortable moment.

Mandy looked at Taylor pleadingly, silently asking her to explain the rest. Gently Taylor shook her head.

"Eddie's been talking to me lately . . . in the halls and sometimes at lunch. Yesterday he sat with me on the bus." This was clearly of monumental significance. "Eddie was the one who encouraged me to try out for the drill team, and when I made it, he said he knew I could do it.''

"That was him on the phone earlier, wasn't it?"

A happy grin touched the teenager's mouth as she nodded. "Yes—he wanted to know if I'd talked to you yet."

"About what?" Russ asked, then almost immediately stiffened. His torso went tense as his eyes narrowed. "You're not going out with that young man, Amanda, and that's the end of it. Fourteen is too young to date, and I don't care what Taylor says!"

If she hadn't been sitting on his lap, Taylor was certain Russ would have leaped to his feet. Framing his face with her hands, she stroked the rigid muscles of his jaw. "There's no need to yell. As it happens, I agree with you."

"You do?"

"Don't look so shocked."

"Then why were you coming to talk to me about it? Because I'll tell you right now, I'm not changing my mind."

"I'm not, either," she said softly, "so relax."

"Mandy?" Russ turned to his sister, his frown threatening a storm unless she explained what she wanted and quickly.

"Well...as you've already guessed, Eddie asked me out on a date. Actually he just wanted me to go to the movies with him."

"No way," Russ said without so much as a pause.

Mandy's teeth appeared over the top of her trembling bottom lip. "I thought you'd feel that way. That's the reason I went to Taylor, but she said that she agreed with you on this issue. Fourteen is too young to date, but while we were talking she came up with a . . . compromise. That is, if you'll agree."

"I said no," Russ returned resolutely.

Taylor felt she should explain. "When I was fourteen, my father—"

"You're from the city," he said in a way that degraded anyone who lived in a town with a population over five hundred. "Folks from the country think differently. I don't expect you to understand."

His harsh words rang in the kitchen like a slap in the face, and they felt like one to Taylor. She blinked back the sharp pain, amazed that he could offend her so easily.

"Russ," Mandy whispered, "that was a terrible thing to say."

"What? That Taylor's from the city? Hell, it's true."

"You're right, of course." She slipped off his lap and looked at Mandy. "Are my clothes in your room?"

The teenager nodded, her look repentant. "I hung them in my closet."

Drawing in a deep breath, Taylor looked to Russ. "I apologize. I should never have involved myself in something that wasn't my affair. I went against my better judgment and I was wrong. Now if you'll excuse me, I'll change clothes and get out of here." The way she felt at the moment, she never intended to come back. What Russ had said was true; he was only repeating what she'd been saying to him from the first. They were fooling each other if they believed there was any future in their relationship. For weeks they'd been building walls around the truth.

Mandy's bedroom was on the main floor, next to the bathroom. Taylor closed the door, walked over to the bed and sat on the end of the mattress. Her hands were trembling, and she felt close to tears. Raised voices came from the kitchen, but Taylor couldn't make out the words, and had no intention of even trying. If anything, she was regretful that she had become another source of discord between brother and sister.

Taylor was dressing when someone tapped politely on the door. "I'll be just a minute," she said, forcing a gay, cheerful note into her voice.

Slipping the dress over her head, Taylor walked barefoot across the floor and opened the door. Mandy came inside, her face red and stained with tears. She sobbed once and slipped her arms around Taylor's waist, burying her face in Taylor's shoulder.

"I'm sorry," she whispered. "I'm really sorry...it was so selfish of me to include you in this. Look what happened. First you fell in that terrible mud—"

"But, remember, I was wearing your clothes."

"I don't care about that." She lifted her head long enough to wipe the moisture from her face. "You could take all my clothes and put them in a mud hole if you wanted."

"If you don't mind, I'd prefer to keep away from any others."

Mandy's responding chuckle sounded suspiciously like another sob. "Russ should never have said what he did."

"But it's true," Taylor said lightly, pretending to dismiss the entire incident.

"Maybe so, but it was the way he said it—as if you're not to be trusted or something. You're the best thing that's ever happened to my foolish brother...and to me. All the kids in school are crazy about you and...and for Russ to say what he did was an insult."

"Don't be so hard on him. You can take the girl out of the city, but you can't take the city out of the girl," she joked, making light of Russ's harsh words.

"He'll be sorry in a little bit," Mandy assured her. "He always is. He's the only man I know who slits his own throat with his tongue."

"There's no need for him to apologize," Taylor said, hugging the teenager close. She broke away, slipped on her shoes and reached for her jacket. She draped the long strap of her purse over her shoulder. "Chin up, kiddo. Everything's going to work out for the best."

Mandy bobbed her head several times, silently agreeing with Taylor.

Russ wasn't anywhere around when Taylor walked through the kitchen and out the back door. For that she was grateful. She opened her car door, but didn't climb inside. Instead she found herself studying the house and the outbuildings that comprised the Lazy P, giving it a final look. Sadness settled over her like a heavy, water-soaked blanket, and she exhaled slowly.

This was her farewell to Russ and to his ranch.

If the day Taylor fell in the mud hole had been filled with problems, Russ decided, the ensuing ones followed suit. Only now, Russ determined, the difficulties he faced were ones of his own making.

Taylor had been on his mind for three days. Not that thinking about the schoolmarm constantly was anything new, but now, every time he did, all he could see were her big blue eyes meeting his, trying so hard to disguise the pain his words had inflicted. He'd been angry with Mandy for going to Taylor, and angry with Taylor for listening.

Unfortunately Russ didn't have time to deal with women problems. Slim and Roy had set up cow camp in the foothills, and Russ and two of his other hands were joining them. They were running cattle, branding the calves born on the range, vaccinating and dehorning them. It would be necessary to trim hoofs, too; otherwise the snow, which was sure to arrive sometime soon, would ball up on their feet.

There had been snow in the mountains overnight, and there was nothing to say the first snowfall of the season couldn't happen any day. With so much to do, he didn't have time to waste. The cattle buyers would start arriving soon, and Russ would be occupied with them, wheeling and dealing to get the best price he could for his beef.

He'd contact Taylor later, he decided, and apologize.

By the time Russ returned to the house, it was after seven and he was exhausted. Mandy was sitting at the kitchen table, doing her homework.

"Any calls?" he asked, hoping Taylor might have contacted him. He knew better, but he liked to think that would be the case.

"None."

Russ frowned. That fool woman was too stubborn for her own good.

"Dinner's in the oven," Mandy said, not looking at him. She closed her book and inserted her papers into her binder.

Russ took the plate from the oven with a pot holder and set it on the table. "I've been thinking over what you suggested about this thing with Eddie," he said while he took down a glass from the cupboard and poured himself some milk.

Mandy's round, hope-filled eyes lifted to search his. "It wouldn't be like a real date. I'd be paying my own way into the movies, and all Eddie and I would be doing is sitting together. It would be just as if we'd accidentally met there. If Eddie wants, I'd let him buy me some popcorn, but only if you think it would be all right."

"I'll drop you off and pick you up at the theater?"

"Right."

Russ pulled out a chair and sat down. "This is a sensible solution," he said as he spread the paper napkin across his lap. "I'm proud of you for thinking of it. This idea shows maturity and insight on your part, and I'm pleased you came up with it."

"I didn't."

Russ finished his first bite and studied his sister, who was standing across the table from him, her hand resting on the back of the chair. "Taylor's the one who mentioned it to me first. She tried to explain it to you.... Actually, we both did, but you wouldn't listen."

The bite of chicken-fried steak stuck halfway down Russ's throat, and he swallowed tightly before he could speak normally. "Taylor came up this this idea?"

"I think her parents were the ones who thought of it because she was telling me that's what they did with her and her sister when they were fourteen and boys began showing some interest in them."

"I see."

"Just think, Russ," Mandy murmured a tad sarcastically. "Taylor's parents are from the big city, and they managed to come up with this stroke of brilliance all on their own. Naw, on second thought, I bet someone from the country suggested it."

Normally Russ wouldn't have tolerated his sister talking to him in that tone of voice. The kid knew all the right buttons to push to raise his hackles. Only this time Russ didn't react as he usually did. The pressure that settled over his chest weighed more than several of the cattle he'd wrestled with that day.

His appetite gone, Russ pushed his plate away, planted his elbows on the table and stared straight ahead while uneasiness filled him.

He'd done it now. Taylor would probably never speak to him again. Unless...

* * *

Another lonely Friday night, Taylor mused as she sat at the kitchen table, a tablet and pen in hand. She owed everyone letters, and there wasn't any better time than the present.

She leaned back in the chair and read the lengthy epistle from Christy, chuckling over her youngest sibling's warmth and wit.

The doorbell chimed and, laying aside the letter, Taylor moved into the living room. A smiling Mandy stood on the other side of the door.

"Mandy? Is everything all right?"

"It's perfect, just perfect. Well, almost..." she said, beaming. She seemed in a hurry and glanced over her shoulder.

Taylor's gaze followed her young friend's, and for the first time she noted Russ's truck parked alongside the curb. He was sitting in the cab.

"Russ said I could meet Eddie at the movie and sit with him, but only under one condition, and I'm afraid that involves you."

Taylor wasn't certain she'd heard Mandy correctly. "I beg your pardon?"

"Russ seems to feel that Eddie and I are going to need a couple of chaperons."

"That's ridiculous."

"No, it isn't," Mandy insisted much too cheerfully to suit Taylor. "At least I don't mind if you guys sit on the other side of the theater from Eddie and me."

"You guys?"

"You and Russ, of course. He said the only way I can do this is if you agree to sit with him during the movie so that he doesn't look like a jerk being there all by himself."

"You can tell your brother for me—"

"Taylor," Mandy cut in, leaning forward to whisper as if there were a chance Russ might possibly overhear. "This is the only way Russ could think of to get you to talk to him again. He's really sorry for the way he acted and the things he said."

"Sending you to do his apologizing for him isn't going to work," Taylor said matter-of-factly. "Neither is this little game of blackmail."

Mandy thought about it for a moment, then nodded abruptly. "You know what? You're absolutely right!" Placing her hands on her hips, she whirled around to face the street. *"Russ!"* she yelled at the top of her lungs. A foghorn couldn't have been any louder.

Russ leaned across the cab of the pickup and rolled down the window.

"If you want to apologize to Taylor, you're going to have to do it yourself!" Mandy shouted. Her voice carried like a boom box, and Taylor was certain half the neighbors must have heard her. Her worst fears were confirmed when she noticed the lady across the street pulling aside her drape and peeking out.

"And furthermore, Taylor says she refuses to be blackmailed."

Taylor was mortified when the doors to two more homes opened and a couple of men stepped onto their porches to investigate the source of all the shouting.

"What are you going to do about it?" Mandy insisted.

By this time Russ had climbed out of the truck. He was wearing the same gray suit jacket with the suede yoke he'd had on the night of the Grange dance.

"Hey, Palmer, what are you going to do to the schoolteacher?" one of Taylor's neighbors heckled.

A couple of others came off their porches and onto the sidewalk. A low murmur followed Russ's progress toward Taylor.

"Hey, Russ, you're going to put her in her place, aren't you?"

Russ didn't answer until he reached the bottom of the steps. He looked straight at Taylor, then leaped up the stairs, taking three at a time. "You want a formal apology, then I'll give you one, but after that we're going to the movies."

Chapter Ten

I'm not going to the movies with you, Russ Palmer, and that's the end of it,'' Taylor vowed, and gently closed the door. Leaning against it, she turned the lock just to be on the safe side and returned to the kitchen where she'd started a letter to her sister.

She'd just sat down when she heard the faint strains of a guitar and someone singing, sadly off key. Good grief, it sounded like . . . Russ. Russ singing?

Deciding the only thing she could do was ignore him, Taylor returned her attention to her letter-writing project.

Apparently Russ wasn't going to be easily foiled, and when she didn't immediately appear, he countered by singing and playing louder. His determination showed through each word of his ridiculously maudlin song. He sounded terrible. Really bad, and his guitar-playing abilities weren't anything to brag about in her letter to her sister, either.

Covering her ears, Taylor scooted as low as she could in her chair, stubbornly ignoring him. The man's nerve was colossal. If she'd learned anything in her short weeks in Cougar Point, it was that cowboys didn't lack for arrogance. To even suggest that she would be willing to forget everything simply because he serenaded her was so ludicrous that Taylor found it downright comical.

It was then that the phone rang. Taylor answered it on the second ring, grinning at Russ's impertinence, despite her irritation.

"For God's sake," her neighbor shouted over the line, "do something, will you? His singing is making my dog howl."

No sooner had Taylor replaced the phone when it rang a second time. "My china's starting to rattle. If he's apologizing, kiss and make up before my crystal cracks." Taylor recognized the voice of Mrs. Fergason, the lady from across the street.

Grinding her teeth with frustration, Taylor tore across the living room and yanked open the door. "Stop!"

Russ took one look at her, paused and grinned broadly. He lowered the guitar, looking more than pleased with himself. "I see you've come to your senses."

"Either stop singing or I'm calling the police. You're disturbing my peace and that of my neighbors. Now kindly leave."

Russ blinked, apparently convinced he'd misunderstood her. "I wish it were that simple, but I owe you an apology and I won't feel right until I clear the air."

"Fine, you've apologized. Now will you kindly go?"

He rubbed his hand down the irregular contours of his jaw. "I can't do that."

"Why not?" Taylor jerked back her head hard enough for it to ache and loudly slapped her hands against the sides of her legs. "I can't believe you. Why are you doing this?"

"Because I'm falling in love with you."

The lump that immediately formed in Taylor's throat would have choked an alligator. This was the last thing she'd wanted. Living in Cougar Point was supposed to give her a chance to heal from one disastrous relationship, not involve her in another.

"Russ," Mandy called, leaning out the window of the truck, "hurry or we'll be late for the movie."

"Are you going or not?" Mrs. Fergason from across the street shouted at the top of her voice. "Decide, will you? *Jeopardy*'s about to start, and I don't want to miss seeing Alex Trebek."

Taylor was still too stunned to react. "Don't love me, Russ. Please don't love me."

"I'm sorry, but it's too late. I knew the minute you went headfirst into that mud hole that we were meant for each other. Now are you going to ruin Mandy's big night with your stubbornness, or are you going to the movie with me?"

If Taylor had had her wits about her she would never have agreed to this blatant form of blackmail, but Russ had taken all the wind from the sails of her righteousness. Before she fully realized exactly how she'd gotten there, she was inside the Cougar Point Theater, sitting in the back row with Russ, munching on hot buttered popcorn.

"We've got to talk," she whispered as the credits started to roll. She'd seen the movie months earlier, and although she'd enjoyed it, she wasn't eager to view it a second time, especially when forced to deal with the bomb Russ had so carelessly dropped at her feet.

Russ's large callused hand reached for hers, closing around her fingers. "We can talk later."

How she managed to sit through the entire feature film was beyond Taylor. Her mind was in a chaotic whirl. All too soon the final scene was showing and the dim lights returned. The theater started to empty.

Mandy raced up the aisle, the famous Eddie at her side. "Would it be all right if we went over to the bowling alley? Chris's mom and dad offered to buy everyone nachos. Lots of other kids are going."

"How long will you be?" Russ asked.

Mandy looked at Eddie. "An hour," the boy said firmly, as though he expected Russ to argue with him. The teenager's Adam's apple bobbed up and down a couple of times. He was over six feet tall and as lean as a telephone pole, yet Mandy looked at him as if he were a Hollywood heartthrob.

"All right," Russ said, apparently surprising them both. "I'll pick you up outside in exactly one hour."

"Thanks," Mandy said, and impulsively kissed Russ's cheek.

"That give us exactly one hour to settle our differences," Russ said, smiling over at Taylor, his eyes filled with silent messages.

By this time Taylor was certain she was suffering from a form of shell shock. It was as if her entire world were moving like the flickering frames in a silent movie. Everything had a jerky feel, and nothing seemed real.

"Where are we going?" she asked when Russ opened the truck door for her.

"Back to your place. Unless you object."

Russ had ignored every one of her objections from the moment they'd met, and there was nothing to prove he was going to change at this late date.

At the rate her evening was going, Taylor half expected her neighbors to file out of their homes and line the sidewalk, offering advice when Russ parked his truck outside her home. But all the excitement earlier in the evening had apparently tired everyone out. It wasn't even nine, and already most of the homes were completely dark.

"I'll make us some coffee," Taylor said, finding her voice. She unlocked the door, but before she could turn on the living-room lights, Russ gently twisted her around and pulled her into his arms.

He closed the front door and pressed her against it. Their eyes adjusted to the dark, and met. "Dear God, you're beautiful," he whispered reverently, as if in awe of her beauty. He lifted his hands to her hair, weaving the thick strands through his long, narrow fingers. Taylor felt powerless to stop him. She closed her eyes and savored the moment. Savored the incredible sensations Russ evoked within her.

"Please don't fall in love with me," she pleaded, remembering the reason for this discussion. "Don't love me."

"I can't help myself," he whispered, kissing the taut line of her jaw. "Trust me, Taylor, I wasn't all that pleased about it myself. You belong in the city."

"Exactly," she said, breathing deeply. It never seemed to fail: Russ would hold her and she'd immediately start to dissolve in his arms. Her breathing became labored, and her heart went on a rampage of its own. She tried to convince herself they were simply dealing with an abundance of hormones, but no matter how many times she told herself that, it didn't matter.

Russ couldn't love her. He just couldn't. Because then Taylor would be forced to examine her feelings for him.

She'd be compelled to face what she intuitively knew would be better left unnamed.

"You're a libber."

"You're a redneck."

"I know," he agreed, continuing to kiss her jawline, his mouth wandering down the side of her neck.

Listing their dissimilarities didn't seem to make much of a difference, however. Russ raised his head and traced the callused pad of his thumb across her lower lip. It was all Taylor could do not to moan. No man had ever evoked such burning need in her.

Taylor captured Russ's finger between her teeth and slowly drew it into her mouth, sucking lightly. He closed his eyes and smiled, then he sighed from deep within his chest.

With his hands cupping her face, he kissed her, and it was incredibly sweet, incredibly sexy. Every time Russ took her into his arms, he reduced all the disparities between them, took everything in their lives and boiled it down to the simple fact that they were man and woman.

His tongue swirled around hers in lazy circles that were nearly her undoing.

She gripped his wrists and held on tightly. "Russ, no more...please." With a strength she didn't know she possessed, Taylor broke off the kiss.

"I've only just begun," he warned.

His lips remained so close to hers that she inhaled his moist, warm breath.

"Why does everything come to this?" she pleaded. Her knees were slightly bent as she struggled to hold on to what little strength she still possessed.

"I don't know," he answered honestly. "I can't seem to keep my hands off you." As though to prove his point, he trailed a row of kisses across the curve of her shoulder while his hands were busy with the buttons of her silk blouse. Then, with maddening, unhurried movements, he unclasped her bra and spilled her full breasts into his palms. Their sighs mingled as Russ slanted his mouth over hers once more.

"Russ..."

"Not here...I know." His voice was so terribly husky Taylor barely recognized it. Without the least bit of trouble, he lifted her into his arms.

"What are you doing?" she demanded.

"Carrying you into the bedroom."

"No," she whispered, close to tears.

"Rhett Butler carried Scarlett into the bedroom—I can't do any less for you. I thought all women, even you feminist types, went in for this romantic stuff."

"We can't do this.... Russ, listen to me. If we make love, we're both going to regret it later." She was nearly frantic, longing to talk some sense into him. Talk some sense into herself. All the while she was chattering away, Russ was walking along the hallway toward her bedroom.

Her weight must have gotten to be too much for him, because he paused and leaned heavily against the wall. Before she could raise an argument, his ravenous mouth sought hers, his lips sliding back and forth over her with mute demand. Whatever objection Taylor was about to raise died the instant his mouth captured hers. She entwined her arms around his neck and boldly kissed him back, sliding her tongue between his lips in a lazy, erotic game.

"I thought that would quiet you down," he murmured triumphantly as he shifted her weight in his arms and carried her directly into the bedroom.

There was ample time to protest, ample time to demand that he stop, but the words, so perfectly formed in her mind, were never spoken. Instead she leaned her head against his shoulders and sighed heavily. She couldn't fight them both.

Gently Russ pressed her against the mattress. Taylor closed her eyes, hating this weakness in her. Savoring this same weakness. "I can't believe we're doing this."

"I can," he rebutted smoothly. "I haven't stopped thinking about it since the day we met. Hell, I haven't been able to stop thinking about *you*," Russ murmured, "day and night, night and day."

She smiled softly up at him and looped her arms around his neck. "You've been on my mind, too."

"I'm glad to hear it. But it's more than that," he continued between kisses. "I can't seem to rid myself of this need for you. I want to make love to you more than I've wanted anything in my life. Right here. Right now."

Taylor felt his moist breath against her cheek and sighed audibly as he began kissing her again, creating magical, mystical sensations. Scorching need.

Taylor's arms and legs felt as if they were liquid; they possessed no strength. Her mouth remained damp and swollen from his kisses when he lifted his head.

He trailed nibbling, biting kisses over her shoulder and lower. Much lower. Pausing, his breathing smooth and even, he reached her breasts, cupping their abundant fullness in his hands. Then he lowered his mouth and leisurely closed his lips around one taut nipple.

Taylor didn't realize her breasts could feel any tighter than they already did, and she whimpered softly at the avalanche of pleasure his lips brought her. He drew one beaded nipple deep into his mouth and laved it generously with his tongue, then sucked lightly.

She threaded her fingers through his hair, holding him against her.

Russ lavished attention on her, gently tugging at her satiny pink nipple between his lips, countering the tenderness with one hard, rough pull. Had Taylor been able to make a single sound she would have gasped with shock at the mild, unexpected pain. His action was immediately followed by a gentler, more tender sucking action. The sensations he produced were incredibly sweet. Incredibly exciting. Incredibly incredible.

She arched her back, seeking more and more. Her hectic movements appeared to please him. He raised his head, and his mouth moved over hers, tasting, kissing, rewarding her.

Her own fingers were busy now, struggling to release the snaps at the front of his shirt. Growing impatient, she gripped the material and pulled, satisfied only when she heard the responding burst as the snaps popped open. With her hands at his shoulders, she awkwardly eased the material halfway down his arms. Russ was apparently just as eager to be unfettered, and jerked off the western-style shirt in one abrupt movement. He tossed it carelessly onto the carpet and leveled his weight over her.

Taylor sighed anew at the satin-rich sensation of his bare skin rubbing against her own. She loved the feel of him, loved the way he held himself so his weight wouldn't be too much for her. She elevated her hips slightly and rotated the lower half of her body against him, parting her legs just enough to cradle the hard ridge of his sex. Desperate to touch him, she ran her long fingers over his bare shoulders, testing the firmness of his sculpted muscles.

No one had ever been so gentle or so patient with her. Ever. This cowman, this self-proclaimed redneck, appealed to all her senses, and she ached for him to possess her completely. All too frequently they'd been at odds with each other. In a battle of wit and words. In a clash of personalities. In a contest of wills.

Russ continued to kiss and hold her, to rain kisses over her face, then nuzzled her neck. Trembling, Taylor tried to immerse herself in his tenderness, but as hard as she tried, she couldn't seem to block out the fact that their lovemaking would only lead to pain. It had been months since she'd seen Mark, and she was still suffering, still aching. How could she do this to herself a second time when she was all too aware of the emotional aftermath?

She'd tried so hard to fight the attraction they shared. Yet here she was in bed, opening herself up to him in ways that would only lead to more pain, more doubts, more questions. She wasn't the type of woman who leaped into bed with a man just because it felt good.

"Russ...no more," she pleaded, pushing with all her strength against the very shoulders she'd been caressing only moments earlier. "Stop...oh please, we have to stop."

He went still, and slowly raised his eyes to meet her. They were darker than she'd ever seen them. Hotter than she'd ever seen them, but not with anger.

"You don't mean that." Lovingly, tenderly, he ran his hands over her face and paused when he discovered the moisture that wet her cheeks. Inhaling deeply, he reversed their positions so that she was sprawled atop him.

"You're crying."

Taylor nodded. She hadn't realized it herself until Russ had caressed her cheeks. His eyes questioned hers, filled with apprehension, misgivings. "I hurt you?"

"No...no." She placed the tips of her fingers on his cheek and slowly shook her head. "I can't make love with you.... I can't."

"Why not?" His voice was little more than a whisper, and gruff with anxiety. "I love you, Taylor." As if to prove his point, he kissed her again, gently, as though frightened that the deep, drugged kisses they'd shared seconds earlier would hurt her.

Twisting her head away, Taylor buried her face in the curve of his neck, dragging deep gulps of oxygen through her lungs. Russ's hands were in her hair, holding her close.

"I don't want you to love me," she sobbed. "If we continue like this, we'll fall in love and that'll only cause problems...not just for me, but for you, too."

"Not necessarily."

How confident he sounded, how secure, when she was neither.

"I've been in love before...and it hurts too damn much." She raised her head and swallowed back a sob. She hesitated and wiped the moisture from her cheek. "His name was Mark—and he's the reason I moved to Montana. I had to get away...and heal.... Instead, I met you."

The sobs came in earnest then. Huge heaving sobs that humiliated and humbled her. She wasn't crying for Mark; she was over him. Over them. Yet the tears fell and the pain gushed forth in an absolution she hadn't expected or wanted. Pain she'd incarcerated behind a wall of smiles, and then lugged across three states.

It was apparent Russ didn't know what to think. He patted her head several times, but he didn't say anything, and she knew her timing couldn't have been worse. Bringing up the subject of Mark in the middle of their lovemaking was insane, but she'd had to stop him. Stop them both. She'd had to do something.

Sobbing still, she rolled off him and the bed. Finding her footing, she gestured in his direction, pantomiming an apology and at the same time pleading with him to go. She needed to be alone.

"I'm not leaving you."

Unable to find the strength to continue standing, Taylor lowered herself down onto the edge of the mattress. "Do you always have to argue with me? Just for once couldn't you do what I want without a lot of discussion?"

"No." He edged himself behind her and wrapped his arms securely around her upper arms, holding her as carefully as he would a newborn. "I love you," he told her once more.

"Please don't."

"The choice was taken from me long ago."

"No...don't even say it. I couldn't bear it if you were to love me—I can't deal with it now. Please, try to understand."

His arms tightened slightly, pulling her back against him. "I wish it weren't so, for your sake, but my heart decided otherwise long before now. I can't change the way I feel now."

"I refuse to love you! Do you understand?" Taylor cried. "Look at us! We're a pair of fools. It won't work, and knowing that, why should we put each other through this? It doesn't make sense! Oh, Russ, please, won't you just leave me alone?"

"Loving you makes sense. We make sense. I'm going to love you, Taylor. Nothing will change that."

"Don't tell me that. I refuse to love you. Do you understand? Nothing has changed. Nothing!"

"It doesn't matter."

If Russ had been angry or unreasonable, it would have helped her. Instead he was gentle. Loving. Concerned.

While she was angry. Extraordinarily angry.

"Kindly leave me alone. Go!" She pointed the direction to the door in case he was unconvinced she meant what she said. "Stay away from me. Understand? I don't want to get involved with you."

Russ seemed to want to argue with her. He studied her for several nerve-racking moments, then sighed, reached for his shirt and stalked out of the room.

The whole house went quiet, like the hush before a storm. Russ had left; he'd done exactly what she'd asked. She should be glad. Instead, the ache inside her increased a hundredfold and the emptiness widened until she felt as if the void were as deep and wide as the Grand Canyon.

Clenching her stomach, Taylor sobbed while she gently rocked. Back and forth. Side to side. She wept for one man, whom she no longer loved. She wept for another she was afraid of loving too much.

She lost track of time. Five minutes could have been fifty-five; she had no way of telling.

A noise in her kitchen alerted her to the fact she wasn't alone. Curious, she righted her clothes, wiped her hands down her face and walked out of the bedroom.

Russ was sitting in the kitchen, his feet balanced on a chair, his ankles crossed. He was leaning back and drinking a cup of coffee. Apparently he'd made it himself.

"You didn't leave?"

"Not yet."

"What about Mandy?"

"I called the bowling alley and told her to kill another hour. She was more than grateful." Dropping his legs, he stood and poured Taylor a mug, then set it down for her. "Are you feeling any better?"

Embarrassed, she looked away and nodded. She would rather he'd left when she'd asked, but that would have caused other problems. Eventually she'd need to explain, and the sooner the better. "I'm . . . sorry. I shouldn't have yelled at you."

"Do you want to talk about it?"

"Not really." She pulled out a chair, sat down and reached for the coffee. Tightly cupping the mug, she warmed her hands with it.

"I suppose I should have suspected something," Russ said after a moment. "Someone like you wouldn't accept a teaching position in this part of the country without a reason. You didn't come to Montana out of a burning desire to learn about life in the backwoods of America."

Her gaze continued to avoid his, but she did manage a smile, although she was certain it was pitifully weak.

"So you were in love with Mark. Tell me what happened."

It was clear, at least to Taylor, that Russ wasn't going to leave her alone until he knew every torrid detail of her shame. How she wished he could leave well enough alone.

"How much do you want to know?"

"Everything. Start at the beginning, the day you met him, and work through to the day you moved to Cougar Point. Tell me everything—don't hold back a single detail."

Taylor closed her eyes, and her shoulders sagged forward. He wouldn't be satisfied with anything less than the whole truth and nothing but the truth. He wanted names, places, dates, details. Gory, pain-filled details. The man was wasted on a cattle ranch; he should have been working for the Internal Revenue Service.

"I can't," she whispered as the ache in her heart increased with the memories. "I'm sorry, Russ. If I were to talk to anyone about Mark, it would be you, but he's behind me now and I'm not about to dredge up all that pain."

"You wouldn't be dredging it up," he assured her. "You carried it along with you like a heavy suitcase all the way to Cougar Point. Get rid of it, Taylor."

"You think it's easy?" she responded tartly. "You're suggesting that I casually take what little remains of my pride and my dignity and spread it across the table for you to examine. I can't do it."

The heat in the kitchen felt stifling all of a sudden. Taylor stood abruptly and started pacing. "I wanted to get away...that's understandable, isn't it? I read everything I could find about Montana, and the idea of living here for a short time appealed to me. I thought...I hoped I could use these months to recharge my emotions, to mend."

"It hasn't worked, has it?"

She hung her head and exhaled slowly. "No."

"Do you know why?"

"Of course I know why," she cried, her voice gaining strength and conviction. "Meeting you has loused up everything. I wasn't in town a week and you were harassing me, goading me. I'd be a thousand times better off if we'd never met. Now here you are talking about loving me, and I'm so afraid I can't think straight anymore."

"Are you looking for an apology?"

"Yes," she cried, then reconsidered and slowly shook her head. "No."

"That's what I thought."

She reached for her coffee, downed a sip and set the mug back on the table. The hot liquid burned her lips and seared its way down the back of her throat. "I met Mark in my fifth year of college while I was student-teaching." She folded her arms around her waist and continued pacing. "His future was bright. Between working and school I didn't have a lot of time for relationships. For the first four years of my college education I might as well have been living in a convent."

"Why was Mark different?"

"I...don't know. I've asked myself the same question a hundred times. He was incredibly good-looking."

"Better looking than me?" Russ challenged.

"Oh, Russ, honestly, I don't know. It isn't as if I have a barometer to gauge the level of cute in handsome men."

"Okay, go on."

"There isn't much to tell you," she said, gesturing weakly with her hands as she continued pacing. "We became...involved, and after a couple of months Mark brought up the idea of us living together."

Russ frowned. "I see."

Taylor was sure he didn't; nevertheless she continued. "I loved him. I honestly loved him, but I couldn't seem to bring myself to move in with him. My parents are traditional, and I'd never come face-to-face with something that countered my upbringing so intensely."

"Mark wanted you to be his 'significant other'?"

"Yes. He wasn't ruling out the idea of marriage, but he wasn't willing to make a commitment to me, either, at least not then."

"Did you agree to this?"

It took Taylor a long moment to answer, and when she did, her voice was low and husky. "No. I needed time to think over the decision, and Mark agreed it was a good idea. He suggested that we not see each other for a week, and I concurred."

"And you decided?"

It seemed as though Russ's question had been shouted at her across a canyon, and the echo reverberated like a sonic boom close to her ears. "Yes...I reached an intelligent, well thought out decision, but it didn't take me a week. In fact, five days was all the time I required. Having made my choice, I decided to contact Mark. I'd missed him so much that I went over to his apartment the following evening after work...." The floor seemed to buckle, and she reached out and gripped the back of the chair so hard her fingers immediately started to ache. "Only Mark wasn't alone—he was making love with a girl from the office." The pain, the humiliation of the moment, was as sharp now as it had been several months earlier. "Correction," she said in a breathy whisper. "In his words, he was 'screwing' the girl from the office. But when he was with me, he was making love."

Russ stood and walked over to her side. As if she were the most priceless, delicate object in the world, he drew her into his arms and held her.

Bunching her hands into tight fists, Taylor resisted his comfort. The burning tears returned in force. Her breath seemed to stick in her throat and released itself with a moan, the kind a trapped and injured animal makes. "You don't understand," she sobbed. "You don't know...no one does. No one ever asked."

"I do," Russ whispered, brushing the tendrils from her face. "You'd decided to move in with him, hadn't you?"

Sobbing and nearly hysterical, Taylor nodded.

Chapter Eleven

Every part of Russ longed to comfort Taylor. He wasn't immune to pain himself. His mother had run off and left him when he was still a child and unable to understand what had driven her away, unable to understand why she hadn't taken him with her. Then several years later his father had met and married Betty. Mandy was born and Russ was just beginning to feel secure and happy when Betty had died. His father had buried himself in his grief and followed not long afterward. Russ had been left to deal with his own anguish, plus that of his young sister, who was equally lost and miserable.

Emotional pain, Russ had learned during the next few years, was a school of higher learning, the kind no ordinary teacher could instruct. It was the place where heaven sagged and earth reached up, leaving a man to find meaning, reconciliation and peace all on his own.

Taylor sobbed softly, clenching him. Russ closed his eyes and held her close. The ache he felt for this woman cut clear through his heart. Taylor had loved another man, loved him still. Someone who didn't deserve her, someone who didn't appreciate the kind of woman she was. The overwhelming need to protect and guard her consumed him.

Lifting her head, Taylor brushed the confusion of hair from her face. "I think you should go."

"No," he answered gently, his hands busy stroking her back. He couldn't leave her. Not now. Not like this.

"Please, Russ, I want to be alone. I need to be alone."

"You'll never be again," he promised her.

Her head sagged, and her long hair fell forward. "You don't understand, do you? I can't ... I won't become involved with you. I'm here to teach, and at the end of my contract I'm leaving. And when I do, I don't want there to be any regrets."

"There won't be. I promise you." Russ tried to reassure her, but when he went to kiss her, she broke away from him and moved to the other side of the kitchen as if the distance alone would keep her from him.

"It would be so easy to let myself fall in love with you," she whispered, and resolutely wiped the moisture from her cheeks.

Witnessing her pain was nearly Russ's undoing. He moved toward her, but for every step he advanced, she retreated two. He hesitated. "All I want to do is love you."

"No," she said firmly, holding out her arm as if that should be enough to stop him. Russ found damn little humor in her pathetic attempt. He wasn't the one who'd cheated on her. He wasn't the one who'd abused her love and her trust. He damn well refused to be the one who suffered as a result of the sins of another.

"Taylor, listen to me."

"No," she said with surprising strength. "There isn't anyone to blame in this but me. From the moment you and I met I realized we were in trouble, and we've both behaved like fools ever since. Me more than you. I've said it once, and apparently you didn't believe me, so I'm saying it again—one last time. I don't want to become involved with you."

"You're already involved."

"I'm not...at least not yet. Please, don't make this any more difficult than it already is. I'm not asking you this time. I'm begging you. If you care about me, if you have any feelings toward me whatsoever, you'll forget you ever knew me, forget we ever met."

Her words formed a long rope that encircled his chest like a lasso and then tightened like a barbed wire around his heart. If he cared for her? Dear God in heaven, he was crazy in love with her. His breath felt frozen in his chest.

"Am I supposed to forget I held you and kissed you, too?"

She nodded wildly. "Please...oh, please."

Russ rubbed a hand over the back of his neck several times while he contemplated her words. "I don't know that I can forget."

"You've got to," she wept, and her shoulders heaved with each pleading syllable. "At least try—and I will, too.... I promise I will." With that she leaned against the kitchen counter, covered her face with both hands and sobbed.

Walking out on her then would have been like taking a branding iron and searing his own flesh. Despite everything she'd claimed, and asked for, Russ moved to her side, gripped her by the shoulders and pulled her against him. She fought him as though he were the one responsible for hurting her so terribly. As if he were the one who'd abused her trust.

Her fists continued to beat against him, but he felt no pain. None. Nothing physical could hurt him as much as her words.

Gripping her by the wrists, he pinned her hands behind her back. She glared up at him, her eyes spitting fire. "Why do you have to make this so damn difficult? Why?"

"Because I don't give up easily. I never have." Not willing to enter into a battle of words with her, Russ hungrily sought her mouth. She twisted her head in an effort to avoid him, first right and then left, but Russ would have none of it. Trapping her wrists with one hand, he freed the other and gripped her chin, stilling her action.

Her deep blue eyes glared up at him as she vented her frustration and her anger with one fiery glare, daring him, taunting him. Russ refused to reconsider. Over the past several months he'd kissed Taylor any number of times, but this kiss was special. If she planned to throw him out of her life, then he fully intended for her to realize exactly what she would be missing.

He raised his hand and glided his fingertips over the soft contours of her face. He traced the stern, unyielding sides of her mouth, and with his hand at the small of her back, he pressed her forward until her body was perfectly molded to him. Her breasts met his chest, and he smiled softly at the way her nipples beaded and stabbed at him through the material of her blouse. With his feet braced slightly apart, the juncture between their legs rubbed against each other, and as he adjusted his height, she was fully aware of his powerful need for her. Then he buried his face in her sweet-smelling hair and inhaled deeply, savoring the special scent that was hers alone.

"Russ," she pleaded, rolling her head to one side, granting him access to her neck, "please don't do this."

He answered by slanting his mouth over hers. His hand freed her wrists as he crushed her against him. The fight had gone out of her, and her arms crept up his chest, pausing at his shoulders, her nails digging hard into his muscles. But Russ felt no pain.

His mouth moved hungrily over hers, and when her lips parted, he swept the inside of her mouth with his tongue.

Taylor reacted instantly with a sharp intake of breath. She wound her arms around his neck and pulled her seductive body hard and high against his own. Her femininity cradled his hardness, and she was soft and yielding in his arms.

Russ never intended the kiss to go so far. Without thought of what he was doing or why, driven by a need he didn't take time to examine, his hands frantically fumbled with the snap of her jeans and slowly lowered the zipper. The sound only added to his desire, his growing need. Shoving the material aside, he eased his hand between the flimsy barrier of her silk panties and her velvety, eager flesh. Taylor seemed to have stopped breathing. Then all at once she heaved one giant breath and slowly, as though against every dictate of her will, she parted her thighs.

Moaning, Russ deftly inserted a finger into the moist, hot folds of her womanhood. For a moment everything went still. The moon, the stars, the universe. He kissed her then, and it was as lusty as any she had ever known.

Taylor broke off the kiss and tossed her head back, gripped his shoulders hard, and of her own accord she started to move her hips, rotating them from side to side, twisting and turning. Her breath, his breath, became pants that echoed each other. Her eyes were squeezed closed as she bit unmercifully into her lower lip and, after a moment, shuddered wildly. Several impatient minutes passed before she began to drift back to earth, where Russ was waiting for her. He wrapped his arms around her and dragged her face to within inches of his own.

"Tell me you don't want this," he demanded in a husky whisper. "Tell me to leave you now."

Her shoulders sagged in abject defeat. "You've always been able to draw a physical response from me. This proves nothing.... Nothing." The words tumbled from her lips like an overturned barrel of apples. They fell hard, bruising his pride, injuring his heart.

Russ frowned and closed his eyes to the frustration that pounded at him like a jackhammer slamming against a slab of concrete.

With the last vestige of his pride intact, Russ moved away from her. "You don't mean that."

She started to sob then, and it took everything within Russ not to race back to her side. Even now the need to console her was nearly his downfall.

"Do I have to walk out on my contract, pack my bags and leave town to convince you I do mean it?" she implored. "Is that what it's going to take?"

"If you want me out of your life, just say so," Russ said, stuffing his hands into his pockets.

"What do you think I've been trying to do for the past several weeks? Stay away from me, Russ. Please. I've got to get my head straight. I'm not ready to fall in love again, not with you, not with anyone. Not... not so soon after Mark. I can't deal with this now... with you now. I may not be able to for a long time."

"All right," he said gruffly. "I get the message. Loud and clear." He stalked out of the kitchen, paused long enough in the living room to reach for his hat, and then he was gone.

But as he closed the door, he heard Taylor's sobs. He forced himself to walk away from her, but he hesitated on the porch and sagged against the pillar by the steps. Regret and pain worked through him before he was able to move.

Once more he was left to find meaning, reconciliation and peace in the aftermath of pain.

"Cody Franklin just pulled into the yard," Mandy told Russ as though it should be earth-shattering news and they should both run for the storm shelter.

Russ's reply was little more than a grumble, although his muscles tensed involuntarily. If Cody was stopping off to talk, Russ damn well knew who the subject was bound to be.

Taylor.

"I don't understand you," Mandy cried, clearly at the end of her wits. "Why don't you just call Taylor and put an end to this nonsense? You've been walking around like a wounded bear all week."

"When I need your advice, I'll ask for it," Russ bit out, and stood up so fast, he nearly toppled the kitchen chair. "Stay out of it, Amanda. This is between me and Taylor."

"She apparently isn't doing any better. She called in sick two days this week."

"How many times are you going to tell me that?" Russ barked. "It doesn't change anything. She doesn't want anything to do with me. Understand? If and when she does, she'll contact me. Until then it's as if we never met."

"Oh, that's real smart," Mandy said, her fists digging into her hipbones. "You're so miserable, it's like having a thundercloud hanging over our lives. You love Taylor and she loves you, so what's the big hang-up?''

"If Taylor feels anything for me, which I sincerely doubt, she'll let *me* know. Until then there's nothing I have to say to her." It gnawed at his soul to admit it, but the truth was the truth no matter how many different ways he chose to examine it. Taylor had claimed she wanted nothing to do with him often enough for him to believe her. He had no other choice.

"Dear Lord, save me from stubborn men," Mandy muttered as she headed for the door, pulling it open for Russ's friend.

"Howdy, Amanda," Cody Franklin said as he walked into the kitchen. He removed his cap and tucked it under his arm. He was dressed in his uniform—green shirt and coat and tan slacks. His gunbelt rode his hips like a second skin, as much a part of him as his arms.

"Hello, Cody," Mandy greeted, and craned her neck toward Russ. "I hope you've come to talk some sense into my bullheaded brother."

Cody looked suspiciously uneasy. "I'll try."

Mandy left the two of them alone, a fact for which Russ was eternally grateful. He didn't need a letter of introduction to deduce the reason for this latest visit on his friend's part. One look at Cody confirmed what Russ had already guessed. The deputy had stopped off as a courtesy before going out with Taylor himself.

"So you intend to date the schoolteacher?" Russ asked without waiting for the exchange of chitchat that was sure to lead to the subject of Taylor.

Cody's eyes just managed to avoid Russ's.

"Frankly, Cody, you don't need my permission. Taylor is her own woman, and if she wants to date you that's her business, not mine."

Having said as much, Russ should have felt relieved, but he didn't. He was a hairbreadth from losing his cool, and knew it, not that it made much difference. He'd been in a rotten mood from the moment he'd left Taylor's nearly a week before, and having Cody stop in unannounced hadn't improved his disposition any.

Cody must have sensed his mood, because he gave Russ a wide berth. He walked over to the cupboard, brought down a mug and poured himself coffee before he turned to face Russ.

"Sit down," Russ snarled, doing so himself. "I'm not going to bite your head off."

Cody grinned at that, and Russ noted for the first time that Cougar Point's deputy sheriff wasn't half bad-looking. Handsome enough to stir any woman's fickle heart. Plenty of women were interested in him, but he took his duties to uphold law and order in the community so seriously that no romantic relationship lasted longer than a couple of months. Now that he thought about it, Cody Franklin didn't smile often enough, and Russ knew why.

The two men went back a long ways, and Russ didn't want their friendship to end because of one stubborn woman. "You're planning on asking Taylor out, aren't you?" he demanded when Cody didn't immediately supply the answers.

Cody twisted around a chair and straddled it. "Actually, I hadn't thought to do anything of the sort. I asked her once already, earlier in the year, and she turned me down. The way I figured it, she wasn't interested. I was willing to leave it at that."

"Then why are you here?"

"Because the schoolteacher phoned me the other day and asked *me* to dinner Friday night." He paused to rub the side of his jaw. "I don't mind telling you, I was taken back with that. I've never had a woman ask me on a date."

"What did you tell her?"

Cody looked uncomfortable as he continued to stroke the side of his jaw. "I said I needed some time to think it over."

"So Taylor's the one who contacted you?" Russ was surprised at how forced his voice sounded.

"I've never had a woman approach me like this," Cody went on to say for the second time. "I'm not sure that I like it, either. It puts me in one hell of a position." He twisted the mug around in his hands several times, as though he couldn't locate the handle. "From what she said, I assume she intends to pay, as well. Hell, I've never had a woman pay for my meal yet, and I'm not about to start now."

"I don't blame you for that," Russ felt obliged to say, although he couldn't help being slightly amused. He didn't need a script to realize what Taylor was doing. She'd asked Cody Franklin to dinner to prove something to herself and possibly to him.

"You've got feelings for the schoolteacher, haven't you?" Cody asked, eyeing him suspiciously.

"You could say that," Russ confirmed, understating his emotions by a country mile. He had feelings all right, but he wasn't willing to have his friend examine the depth of them.

Cody grinned, revealing even white teeth. Crow's-feet marked the edges of his eyes. "So, what do you want me to say to her?"

"That you'll be happy to let her take you to dinner."

Cody hesitated before taking a sip of his coffee, as if that short amount of time would give order to his troubled thoughts. "You don't mean that."

"I do. Trust me, Cody, I've never been more serious in my life."

"But—"

"Taylor Manning doesn't want to have anything to do with me."

"And you believe her?"

Russ shrugged. "The way I see it, I don't have any choice. If she wants to go out with you, fine. That's her choice."

Cody shook his head. "I can't believe I'm hearing you right."

"You did. Trust me, dealing with this woman isn't easy."

Sipping from his coffee, Cody set it on the table and stood. "All right, but I have the feeling you're going to regret this."

Cody Franklin was as nice a man as Taylor had ever met. And a gentleman to boot. He'd arrived promptly at seven, dressed in a suit and tie. He really was handsome. Considerate. And Taylor was badly in need of some tender loving care. She'd just spent the most miserable week of her life, and an evening with a man who didn't pose the least bit of threat was exactly what she needed to pull herself out of this emotional slump. At least that was what she kept telling herself.

"I hope I'm not too early," Cody said, stepping into her home and glancing around. Apparently he approved of what he saw, because he shared a gentle smile with her.

"No, this is perfect." She reached for her coat, but Cody took it from her hands and held it open for her so she could slip her arms inside. That done, she reached for her purse.

"Before we leave," he said, and cleared his throat, "there's something I'd like understood. If we go to dinner, I pay the tab."

"But I was the one who invited you," Taylor reminded him, somewhat surprised at the vehemence with which he spoke.

"I pay or we don't go."

Taylor couldn't see any point in arguing. She'd butted up against stubborn male pride with Russ often enough to know it wasn't going to do her any good. "If you insist."

"I do."

Once that subject was cleared, they managed to carry on a decent conversation while Cody drove to the restaurant. He chose to eat at Larry's Place, the one halfway decent diner in town. Taylor hadn't eaten there before, but she'd heard the food was good, and the company was certainly right. As she suspected, a night out was exactly what she needed. For the first time in a week she found herself smiling and talkative.

The hostess escorted them to a table, and they were handed menus. It took Taylor only a moment to decide. Her appetite had been nil for days, and she was determined to enjoy this evening no matter what.

"Hello, Cody. Taylor."

Russ's voice came at her like boxing gloves. She sucked in a deep breath before turning toward the man who had dominated her thoughts all week. "Hello, Russ."

"Russ," Cody said, standing. The two exchanged handshakes. "It's good to see you again, Mary Lu."

"Have you met Taylor Manning?" Russ asked of his date. His hand was casually draped over the other woman's shoulder as he smiled down on her. "Taylor's the new schoolteacher."

"Pleased, I'm sure," Mary Lu said, sounding exactly that.

Taylor smiled and nodded. The woman didn't reveal a single shred of jealousy, she mused darkly. Surely by now everyone in town knew that there was something going on between her and Russ. The least the other woman could do was look a little threatened. But then why should she? Mary Lu was the one with Russ. Taylor was the one with Cody Franklin.

Cody reclaimed his seat. "Would you two care to join us?"

Taylor's heart shot upward, catching halfway up her throat as alarm filled her. Seeing Russ with another woman was painful enough without being forced to make polite conversation with the couple throughout the remainder of the evening.

"Another time," Russ said after a moment. His thoughts apparently reflected her own.

Taylor was so grateful, she nearly leaped from her chair, threw her arms around Russ's neck and thanked him with a kiss. It wasn't until Russ had left the table that she realized how tight and tense she'd been holding herself. Smiling in Cody's direction, she forced herself to relax. Pressing her elbows on the tabletop, she leaned toward her date. "So how long have you been in law enforcement?"

"Since I graduated from college," he answered, but his concentration wasn't focused on her. Instead, his gaze followed Russ and Mary Lu to the other side of the restaurant.

His frown disturbed her. "Is something wrong?"

"I don't know yet."

Taylor sighed and reached for her water glass. This whole evening was a mistake. She'd phoned and asked Cody to dinner for two important reasons. The first and foremost was simply because she was lonely, and the thought of spending another weekend alone was more than she could bear. The second and less important reason was to prove something to herself, and possibly to Russ. Only what she'd hoped to accomplish was lost on her at the moment.

Cody reached for his coffee. "You're in love with him, aren't you?"

This man certainly didn't pull any punches. The least he could have done was lead into the subject of Russ Palmer with a little more tact. Taylor toyed with the idea of pretending she didn't know who he was talking about, but that would have been ridiculous.

She lowered her gaze to the tablecloth, which was protected by a thick sheet of polyethylene. "I don't know if I love him or not."

"What's there to know? I saw the look in your eyes just now. Russ walked in with Mary Lu, and I swear you nearly keeled over."

"You're wrong. I was mildly surprised, that's all."

"It bothers you that he's with Mary Lu?"

A smile touched the edges of her mouth while she considered the question. "Not really. I wasn't expecting to see him. If I reacted, which I don't think I did, it was due to that and that alone."

"So what are you going to do about it?"

"Do about what?" Taylor wasn't sure she understood the question.

"The way you feel for Russ."

"I'm not going to do anything." She didn't need time to think over that decision. It had been made for her weeks earlier. All the arguments she'd put forth, time and time again, crowded her mind. They shouted back and forth to each other, causing distant echoes in the deepest chambers of her mind. Yet she couldn't force her eyes away from Russ, couldn't stop gazing at him with an emotional hunger that left her trembling and weak.

"He loves you, too," Cody whispered. He reached across the table and took hold of her hand. "I don't know what it is that drove you two apart, but I'm here to tell you right now, it's eating him alive." His smile was gentle, concerned. "It seems to be having the same effect on you, too."

"It's not that simple," she whispered.

A long moment passed before Cody spoke a second time. "Nothing worthwhile ever is."

"Taylor, do you realize what time of the night it is?" her sister, Christy, groaned after she answered the phone on the fifth ring.

"I'm sorry... I should have checked," Taylor whispered, feeling utterly foolish and completely miserable.

Christy's loud yawn sounded over the wire. "It's after three! What are you doing phoning at this ungodly hour? Are you all right? You're not in any trouble, are you?"

If only Christy knew! "I... was calling to see if you were going to be free next weekend."

"Are you flying home? Oh, Taylor, it would be so good to see you again. I can't believe how much I miss you. Paul, Jason and Rich, too. Mom and Dad don't say much, but everyone knows they feel the same way."

"Don't get your hopes up. I'll be in Reno, and I thought that, well... I was hoping that I could talk you into joining me. As I recall, there are a bunch of cheap flights out of Sea-Tac and I thought you could meet me in Nevada."

Christy released her breath on a slow, disgruntled sigh. "I can't. I'm really sorry, but there isn't any way I could swing it at this late date. What will you be doing in Reno?"

"Nothing much. The drill team is competing there, and I volunteered to be a chaperon . . . but apparently the team will be tied up for two days and I'm going to have a lot of time to kill. I thought it would be fun if we got together."

"All right, Taylor," Christy said after a tension-filled moment. "What's wrong? And don't try to feed me that line about nothing troubling you. The last time you called me at three o'clock in the morning was when . . . I'm sure you remember."

"This doesn't have anything to do with Mark."

"Thank God for that." Her voice lowered slightly with concern. "What's wrong?"

Taylor reached for a tissue and loudly blew her nose. "I . . . think I'm in love."

Christy groaned. "You've got to be kidding. Who?"

"His name is Russ Palmer and he owns a cattle ranch."

"I was afraid of that. I read your last letter to Mom and Dad and it was full of that cowboy! It was Russ this and Mandy that. Taylor, dear heart, take control of yourself. You don't want to spend the rest of your life on a ranch out in the wilds of Montana, do you?"

"Of course not. Trust me, I'm not all that keen on this myself," Taylor sobbed. "The last thing I even intended to do was fall in love—especially with someone who thinks just like Dad."

"Your cowboy is convinced women shouldn't have the right to vote?" Christy asked, aghast.

Taylor started to laugh even while she was crying. "He said he doesn't care if we vote. It's females holding public office that bothers him."

"Dear merciful God. Listen, Taylor, you're my sister and my dearest friend. What you feel isn't love. It's a natural and common emotion following the breakup of any romance."

"That's what I thought . . . at first."

"You weren't wrong. For the majority of your life your judgment was as sound as a judge's. Nothing has changed all that much. When you come out of a long-term relationship, there's an emptiness that's left and the normal reaction is to immediately fill that emptiness."

"I don't think that applies to this case," Taylor argued. In the beginning she'd assumed the same thing, but not any longer. This ache she felt went deeper than anything she'd known.

"You've spent the past six weeks in a town where no merchants accept American Express," Christy reminded her. "Trust me, Taylor, this thing with the cowboy is all due to what happened with Mark. You're away from your family for the first time. You're lonely and vulnerable, and it's only natural to find yourself attracted to another man. I know I would if the situation were reversed."

"You would?"

"Of course," Christy said smoothly and with conviction. "Just hold on for another week, and once you're in Reno, where there are real stores and real people, then you can reevaluate your feelings. I'm sure the crisp, clean air will help clear your mind."

"Do you honestly think so?"

"I know so," Christy said without revealing the least qualm. "Now take two aspirin, go to bed and call me next week when you get back from Reno. Ten to one you're going to think a whole lot differently than you do tonight."

"All right," Taylor said, and exhaled sharply. After a few moments she replaced the receiver, convinced her sister was right.

The next week flew past, the days blending smoothly into each other as Taylor threw herself into her job. Friday afternoon, her suitcases packed, she headed for the school bus and the twenty girls that comprised the Cougar Point High School Drill Team.

The first girl she saw was Mandy, who flew across the yard and hugged Taylor close. "I'm so pleased you're going with us."

"Me, too," Taylor said, meaning it.

Mandy reached for Taylor's suitcase, setting it beside the others. "Everyone's here except the driver." She paused and rolled her eyes. "But then he's always late."

The girls gathered around Taylor, and soon they were chatting away like old friends. Taylor knew a majority of the team members as well as their coach.

"Is everyone ready?" a male voice called out.

Taylor recognized it immediately as Russ's. She swallowed tightly and turned toward him, frowning. "What are you doing here?" she demanded.

He tossed one suitcase into the compartment on the side of the bus. "The same thing as you," he countered without the least bit of animosity. "You're a chaperon, and I happen to be driving the bus."

Chapter Twelve

It wasn't the twenty boisterous, exuberant high school girls who were driving Russ crazy. They sang, they cheered and they shouted as he drove the school bus across three states.

No, it wasn't the girls who were giving him trouble—it was Taylor. Taylor, who laughed and sang. Taylor, who joked and teased as if she hadn't a care in the world.

Each and every one of those high school girls adored her. The problem was—so did Russ.

Other than their brief exchange before they'd boarded the bus, she hadn't said more than a handful of words to him. True, there hadn't been a whole lot of opportunity. They'd stopped in Billings for something to eat and she'd sat in a booth surrounded by teenagers. Russ had been left to eat with Carol Fischer, the drill team coach, and another of the chaperons. Carol and he had exchanged a handful of pleasantries, but the entire time they were eating, Russ had found his gaze drawn again and again to the table next to his where Taylor was seated.

The woman was slowly but surely driving him crazy. If matters continued the way they had for the past two weeks, Russ was likely to find himself a candidate for the loony bin by the end of his four-day venture.

He would have liked nothing better than to get Taylor alone for a few hours. Then, and only then, would he have the chance to talk some sense into that stubborn head of hers.

Okay, she'd made a mistake and fallen in love with the wrong man. Everyone suffered an error in judgment at one time in their lives, but that was in the past and Russ was very much in the present. Although he told himself exactly this a hundred different times and in as many different ways, the thought of Taylor aching, wanting, crying over another man felt like the serrated edges of a knife slicing directly into his heart. It hurt so damn much that for a moment or two he wasn't able to breathe normally. Hell, he hadn't been breathing normally from the second he'd stumbled upon Taylor in the five-and-dime last September.

The long, lonely miles sped past. The girls gave up singing even before they left Montana. Around midnight the only one aboard the bus who wasn't sleeping was Russ.

"Do you want some coffee?"

The soft female voice from behind him sounded suspiciously like an angel's, Russ mused, grinning, when in actuality it belonged to Taylor.

"Russ?"

"Please." He waited to speak until she'd poured him some and he'd sipped it, appreciating the way it revived him. "I thought everyone was asleep."

"They are."

"What's keeping you awake?" He'd love it if she admitted he'd been in her thoughts for two desolate weeks and that she couldn't let another hour pass, or even another second to mark time without telling him how she felt.

"I never could sleep in a moving vehicle."

"Oh," he said, doing a poor job of disguising his disappointment. He should know by now Taylor wasn't going to fulfill his fantasies by saying all the things he longed to hear.

"How have you been?"

Two weeks, he mused darkly, frowning. They'd barely said a word to each other in all that time and she was asking about his general health!

Briefly he wondered what she'd say if he told her he wasn't sleeping well, his mood was sour and he couldn't sit down to a single meal without suffering from indigestion afterward. All these ailments he attributed entirely to her bullheadedness.

"I'm fine," he grumbled instead. "How about you?"

"Fine, just fine."

"Now that we've got that settled, what else would you like to talk about? The weather seems a safe enough subject, doesn't it?"

"I . . . I think I'll go back and check on the girls."

"You do that," he muttered, then immediately wanted to kick himself for being such an idiot. At least Taylor had been willing to talk to him, which was one hell of a lot better than the strained silence that had existed between them up until this point.

It wasn't until midafternoon the following day that they pulled into the congested streets of Reno. The girls were leaning out the window, shouting at tourists, while Carol and the other adults attempted to quiet down their rampant enthusiasm.

Carol and Russ had traded off driving, but like Taylor, Russ wasn't one to sleep well in a moving vehicle. He leaned back, shoved his hat low over his face and did a fair job of pretending, but he hadn't slept a wink in well over twenty-four hours.

When Russ pulled into the parking lot of Circus Circus, the hotel where they were booked, he heaved a giant sigh of relief. He was exhausted, mentally and physically. With the help of two bellboys, he unloaded the ton of luggage the girls had found indispensable for this short trip. While he was busy with that, Carol and the other chaperons, assisted by the entire drill team, checked in. By the time he was finished, Carol handed him his room key and suggested he get some sleep.

Russ didn't need to be urged twice. He damn near fell asleep in the elevator on the way up to his floor. Taylor and several of the girls rode up with him, and just before he entered his room, Russ noted that she had been assigned one on the same floor.

Some of the aching tiredness left him when he realized Taylor would be sleeping down the hall from him. Not bothering to unpack his bag he tossed his hat onto the small table and collapsed on top of the mattress. Bunching up the pillow, he closed his eyes and savored the quiet, the peace. It wasn't until sleep crowded the edges of his mind that he realized the lazy grin he wore was due to the fact that he had two whole days in which to convince Taylor she was in love with him.

Taylor couldn't remember a time when she was more exhausted. Other than brief stops the bus had spent nearly twenty hours on the road, and she hadn't gotten more than a catnap the entire distance. Carol, bless her dear heart, had insisted that Taylor go upstairs to bed while she and the assistant coach, who was also serving as a chaperon, managed the girls. Taylor didn't offer a single argument.

From the moment they pulled into the hotel, the girls' schedule was jam-packed. In less than two hours they were meeting with several of the other out-of-state teams, who would also be competing the following day, for a social. Then, the first thing the next morning, Carol would be driving the drill team to a local high school and they'd be sequestered the entire day until their performance, which was scheduled late that evening. After a good night's sleep, they'd be back on the road again, heading home to Montana.

Yawning, Taylor ran a tub of hot bathwater and soaked in it, struggling the entire time to stay awake. When she was finished, she crawled between clean, crisp sheets, already half asleep.

There was noise and confusion around her for part of the time, since her room adjoined one with teenagers, but she hardly noticed. She woke at eight the following morning, just in time to see the team off and wish them well.

"You're coming to watch us, aren't you?" Mandy pleaded.

"Wild horses couldn't keep me away," Taylor promised.

"Do you think Russ will want to come?"

Taylor nodded. "I'm sure of it."

Beaming, Mandy hugged Taylor close and then rushed to join her teammates.

Once the Cougar Point High School Drill Team had departed the hotel, Taylor wandered downstairs, where a majority of the gambling took place. Bells jingled and smoke rose as a sacrificial offering to the unpredictable gods of good fortune and chance. Row upon row of slot machines lined the brightest, reddest carpeting Taylor had ever seen.

She had never been one to gamble much, but the excitement that crackled across the room like static electricity lured her toward the slot machines.

Trading her hard-earned cash for several rolls of nickels, she reached for a cardboard container and picked out a one-armed bandit at the end of a long row of identical machines.

"A fool and her money are soon parted," she muttered, pulling up a stool and plopping herself down.

She inserted three nickels and gingerly pulled down on the handle. Oranges, plums and cherries whirled around in a blur, then came to an abrupt halt.

Nothing.

She tried again and again and was rewarded by several minor wins. Two nickels here, ten there.

Someone slid onto the stool next to hers, and when she glanced over, a ready smile on her lips, her eyes clashed with Russ's. He looked well rested and so devastatingly handsome that her breath jammed in her throat from just looking at him. The lazy, off-center grin that he offered her was more potent than any drink she could have requested.

"How are you doing?" he asked.

"Fine...good, real good." She quickly plopped three more coins into the appropriate slot and pulled the lever with enough energy to dismantle the machine.

"How much have you won?"

She glanced down at the small pile of nickels and realized that he hadn't been inquiring about the state of her health, but on her luck.

"Actually, I think I'm out a couple of bucks."

He grinned. "I'm down about the same. I don't suppose I could talk you into having something to eat with me? You wouldn't consider that a breach of goodwill, would you?''

"I…think that would be fine." Taylor didn't know how a grown woman, a college graduate to boot, could be so flustered around one man. The way her heart was jitterbugging around inside her chest, one would assume Russ had asked her to join him in bed instead of asking her to sit across the table from him in a restaurant.

Neither one of them appeared to have much to say until after they were seated by the hostess and handed menus.

Russ chose quickly and set his aside. "So how did your dinner with Cody Franklin go last weekend?"

"Cody's a wonderful man," she answered, glancing over the top of the plastic-coated menu. Their eyes met briefly, and Taylor noted that Russ's had darkened. Quickly she switched her gaze back to the list of breakfast entrées.

"Then you plan on seeing him again?" Russ demanded. Then he shook his head. "I'm sorry. I didn't have any right to ask you that. Whom you choose to date is your business."

Actually, she'd decided not to date Cody again, but not because she hadn't enjoyed his company. The sheriff's deputy had been the perfect gentleman all evening. After they'd left the restaurant, she'd invited him in for coffee and he'd accepted, but to her dismay she discovered that their entire conversation then, as it had through most of dinner, centered on Russ. Cody hadn't kissed her goodnight, nor had he asked her out again. Why should he, Taylor mused? She'd spent the entire evening with one man, longing to be with another.

The waitress came by for the order and filled their coffee cups. Taylor took a sip of hers, and decided if Russ could question her, then she should feel free to inquire about his own evening out. She carefully returned the cup to the saucer. "How was your dinner with Mary Lu Randall?"

"Great," Russ answered quickly. "She's a wonderful woman. The salt of the earth."

Taylor's throat constricted painfully as she nodded. Everything Russ said was the gospel truth. Mary Lu Randall was known as a generous, unassuming woman.

"I won't be seeing her again, though," Russ muttered, drinking his coffee.

Against everything she'd striven to prove to this man, Taylor sighed with relief. "You won't? Why not?"

Russ set his coffee cup down hard enough to attract attention. The sound of ceramic scraping against ceramic caused several heads to turn in their direction. Russ glanced apologetically at those around him.

"Why?" he demanded in a heated whisper. "Do you honestly need me to explain the reason I won't be dating Mary Lu again?" He tossed his head back and glared at the ceiling as though silently pleading for patience. "Because I'm in love with you is *why*. In addition, you've ruined me for just about any other woman I might happen to meet."

"I've ruined you?" she echoed vehemently. She leaned toward him, managing to keep her voice low enough not to attract attention.

The waitress delivered their meals, and Russ dug into the fried eggs as though he hadn't eaten in a week. He'd finished off both eggs before Taylor had finished spreading jelly across her toast, which she did with sharp, jagged movements.

"I would have thought Mary Lu was perfect for you," she said, unwilling to let the subject drop. "She's sweet and gentle and *submissive*, and we both know how important that is to a man of your persuasion.''

"I used to think that was what I wanted until I met you," he mumbled, and stabbed his fork into his fried potatoes. "I'll be damned if you didn't ruin me for decent women."

"Ruined you for decent women?" Taylor cried, not caring whose attention she drew.

"That's right. *You.* This is all your fault, with your feminist talk. No woman ever challenged and dared me the way you do, and I'm having one hell of a time adjusting my thinking. Compared to you, every other woman has the same appeal as watered-down soup." He jammed his index finger against the top of the table before continuing. "Mary Lu's probably one of the nicest women in Cougar Point, and any man she married would consider himself damn lucky."

"But it won't be you," Taylor stated, hating the way her heart gladdened with the information.

"How can it be when I'm so crazy about you?"

The irritation drained out of Taylor as quickly as it had risen. She set her slice of toast aside and dropped her gaze. Sadness permeated her, and she discovered she was close to tears. "I wish you wouldn't say that."

"Why? Because you don't like hearing it? Fine, I won't say it again, but that isn't going to change a damn thing. If you want to put us both through this hell, then go ahead. There isn't a thing I can do to stop you, but I love you, Taylor, and that's not going to change. Not for one hell of a long time."

"But I don't want you to love me."

"Don't you think I know that? Trust me, lady, if I had my choice, you're the last woman I'd willingly fall in love with. Do you honestly think I need this aggravation in my life? If so, guess again.''

"There's no need to be so angry.''

Russ pushed his near-empty plate aside and downed the last of his coffee in a single gulp, apparently doing his best to ignore her.

"Thank you for breakfast,'' Taylor said, pushing her own plate aside after a moment. She'd only managed a handful of bites. The toast she'd so carefully spread with jelly remained untouched.

"You're welcome.'' Leaning back in his chair, Russ rubbed a hand over his eyes. When he drew his hand away, it was clear that he was forcing himself to put their disagreement behind him. He smiled and lowered his gaze. "What are your plans for today?''

"The first thing I'm going to do is shop. There's a special fingernail hardener I need to find with epoxy,'' she said, glancing down at her carefully groomed nails. "Not a single store in Cougar Point carries it.''

"I thought they used epoxy in glue.'' Russ frowned. "If you want to go spreading that stuff all over your pretty nails, far be it for me to stop you.''

"Thank you,'' she said graciously, resisting the urge to roll her eyes. "After that, I thought, since I was in town, I'd pick up a few other things just for the sheer joy of using my American Express.''

Russ chuckled. "Would you mind if I tagged along? I don't have anything better to do.''

It didn't take Taylor long to decide, although he made it sound as if it were a choice between shopping with her and visiting the dentist. "I'd enjoy it very much.''

Over the course of the past few weeks and all the minor disagreements that had plagued them, Taylor had forgotten what pleasant company Russ could be. He was good-natured and patient to a fault as she dragged him from one store to the next. He was more than tolerant while she tried on a series of dresses, and after she chose one, he went with her to the shoe department and helped her pick out a comfortable pair of heels.

Taylor tried to return the favor and helped him choose new work shirts. Russ seemed to be of the opinion that if he found one shirt that suited him, he might as well buy five exactly like it. Taylor took delight in convincing him otherwise.

"Where would you like to go for lunch?" Russ asked four hours later. His arms were loaded with a large number of packages as he led the way down the street.

"Since you asked," Taylor said, smiling up at him, "I'm dying for a good pepperoni pizza, only—"

"Only what?"

"Only my favorite pizza place doesn't have any inside seating."

Russ looked at her as if she were deranged. "How the hell do they do business then?"

"It's take-out and delivery only."

"All right," he said, mulling over this information. "Then I suggest we go back to the hotel. You can drop off the packages in your room while I phone and order one large pepperoni pizza."

Taylor agreed without realizing what she'd done until it was too late. After returning to her room, she dropped her packages on top of the double bed, then sat on the edge of the mattress while she mulled over this latest development. She'd willingly agreed to join Russ in his room. In the middle of the day. With no one else around.

Walking into the bathroom, she ran a brush through her hair. She toyed with the idea of finding an excuse, phoning Russ's room and canceling the whole thing. The hotel was filled with restaurants. The food was good and so reasonably priced that it was a shame to order out.

Taylor slumped against the side of the bathroom sink and dejectedly closed her eyes. Who was she kidding? Certainly not herself. She was in love with Russ and had been for weeks. They had no business falling in love, but it had happened, and instead of fighting it so hard she should be grateful. Her attitude should be one of thanksgiving to have happened upon a man as fundamentally honest as Russ. Comparing the cattleman to Mark made her male chauvinist rancher look like a knight in shining armor.

Five minutes later she knocked on Russ's door. He let her in and had apparently been having second thoughts of his own. He marched to the other side of the room as though he feared she was carrying a dangerous Third World virus.

"I phoned that pizza place and ordered," he said, striving to sound casual and failing. He tucked his hands into his pockets as if he suddenly didn't know what to do with them. "They said they'd be here in thirty minutes or less." As if it were of vital importance, he checked his watch. "That gives them nearly twenty-five minutes."

"Good," Taylor said, walking farther into the room. His was almost identical to her own. One queen-size bed, a dresser, one small table and two chairs.

"Make yourself at home," he said, pulling over a chair. Then he walked around the bed as if they should both pretend it wasn't there.

"That was quite a morning we had, wasn't it?" he asked, rubbing his palms together. Heaving a giant sigh, he whirled around and faced her. "Listen, Taylor, this isn't going to work. If you want to have your pizza fine, but I've got to get the hell out of here."

"You don't have to leave," she said as she sauntered across the room, making sure her hips swayed just a fraction more than normal. When she turned to look at Russ, she was well rewarded for the little extra she'd put into her walk. His jaw was tight, and the edges around his mouth had whitened. His hands were knotted into fists at his sides.

"I...don't think you understand," Russ ground out.

She moved close so that she was almost directly in front of him. Standing on the balls of her feet, she raised her arms and looped them around his neck, then molded her body against his.

Russ held himself completely rigid. He raised his hands and closed them around her wrists, ready to pull her away from him. For some unexplained reason he hesitated. His gaze was hot and questioning when it locked with hers. "Just what kind of game are you playing?"

"The seductress. How am I doing?"

Russ's gaze narrowed, and she noted that his breathing had become short and choppy. "Good. Real good."

She sighed and sagged against him. "Did you notice that I'm not wearing a bra?"

"I noticed first thing," he responded, not sounding anything like himself. When she least expected it, he startled her by gripping her by the shoulders and pushing her away from him.

Taylor gasped. He didn't hurt her as much as surprise her. His eyes darkened, and he glared down on her, his look a mixture of doubt and wonder.

"What are you saying? That you want us to make love? Is that it?"

She didn't respond right away, not because she didn't know the answer. It was just that saying it out loud, admitting that making love was exactly what she'd had in mind, sounded so cold and calculating.

"Do you love me?"

Once more she found herself lost, the words confusing her before they even reached her lips. Before she could tell him everything, before she could explain everything that was in her heart, Russ released a jagged sigh and hauled her back into his arms.

His hands were in her hair, and his mouth was seeking out hers. "It doesn't matter," he whispered brokenly. "I love you enough for the both of us. It doesn't matter," he said again, just before his hungry lips claimed hers.

The passion between them was explosive. A forest fire of sensation seared her senses. Tears clouded her eyes and fell without restraint down her face. But these were tears of joy, tears of thanksgiving and discovery, surging deep from within her heart.

"I love you, I love you," she chanted silently as she felt the tremors that went through Russ. He pulled her flush against him and held on to her as if he'd jerked her from the jaws of death and feared losing her a second time.

Taylor buried her face in the column of his neck, and her breath fanned his throat. Unable to hold still, she moved against him, and her nipples, hard with need, stabbed at him through the silklike material of her blouse, while the lower halves of their bodies strained against each other.

Russ's mouth was hard over hers, masterful, passionate, his need as fierce and demanding as her own. Feverishly he tore his mouth from hers, lifted her into his arms and carried her the three steps to the queen-size bed. He placed her on the mattress as though she were made of the finest, most delicate porcelain.

With one knee pressed against the edge of the bed, he leaned forward and paused. Once more he amazed her by hesitating and closing his eyes. For the longest moment he didn't move.

"Russ?" she whispered, concerned. "What's wrong?"

The merest hint of a smile turned up the edges of his mouth. He leaned forward enough to press a small portion of his body over hers. With infinite care he brushed the hair from her brow, and his callused, work-roughened hands shook slightly, she noted.

"Russ?" she repeated, growing alarmed. Her hands framed his face, and he dragged her palm across his cheek to his lips and kissed the inside of her hand.

"I need to explain something first," he whispered, and the words seemed to be pulled from the farthest corner of his soul. "If we make love now, there'll be no turning back."

Taylor blinked, not certain she understood him. She heard the desperation in his voice, read the havoc in his handsome features and wondered at the source of his discontent.

Taylor's mind was reeling, her thoughts jumbled. Had she been able to speak she was confident her words would have made no sense.

Russ lowered his mouth to hers, but his kiss was featherlight. "Look at me," he whispered, and his voice wobbled slightly. "I want you so much I'm shaking like a newborn calf. All these weeks I've dreamed of this moment, dreamed of making you mine, and once the time arrives, I discover... I can't."

Not according to the hot shaft of evidence pressing against her thigh. Taylor didn't know a delicate, or even an indelicate way, of mentioning the fact.

"I know your career is important to you, and it should be. You worked too hard to gain your education to give it up now," he said as though he'd reached a major decision.

"That's r-right," Taylor returned, frowning.

Gripping her hand on his own, Russ brought her fingertips to his lips and kissed them gently. "And another thing..."

"There's more?"

"Lots more," he whispered, grinning down on her. His mouth brushed hers again in a lazy, affectionate kiss. He dragged a breath between his teeth before continuing. "I know you haven't come to appreciate Cougar Point yet, but that's all right. I promise you will in time. There's something about standing outside on a crisp autumn night and feeling the moonlight on your face. Or hearing the crunch of snow under your boots in winter. In spring it's kittens, and the rush of wind as it blows over the treetops. Those are the things I love most. Like the song, they're my favorite things."

Taylor frowned, lost in confusion. The last thing she remembered was Russ telling her that it didn't matter if she loved him, because he was so crazy about her. Then he started listing a series of very sweet enjoyments, but for the life of her, Taylor couldn't understand where their conversation was leading.

Her hands went back to his face, cupping his head as she studied him, seeking some meaning to his words. "Why are you telling me all this?"

"Because I want you to love them as much as I do. I want you to love the country. Cougar Point will never rival Seattle. It won't even rival Reno, but it's a good place to live, a good place to raise a family."

Taylor had no argument with that. None. From the first, she'd noted how strong the sense of family was in the small community. "In the beginning I was so lost. Moving to

Montana was like visiting a foreign country. Time seemed to have been turned back thirty years."

"What about the ranch life?"

Again she wasn't entirely sure what he was asking. "In many ways it's beautiful. I never thought I could say that and mean it. At first all I saw was the barrenness of the land, the harshness, and how unforgiving it could be. I saw how hard you and the others worked to eke out a life for your cattle. How busy you were each season. I learned a little of the problems and wondered why anyone would bother when ranching was such a demanding way of life."

"And now?"

"Now...there's still a great deal I don't understand, and I probably never will, but there's peace. There's contentment, too, in knowing you've worked hard, and the rewards are well deserved." She hesitated, surprised at how well formed her thoughts actually were since she'd never voiced them before this moment. "I moved to Cougar Point looking for one thing and found something else entirely. In the past few weeks I've learned a good deal about what's important in life and what isn't."

Russ smiled and rewarded her with a lengthy kiss that sapped her energy. Reversing their positions, Russ brought her on top of him and hugged her around the middle. "Now that we've got that subject all clear, I want you to know that I consider babies a woman's business...."

Bracing her hands against his chest, Taylor lifted her head. "What are you talking about? I didn't want to say anything because you seemed to have a lot that needed to be said, but quite honestly, Russ, I'm at a loss as to where this conversation is leading."

His eyes rounded and his mouth dropped open. "You are?"

"Yes."

"Good grief, I thought you knew all along. I'm asking you to marry me."

Chapter Thirteen

Marriage!" Taylor cried, stunned. She climbed off the bed so fast, she nearly stumbled onto the carpeting. "You're joking."

"Trust me, a man doesn't joke about something this important."

All at once Taylor's knees didn't feel as if they would support her any longer, and she slumped onto the end of the mattress. Although she hadn't done anything physically strenuous, she felt breathless and light-headed. She pressed her hand over her heart in an effort to calm its erratic beating, but it didn't seem to help.

"Taylor, what's wrong?" Russ knelt down in front of her and gripped both her hands in his own. "You look like you're about to faint."

"Don't be ridiculous."

"What's wrong?"

She twisted around and pointed at his door. "When I walked in this room, I wasn't thinking about the two of us getting married."

"Do you mean to say you came here after my body?"

"Don't go all righteous on me," she muttered. "You've been after mine for weeks."

"I've reconsidered," Russ said with infuriating calm. "I want more than an occasional tumble with you. A whole lot more."

"Isn't marriage carrying this a tad too far?"

"No. Is it so wrong to want to wake up in the morning with you at my side?"

"You shouldn't hit a girl with this kind of talk. I'm not prepared for it." She pulled her hands from his and waved them dramatically. "Out of the blue he starts talking about marriage."

Russ ignored her small outburst. "When I come into the house after a hard day's labor, it's you I want to find waiting for me."

Taylor's gaze narrowed. "I suppose it's me you want cooking your dinner and laundering your clothes!"

"Yes," he returned matter-of-factly. "Because I'll have spent my life's blood for the past twelve or more hours building a good life for us. If washing a load of work clothes troubles you so much, I'll bring someone in. I don't want to marry you for your domestic talents."

He was serious. Dead serious. "Russ," she whispered, running her hands down the sides of his face, "marriage isn't something we should discuss now. Let's talk about it later...much, much later." Leaning forward, she slanted her mouth over his, giving him her tongue. Russ resisted her at first but quickly surrendered. His response was gratifying.

He wrapped his arms around her, and his returning kiss was urgent, plundering with unleashed passion. As the kissing intensified, Russ eased her back onto the bed and positioned himself above her.

Taylor's hands were busy with the fasteners of his shirt. Once the snaps were open, she ran her fingers over the corded muscles, reveling in the hard, rugged feel of him.

"Taylor..." He lifted his head and groaned. He looked like a man who didn't know what he wanted to do, a man trapped in one world, seeking entrance into another. His eyes were pinched shut.

Taylor had no answers to give him. All she knew was that she was tired of fighting this feeling, tired of living a life filled with denial. She hadn't meant to fall in love with Russ Palmer, but she had. Her fingers tangled in his hair as she directed his lips back to hers.

She yearned for more of his mouth, more of him. When he kissed her again, she felt it in every part of her body, from the crown of her head all the way to the soles of her feet.

Russ's hands were equally busy, fondling her breasts, working feverishly to free her from the restraints of her blouse. The whole time he was struggling with the tiny pearl buttons, his mouth was devouring hers.

Once her blouse was unfastened, he pulled it open and sighed as he cupped a breast, molding it to fit inside his palm. His hungry, eager lips followed a downward progression, and he drew her nipple into his mouth and sucked greedily. With each gentle tug of his mouth, Taylor rolled her head against the mattress. She threaded her fingers through his hair, loving the feel of his skin against her own, his wonderful mouth and all the hot sensations he created within her.

The pleasure he offered, the need he created were so potent that Taylor's hips started to buckle. Russ found the waistband of her wool slacks and eased it down. In an effort to aid him, Taylor lifted her hips, and she sighed as the material whispered its way over her buttocks and down her thighs.

Once more she raised her hips and moved against him. Russ tore his lips from hers and groaned. Taking her hand in his, he eased it down and pressed her open palm against the bulge in his pants. Soon it was Taylor who was groaning as she gave him the pleasure he craved.

"Taylor." He hissed her name between clenched teeth. "No more..."

She patently ignored him, and he sighed anew. Lifting his head, Russ ground his teeth and slowly shook his head in a silent plea for her to cease.

Taylor gazed into his tortured face and smiled softly. "I want you so much," she whispered. "Don't make me wait...don't make me wait."

Russ slipped his fingers inside her silk panties, and she released a ragged breath and opened herself to him. His own breathing was labored, and he was making low, incoherent sounds when he rested the heel of his hand at the apex of her womanhood. Taylor's teeth marked her lower lip as he delicately parted her and slipped one finger inside.

Taylor thought she would faint, the pleasure was so keen. She moved against him, melting with need. He gave her everything she yearned for and more.

When she least expected it, he levered himself up and started kissing her in a fierce and raging storm of his own, and then without warning, he rolled away from her.

Shocked, Taylor sat upright. Russ had tossed his arms out to the sides, and with his eyes tightly closed, he dragged in deep, even breaths in a monumental effort to bring himself back under control.

With shaking hands, Taylor adjusted her clothes. "Russ?" she asked once she was finished. She ran her fingers through his hair and lightly kissed him. "Why did you stop?"

"I already told you. If we're going to make love, even once, there's no turning back. I've got to have more from you than your body.... I want you for my wife."

"Does it have to be all or nothing?"

"Yes," he returned forcefully, "although God knows you make me want you until I'm insane with it."

"But why talk about marriage now?" she asked gently. "Isn't that something we could consider later?"

"No... it'll be too late to think about it afterward," he said fervently. "If we're going to make love, then there's got to be a commitment between us."

"But, Russ..." She wasn't sure why she was fighting him so hard; the reasons had escaped her. She'd already admitted she loved him, and if she'd taken that step, then accepting responsibility for their feelings would be the next logical phase. Only she'd just learned to walk and Russ was talking about signing her up for a marathon.

Russ sat up and gripped her by the shoulders. "I realize things are done differently in the city. Men and women change partners as often as they do their sheets. I've read about the 'swinging singles,' the 'headhunters in a land of search-and-seizure.'"

"That's not true," Taylor argued heatedly. "At least not with me. There's only been one other man in my life, and it was the biggest mistake I've ever made."

"Good, then don't repeat it. I'm offering you what Mark never would have, because I refuse to suggest anything less. When we make love, I don't want there to be any doubt in your mind of my commitment to you. It's complete and total. When I told you I loved you, that wasn't a momentary thing based on physical attraction or a case of overactive hormones. It's something that's been cultivating and blossoming from the first moment we met. It's not going to change or go away. I love you, and it's the first time I've ever said that to a woman and truly meant it."

A hard lump formed in Taylor's throat, and tears brimmed in her eyes. "But we're different."

"Of course we are," Russ said, tucking both her hands between his. "That's the crazy part of all this. At first I thought those differences would doom any chance of a lasting relationship between us. The way I figured it, we didn't have any business linking our lives together when our views are so far apart. Then I realized that knowing you, fighting with you, has brought balance into my life. You've shown me and taught me things I needed to know. There's a lot I disagree with yet, but those issues are things we can face when they arise. Basically I'm coming around to your way of thinking."

That was news to Taylor. He still seemed as obstinate as ever in several areas. But then again, he had allowed Mandy to wear makeup and he had changed his opinion about the drill team uniform and even agreed to her compromise on the dating issue. There had been other changes, too. Subtle ones. When she argued with him, Russ listened and weighed her argument, which was something she'd never gotten her father to do. Her mother had always lent a willing ear, but never her father.

"I can see the changes in you, too," Russ continued. "Remember how you felt when you first moved to Cougar Point? As I recall, you claimed it was the farthest corner of the known world. Just a moment ago you were telling me you've come to appreciate some of the qualities of small-town living. True, no merchant in town is likely to accept American Express in our lifetime, but who knows. If you really get a craving to use that card, Billings isn't all that far.''

''Three and a half hours,'' she muttered, resisting the urge to laugh. Dear sweet heaven, she was actually considering this crazy proposal of his. What he said about Mark had hit home. The months apart had given her perspective. Russ was right. Mark would never have married her.

''Billings is only three hours, four at the most, and that isn't far,'' he explained eagerly. ''If you like, we'll make a weekend trip of it and spend our days shopping and our nights making love. I'm willing to compromise with you. If doing housework offends you—''

''That's not it!''

''Then what is?''

For the life of her, Taylor couldn't think of a single argument that made the least bit of sense. She stuck with one that was tried and true. ''It's the idea of the woman having to work for a wage and then being expected to do everything else at home in addition. If a wife works outside the home, her husband should lend a hand with the housework and the rearing of the children.''

''I agree,'' Russ murmured, although it looked as if he had to swallow a watermelon whole to do so. ''But that's also the reason I feel a mother's place is in the home.''

''Oh, please, let's not get into that again.''

''Right,'' Russ agreed emphatically. ''We could inadvertently start another war, and the last thing I want to do is fight with you. I love you, Taylor. God help me, but it's true.''

She lifted her hand and caressed the side of his face. "I love you, too."

Russ captured her right hand, pressing his own over hers, and then sighed deeply. "I knew you did. I couldn't believe otherwise because it hurt too damn much. I swear to you, Taylor, I've never been a jealous man, but when you were having dinner with Cody Franklin last weekend, it took every ounce of restraint I possess not to march across that restaurant and claim you as mine."

Taylor smiled and leaned forward until their foreheads touched. Her lips lightly brushed his. "I'm not much for the green-eyed monster myself, but Mary Lu Randall should consider herself a lucky woman. I felt like tearing her hair out."

"Does this mean you're willing to marry me?"

Taylor closed her eyes and waited for a list of sound, rational arguments to convince her otherwise. To her surprise there were none. "Yes . . . I'm willing to consider it."

With a triumphant shout loud enough to crack the windows, Russ bolted to his feet, hauling her with him. With his arm at her waist, he whirled her around and around until Taylor, laughing, begged him to stop.

Instead, he lifted her higher and higher until she braced her hands against the tops of his shoulders and tossed back her head. Together they went crashing down onto the bed.

The knock on the door caught them both by surprise. Taylor's round eyes found Russ's. She didn't even want to imagine who stood on the other side.

"Who is it?" Russ demanded.

Taylor hurriedly arranged her clothes and paused to smile when she realized it was the boy delivering the pizza. She'd completely forgotten about it.

Russ paid for their meal and brought the thick cardboard box and a stack of napkins inside. The scent of pepperoni and melting cheese filled the small hotel room. Taylor felt weak with need of her favorite pizza.

Taking the box from Russ, she put it on the table and immediately opened it. She was grateful for the napkins the delivery boy had included, and pulled a hot slice free for Russ. Next she helped herself, savoring the first delicious bite.

"Taylor," Russ groaned, sitting in the chair across from her, "we're having the most important discussion of our lives. How can you eat at a time like this?"

"The pizza is hot *now*," she explained, and immediately gobbled down two extra bites, lest he convince her to put it aside.

"I suppose we're going to have to figure out a way of getting your pizza fix, too, aren't we?"

She nodded eagerly. "At least once a month, please." She paused and closed her eyes, her shoulders sagging with the action. "Oh, my goodness, I'd forgotten how good a pizza could taste. Russ, I'm sorry, but I can't marry you unless we arrange for me to have a decent pepperoni pizza every few weeks."

"The bowling alley—"

"Makes a great breakfast, but someone has got to let those people know good pizza is made fresh and doesn't come out of the freezer compartment."

Russ jammed his fingers through his hair. "I'll do what I can. Anything else?"

"When are we going to announce the engagement? Christmas time?"

Russ stood abruptly and started pacing in rough, uneven steps. He didn't look toward her and seemed to be composing his thoughts.

"Russ?"

He turned hastily to face her. "I want us to get married this afternoon. I realize you're entitled to a big wedding with all the trimmings and the dinner and dancing and everything else you want, but damn it all, Taylor, we could be married within the hour if you'd agree."

The pizza that had seemed so important a few moments before was forgotten. "You want us to get married *now? Today?*"

"We're in Reno, aren't we? What else do folks do in this town?"

She shrugged, and when she started to speak, her voice came out sounding as though she'd suddenly been struck with laryngitis. "I understand gambling is a big interest."

"Okay," Russ said, rubbing the side of his jaw, clearly calling upon all his powers of self-control. "Rushing you wouldn't be fair. I've been thinking about us getting married for weeks, and it's coming at you out of the blue. If you want to wait until Christmas, then fine. I can accept that. I don't like it, and God knows how I'm going to keep my hands off you until then, but I'll try."

"You know what they say: marry in haste, repent at leisure," she felt obliged to remind him.

"Right," Russ returned with a complete and total lack of conviction. "When we look back on your wedding day, I don't want there to be any regrets. None."

"I certainly wouldn't want you to have any, either."

"The best thing to do is take this nice and slow," he said, raising both hands. "You're a teacher and tend to be methodical, and although you've seen evidence to the contrary, I'm not normally one to act on impulse, at least not often."

"I don't think you heard me correctly," Taylor murmured, because he really had misunderstood her. "I thought we'd *announce* our engagement this Christmas."

Russ whirled around and stared at her, looking all the more disgruntled. "Are you thinking you'd like to be a traditional June bride?"

"It makes sense, doesn't it? School will be out but... then I'm not much of a traditionalist."

He grinned at that, bent forward and kissed her. He appeared to have trouble pulling away from her. "You're more of one than you realize, otherwise you wouldn't have had any qualms about moving in with Mark." Once more he knelt down in front of her. "I want to do everything right for you, Taylor. Set the date for the wedding any day you want."

His eyes were filled with such intensity that Taylor found herself mesmerized by the love she found there. "I don't know..." she whispered, feeling herself lulled by his willingness to commit his life to her. "We're both in Reno now. We're in love, but there are problems...."

"Nothing we can't settle," he suggested with an eagerness that brought a smile to her lips.

Closing her eyes, Taylor leaned forward and looped her arms around Russ's neck. "Are you sure you really want to marry me? You haven't met a single member of my family, and my father's opinionated enough to test the saints."

"It's not your family I'm marrying—it's you." He drew her hand to his mouth and kissed her knuckles. "As for if I'm sure about marrying you, I've never been more confident of anything in my life."

Despite everything, Taylor felt utterly certain herself. "Now that you mention it, today does have appeal, doesn't it?"

"Yesterday had appeal, too, as does tomorrow and all the tomorrows for the rest of my life."

"Oh, Russ, sometimes you say the most beautiful things."

"I do?" He seemed completely surprised by that. "I wasn't trying." Tucking his hands at the small of her back, he drew her forward until she was perched on the very edge of the chair. "I love you, Taylor, and I'm going to love you all the days of my life." His mouth captured hers, and he worshiped her in a single kiss.

When he pulled away, Taylor felt like clay in his arms, her will shaped and molded by his. "I'll wear my new dress."

"One more question," he whispered close to her ear. "Are you on birth control?"

Her eyes flew open. "No. Are you?"

He jerked his head back and stared at her, openmouthed. Then his face relaxed into a lazy smile. "I'm beginning to know you, Taylor Manning, soon to be Taylor Palmer. You're telling me birth control isn't completely a woman's responsibility."

She rewarded him with a long, slow, leisurely kiss.

"I'll stop off at the drugstore," he murmured when she'd finished.

"No," she whispered between nibbling kisses. "I don't want you to."

"But you might get pregnant."

"Yes, I know." She found his earlobe and sucked at it gently. "I'd like it if I did. What about you?"

"I'd like it, too.... Dear God, Taylor," he moaned, "stop now while I've still got my sanity."

She continued to press her breasts against him, loving the feel, savoring the sensations the action aroused.

"Taylor," Russ groaned once more. "Stop...please."

"In a moment," she pleaded.

"Now." He gripped her around the waist and pulled back. His shoulders heaved once as if the struggle to resist her demanded a herculean effort.

He stood and gripped the back of the chair. "I'll go find us a preacher," he said, and his voice shook. "Can you be ready in an hour?"

Taylor stood in the foyer of the wedding chapel, clenching a bouquet of small pink rosebuds in her hand. The minister who'd married her pointed out the line on the wedding certificate where she was supposed to sign. Taylor did so with a flair, then smiled at her husband and handed him the pen. Russ in turn gave the pen to the receptionist and clerk who'd agreed to serve as witnesses.

Russ hurriedly signed the document, and when he finished, he turned to the man of God, shook his hand and then directed Taylor out of the chapel.

"I don't think I've ever seen you more beautiful," he said, tucking his hand around her waist and drawing her close to him. His eyes shone with a golden light that had been transmitted straight from his heart, the message of joy transparent.

"I don't think I've ever seen you more handsome," Taylor told him.

His eyes didn't stray from her. "What would you like to do next? Have dinner? See a show? I understand some of the biggest names in Hollywood are in town."

Taylor chuckled. "You've got to be kidding. You know what I want because it's the same thing you want. Besides, we've only got a few hours."

"A few hours. Why?"

"Because," she said, leaning forward to lightly press her mouth over his, "the drill team is scheduled to perform at eight, and Mandy would never forgive us if we weren't there for her big moment.''

Russ grumbled something under his breath and quickened his pace, leading her back to the hotel.

"You seem to be a might eager, Mr. Palmer," she said as they stepped into the hotel elevator.

"Move your hips against me like that one more time and I'll be forced to show you exactly how eager I can be."

"And I'd be willing to let you."

Russ reached for her then, dragging her flush against him. His mouth captured hers, and he gave her a prolonged glimpse of the pleasure that awaited her. The elevator had stopped at their floor, and the doors had glided open before either of them were aware of it.

As soon as they stepped into the long, narrow hallway, Russ paused and lifted her into his arms. "You didn't get the big fancy wedding, with the bridesmaids and orange blossoms and the organ music, but there are some traditions I can and will provide."

However, opening the door with Taylor in his arms proved to be awkward, and after a frustrating moment, Russ, grumbling under his breath, tossed her over his shoulder as if she weighed no more than a bag of grain.

"Russ," Taylor cried, "put me down this minute."

"Be patient," he said, squatting down in an effort to insert the key into the lock. Apparently he was having some trouble, because it was taking him forever.

A middle-aged couple strolled past, and mortified, Taylor covered her face with both hands.

"Dear," the older woman whispered to Taylor, "do you need help?"

"Not really," she answered. "Just don't ever let your daughters grow up to marry cowboys."

"You're recently married?" the woman asked as if it were the most romantic thing she'd ever heard. "Did you hear that, John? They just got married."

The door opened, and Russ walked inside with Taylor still dangling from his shoulder. "We've been married for all of about fifteen minutes," Russ advised the couple. "Now, if you'll excuse us, we're going to have our honeymoon." With that he shut the door.

"Russ Palmer, put me down."

"With pleasure."

He walked over to the bed and released her. Taylor went flying backward, a cry hovering on her lips. Chuckling, Russ lowered himself over her.

"Was that really necessary?" she demanded, feigning indignation.

"If I wanted to get you inside this room in one piece, it was. And trust me, I wanted you in one piece."

A smile twitched at the edges of Taylor's mouth.

"Oh, Taylor," Russ groaned, "I'm so crazy about you." He set his long fingers in the thickness of her hair and pulled her head up to receive his kiss. His mouth was hard over her own, hard with passion, hard with need.

"Oh, sweet Taylor," he murmured as he tore his mouth free and nestled his face in the delicate curve of her neck. He kissed her there, his lips hot and moist. His hands were eager yet gentle as he helped her stand and slip out of her dress. It fell to the floor in a pool of silk and lace. He picked it up and set it aside.

Taylor stood before him, proud and regal in her chemise and tap pants. The coral crowns of her nipples stood out through the sheer material. Russ had barely touched her, and already Taylor was tingling with sensation.

Stepping back, he gazed at her, and he seemed to have lost his voice. He touched her gently, reverently running his hands down the silky smooth texture of her undergarments.

He reached for the hem of the chemise, and like a child being undressed, Taylor raised her arms. He removed her top and folded it over the back of the chair.

Taylor arched her back to him, thrusting forth her breasts, silently offering herself to him. Russ didn't require a second invitation. He growled low in his throat, a primal animal sound that was so earthy, so pagan and sensual that Taylor all but swayed into his arms at the very sound of it. Her head fell back, and her thick, luxuriant hair swung down to the small of her back.

Taking her by the shoulders, Russ pressed her down onto the bed. He removed the tap pants and her panty hose, then quickly undressed himself, taking none of the care with his own clothes that he had with hers.

He joined her and kissed her hungrily several times before lowering his head to her breasts, which by now were pulsating with need, craving his mouth. He seemed determined not to disappoint her. His tongue flicked over the pearled tip of one breast, and Taylor felt a shimmering spark of desire shoot through her like the flashing beam from a laser. She raised one knee and buckled her hips upward.

Russ continued to work his magic on her until Taylor became a whimpering mass of need.

Their mouths met once more in another kiss so hot, it threatened to consume them both.

"Russ, please don't make me wait any longer," she pleaded, her words so unintelligible she could barely understand them herself.

He placed his hand on her upper thigh and eased her legs apart with his fingers. He separated her and probed lightly between the moist folds of her womanhood until she thought she would die if he didn't make love to her soon. At the same time he lowered his head to cover her breast with his mouth.

His finger continued its magical manipulation as his tongue deftly caressed her nipple. Twin sensations brought her to a climax so strong, so splendid and so scalding that she twisted restlessly and embedded her fingers in his hair.

When the ripples of pleasure had started to abate, Russ introduced another. Poised above her, his eyes holding hers, the tip of his manhood penetrated her.

Slowly, so very slowly, Russ closed his eyes, his pleasure apparently as keen as her own.

"Oh, Russ," she breathed, lost in sensation.

He slowly lowered his body until he filled her. Thoroughly. Completely. He was hard and smooth. Thick and warm. Then, with the greatest care, he started to move. Each stroke led her farther into the Garden of Eden, past the gates of Paradise into a universe so bright that the light blinded her senses. Her body responded naturally of its own accord, mimicking each motion of his.

Russ's release came seconds after her own. He collapsed on top of her, then rolled to the side, taking her with him. "I love you," he whispered after a breathless moment, and kissed her softly.

"I love you, husband of mine," she whispered back.

Russ brushed a stray tear from her eye, and his fingers lingered on her face before tangling with her hair, drawing the thickness over her shoulders. Their eyes met and locked.

"I'll love you on my dying day," Russ vowed.

Taylor arched one delicate brow and laughed softly. "I don't think it's polite to make love to a woman and then speak of dying."

"It is after making love to you. I could have died of pleasure. We waited too long, love. I was ready to explode the minute I entered you."

Her answering smile was languid. "What do you suggest?"

"There's only one thing to do."

"Yes?"

Quickly Russ rolled her onto her back. "Make love again."

An hour later, just before they were ready to leave for the drill team performance, Taylor used the phone in Russ's room to call her family.

Russ stood behind her, his hands smoothing her shoulders. Without her ever having said a word, Russ seemed to know how difficult this discussion would be for her.

"Mom?" she said excitedly when her mother answered. "If Dad's home, get him on the other phone. I've got some important news."

Taylor heard her mother's hurried call for Eric Manning. Within a minute, Taylor's father was on an extension.

"Taylor," her father's voice boomed over the long-distance line as strong as if he were in the next room, "what is it? Is anything wrong? Listen, I've been reading between the lines in your letters, and I'm worried about you and this cowpoke. Christy said something about you calling and talking to her, but she never said exactly why, other than the fact you were having trouble with that cowboy."

"Dad...stop a minute, will you?"

"Just a minute. Now you listen to me. If he gives you any more problems, I want you to let me know because your brothers and I will deal with him."

"Eric," her mother interrupted, "Taylor called because she has some news."

It took Taylor a tense moment to compose herself.

"Mom and Dad," she said after swallowing tightly, "congratulations are in order.... I was married today." A second of stunned silence followed her announcement. "I'm afraid I married that pesky cowboy." With that, she handed the receiver to Russ.

Chapter Fourteen

Russ took the telephone receiver out of Taylor's hand, wondering at the way her brow had condensed into a brooding frown. It looked for a moment as if she wanted to advise him, but there wasn't time.

"Hello," Russ said. "I'm Russ Palmer."

"What the hell have you done?" a loud male voice shouted at him.

Russ moved the phone away from his ear in a reflexive action. "I married your daughter," Russ explained, doing his best to keep his tone even and controlled. He didn't much take to being yelled at, but he could understand Eric Manning's feelings.

"Taylor's just broken off one relationship, and the last thing she should do is get involved in another, especially with . . ."

"A cowboy," Russ finished for him. Taylor was sitting on the edge of the mattress, her hands clenched tightly in her lap, her deep blue eyes staring up at him.

"I swear that girl of mine should have her head examined. She clearly doesn't realize what she's done...."

A soft, feminine voice interrupted the tirade. "Eric, dear, all this shouting isn't going to settle anything. They're already married. Didn't you hear Taylor tell you so herself?"

"And we fully intend to stay married," Russ added, in case there was any doubt in the older man's mind.

"It's too soon," Taylor's father continued, his tone less menacing. "Surely you realize she married you on the rebound. You may be a perfectly fine young man, but my daughter—"

"Is twenty-six and old enough to know her own mind."

"She's always been a hothead. No doubt her sister told her I was dead set against her having anything to do with you."

"I can understand your concern," Russ said, now that the edge of his anger had worn off. "You don't know me from Adam."

"What about your family?" Eric thundered anew. "What do they have to say about this?"

"The only family I have is a younger half sister. We haven't told her yet, but Mandy will be delighted."

"You don't have any family?" Eric shouted. "How the hell are you supposed to know what's right without parents? By the way, just how old are you?"

"Thirty-five."

"Thirty-five! You're nine years older than Taylor— that's too much."

"Now, Eric," Elizabeth Manning broke in. "You're being ridiculous. If you recall, you're seven years older than I am. Russ, you'll have to excuse my husband's temper. It's just that he loves Taylor and is terribly proud of her, except he has trouble letting her know that."

"You don't need to go telling him that."

"Russ is family, dear."

"Not if I have anything to say about it."

"Frankly, Mr. Manning," Russ said firmly, "you don't. The deed is done. Signed, sealed and delivered."

"We'll just see about that."

"Stop it now, the pair of you. Eric, either you be civil to Taylor's husband or you can get off the phone. I won't have you speaking that way to him." Her words were followed by the click of a telephone receiver.

Russ waited a moment to compose himself. Taylor had mentioned the type of man her father was more than once, but butting heads with the older man proved to be more of a challenge than Russ had anticipated.

"Mrs. Manning, believe me, I can understand your concern, and I can't say that I blame you. But I want you to know I love Taylor, and I have every intention of being a good husband."

"I'm sure you will. Please forgive my husband. Personally I think he was disappointed because he didn't get to walk Taylor down the aisle. Only one of our sons is married, and I think Eric was looking forward to taking part in a wedding for one of his daughters."

"I'm sorry to have cheated him out of that."

"Don't be too concerned. There's always Christy, and we expect she'll be engaged soon to an attorney friend of hers. Now, before you think the worst of us, I want to offer you a hearty welcome into the family, such as it is."

"Thank you," Russ said, and smiled reassuringly at Taylor, who was looking more concerned by the minute.

"Would you mind putting Taylor back on the line?"

"Of course not." Russ's eyes found Taylor's as he held the receiver out to her. "Your mother wants to talk to you."

"Was it bad?" she whispered, sounding guilty when she had no reason to feel so.

"No, I think your father and I will get along just fine."

"The two of you are quite a bit alike."

Russ had to mull that over for a moment. It had probably been a good thing that Russ had first been introduced to Taylor's father over the telephone. Had they met in person it was likely that they would have swung at each other.

Taylor took the telephone and visibly relaxed as she started talking to her mother. Russ was relieved to see her good spirits return. This was their day, the one he'd been thinking about for weeks, and he didn't want anything or anyone to ruin it.

The problem, Russ decided an hour later, was that he'd forgotten about Mandy, his cantankerous, bullheaded younger sister.

"You did what?" the teenager screeched in outrage.

"We got married," Taylor explained softly, holding out her ring finger, adorned with a simple gold band, as proof. It was apparent that she was equally surprised by his sister's response. "I thought you'd be pleased."

"You did it without even talking to me?" Mandy cried. She braced her hands on her hips as though she were the adult and they were the children, and both he and Taylor were badly in need of a lecture. "I can't believe the two of you." She whirled around and confronted Carol Fischer. "Did you hear what these two just did?" Mandy demanded.

Carol had trouble containing a grin. "Yes, I did," she said, and stepped forward to hug Taylor. "Congratulations."

"You didn't so much as consult me," Mandy reminded him, her eyes narrowing. "Can you imagine how I feel? I'm your sister, damn it, and I should have been in on this from the first. Good grief, you wouldn't have even met Taylor if it hadn't been for me!"

"Do you mind so terribly much?" Taylor asked softly.

"Of course I don't mind. Marrying you is probably the smartest thing Russ has done in his entire sorry life. It's just that..." She paused, and tears clouded her pretty green eyes. "I would have liked to have been there. You couldn't have waited until after the drill team performance?"

"Yes, we could have. We should have," Russ agreed, stepping closer to his sister. "I'm sorry if we offended you. That wasn't our intention."

"We were so lost in each other that we forgot everyone else," Taylor explained.

"I can't believe it. When we left this morning, you were barely talking to each other, and the next thing I know, you're married. I just don't understand it."

Taylor slipped her arm around Mandy's shoulders. "I've been in love with your brother from the first, but I was fighting it because... well, because I didn't think I'd fit into his life. Then we started talking and I realized I couldn't even remember why I was fighting him so hard when I love him so much. I realize this probably doesn't make a whole lot of sense to you, and I'm sorry."

Mandy lifted one shoulder in a halfhearted shrug. "In a way it does make sense. I just wish to heaven that you could have waited a little while longer. I would have liked to throw rice or birdseed or something."

"We were just thinking about going out for a wedding dinner. We'd like it if you came."

With her arms folded just below her breasts, Mandy cocked her head to one side. "Are you sure I wouldn't be intruding?"

"More than sure," Russ assured her. "I'm going to order a bottle of champagne and you can have a virgin daiquiri if you want. It isn't every day a brother can share his wedding dinner with his sister, and we have a good deal to celebrate, don't we? In fact, Taylor's and my wedding day wouldn't be complete if it weren't for you being here to share part of it with us."

"You're just saying that," Mandy informed him with a regal tilt to her chin. "However, I'm going to let you get away with it because I really am pleased." She dropped her arms and threw herself against Russ with such force that he nearly toppled backward. "Hey," she cried, wiping the tears from her cheeks with the back of her hand, "did you see how great the team did? Aren't we fabulous?" She didn't wait for a response, but reached for Taylor, looping an arm around Russ's waist and the other around Taylor's. "Now listen," she said, growing serious once more. "There's something I want understood. If you're going to start having babies, I want to be consulted. Understand?"

Three weeks later, early on a Saturday morning, Taylor nestled close to her husband under a layer of thick quilts, seeking his warmth. When she'd first arrived in Montana,

Russ had warned her about the winters, but nothing could have prepared her for the bitter cold that had descended upon them in the past ten days.

Russ stirred, rolled over and pulled her into his arms. Taylor smiled contentedly as she repositioned herself so her head rested on his firm shoulder. She pressed her hands over his chest. Married life certainly seemed to agree with him. She knew it agreed with her. From the moment they'd spoken their vows in Reno, Russ had been a devoted and loving husband. The accent should rest on the word *loving*. He couldn't seem to get enough of her, which was fine with Taylor, since she couldn't seem to get enough of him, either.

With Mandy living with them, it sometimes became downright embarrassing. More than one night after their return, Russ had insisted he was exhausted and dragged Taylor upstairs practically before they'd finished with the dinner dishes. Mandy loved to tease Russ about his sudden need for extra sleep since he'd returned from Reno.

At one point Taylor had felt it was necessary to talk to Russ's sister. Her fear was that the teenager would feel she was excluded, and that was the last thing Taylor wanted for Mandy.

"Are you kidding?" Mandy had said, sharing a smile with Taylor. "I think getting married has been the best thing that's happened to Russ. He should have done it years ago. He's too mellow to want to fight with me anymore. Keep him happy, okay? Because when he's happy, I'm happy."

Keeping Russ happy had done Taylor a world of good, too, and in the process she was delirious with satisfaction herself. Every now and again they clashed over one issue or another, but that was to be expected. Both seemed willing, however, to listen to each other's point of view.

"Good morning," Russ whispered close to her ear. His hand found her breast, and she sighed at the instant surge of pleasure.

"They seem fuller," he whispered.

"And well they should with all the attention you've been giving them the past few weeks."

"I . . . don't mean that kind of full. They're really *full.*"

"I know what you're thinking," she said, snuggling closer. "But it's much too soon to make that kind of assumption."

"Taylor," Russ groaned, kissing her hungrily. "We haven't used an ounce of prevention. Not once. Have you . . . you know, started yet?"

"Not yet, but I'm often a few days late."

Russ smoothed the hair about her face. "You know the problem, don't you?"

"The problem is you and your lusty ways," she muttered.

"You've never complained before."

"I'm not complaining now. I'm just letting you know what the problem is."

"Actually, I believe it's your parents. They're due to arrive next week for Thanksgiving, and you don't want to have to tell them that you're pregnant."

"My father will assume the worst."

"Let him, but we know the truth."

"You don't know my father. He's always been ridiculously protective of us girls, and if he even suspects that I was pregnant before we were married, he's going to raise the roof."

"Do you think I care?" Tenderly Russ planted his hand over her abdomen, and the smile that settled over his face was full and filled with an abundance of pride. "I bet this baby's a boy."

"What a terrible chauvinistic thing to say."

"I can't help it. Every time I think about you having my son I get all warm and tingly inside. I still have trouble believing we're actually married. It seems like a dream."

"We could very well have a girl. In fact, I'd be more than pleased if we did."

"So you're willing to admit you might be expecting."

Taylor was expecting all right, but not the way Russ implied. The minute her parents arrived there was bound to be trouble. Not once since she'd phoned to tell her mom and dad that she and Russ had married had Taylor spoken to her father. Her mother had phoned about the possibility of visiting for Thanksgiving, and Taylor had readily agreed. But she knew the real reason for this visit, and that was for her father to confront Russ about their rushed marriage. Several times in the past three weeks Taylor had tried to prepare Russ for the meeting, but he seemed to let everything she said roll off him like water on an oil-slick surface. Either he wasn't concerned or he was living in a dreamworld. After doing battle with her father for most of her life, Taylor was nervous. Seldom did she back down from Eric Manning, but this was different. She wanted her family to love and appreciate Russ the way she did.

It wasn't that her father was such a monster, but he tended to be opinionated and hotheaded, especially when it came to his daughters. After Taylor had broken up with Mark, her father had taken pains to introduce her to a handful of eligible young men. All of them were professionals. Taylor didn't doubt for a moment that her father would consider Russ an inappropriate husband for her.

"And for another thing," she said stiffly, reminding him of his ridiculous statement when they were discussing marriage, "babies are not a woman's business."

"Oh? And what am I supposed to do?"

"Plenty!"

"Come on, Taylor, be sensible. There's not a whole lot I can do with a baby. They're too tiny."

"You can change a diaper."

"You've got to be kidding."

"You're the one who was so eager to get me pregnant, and now that I am you're going to abandon me." She rolled away from him and buried her face in her pillow. The tears that sprang to her eyes were utterly nonsensical. Even if she was pregnant, it would be months until the baby was born, and there was plenty of time to deal with the issue of Russ's role as a parent.

"Taylor?" Russ asked softly, his hand on her shoulder. "Are you crying?"

She refused to admit it. "Of course not."

"I've been doing a little reading about pregnancy and birth, and from everything I've seen so far, tears are perfectly normal. The experts claim that a woman can become highly emotional during this time."

"I suppose you're going to be quoting statistics to me throughout the next eight months," she said, then immediately regretted her waspish tone. Twisting back around, she sobbed and looped her arms around Russ's neck. "I'm sorry...I didn't mean that. It's just that I'm worried about you meeting Dad."

Russ gently kissed the tip of her nose. "There isn't going to be any problem, sweetheart. I promise you."

"You can't say that—you don't know my dad."

"I won't let there be a problem. We have one very important thing in common, and that's the fact that we both love you. Two men of similar persuasion are going to get along famously. Didn't you tell me he's a chauvinist, too?"

"Yes—just as bad as you."

"Stop borrowing trouble, all right?"

She nodded, and released a ragged sigh. "Okay, but I don't think we should say anything about the possibility of me being pregnant until after Christmas. Agreed?"

"If that's the way you want to handle it." He eased her more fully into the circle of his arms. "But I'm afraid I might inadvertently give something away. Damn it all, Taylor. I'm so happy about it I have trouble not bursting out and shouting every time I think about us having a son."

"We're having a daughter first."

"Son."

"It's ridiculous to argue about it."

"You're right, especially when it's my son growing inside you. Good Lord, the very thought excites me."

"I think I'd better tell Mandy. Otherwise we'll be subjected to the Wrath of Khan for a second time. As I recall, we were given specific instructions to clear the idea of any additions to the family with her first."

"I already told her."

"Russ?" Taylor levered herself up on one elbow.

"I hadn't intended to, but we were sitting at the table one afternoon and apparently I was wearing a silly grin."

"It was probably more of a satisfied smirk," Taylor interrupted. Then she said, "Go on."

"Anyway, I was sitting there minding my own business and she strolled up to me and wanted to know what I found so funny. Of course, I said I didn't find anything amusing, and before I knew it, I was telling her about the book I'd picked up at the library about pregnancy and birth and how I thought you were going to have a baby. She was delighted. By the way, I told her the baby's a boy.''

"Russ, you don't know that."

"Somehow I do. Deep in my heart I know he's a boy. Do you think your father will settle down a little if we promise to give the baby some family name of yours?''

"We've got to get him accustomed to the fact we're married first."

"Right," Russ grumbled. "I forgot." He reached for her and pulled her close to him. "If you're looking for ways to tame the wild beast, I might be able to offer a few suggestions on how to tame me.'' He wiggled his thick eyebrows back and forth several times.

Giggling, Taylor encircled his neck with her arms. "I tamed you a long time ago."

"That you have," he whispered as his mouth sought hers. "That you have."

The Wednesday before Thanksgiving Eric and Elizabeth Manning pulled their thirty-foot RV into the yard of the Lazy P.

Since school had been dismissed at noon, Taylor was home. The instant Taylor recognized the vehicle, she called out to Russ, threw open the back door and flew down the stairs, hardly taking time to button up her coat. Russ followed directly behind her.

Standing on the top step, Russ felt Eric Manning's eyes search him out. The two men quickly sized each other up. Russ slowly descended the stairs. He waited until Taylor had enthusiastically welcomed each of her parents before he placed his arm protectively around her shoulders.

If her parents didn't immediately guess she was pregnant, it would be a miracle. Taylor positively glowed. She had from the moment she'd agreed to marry him. The way Russ figured it, he should be the one beaming. Only rarely in his life had he ever been this happy, this content. Taylor had filled all the dark, lonely corners of his life.

He hadn't been joking when he told her he got all warm and tingly every time he thought about the child growing beneath her heart. At odd moments of the day he'd think about Taylor and how much he loved her, and he'd get all mushy and weak inside. Some nights he'd lie awake and cherish these peaceful moments with Taylor sleeping at his side. She'd been doing a lot of that lately. The books had told him she'd be extra tired. He would prefer it if she'd quit work, but the one time he had suggested it, she'd almost bitten his head off. Moodiness. That was something else the books had addressed. Russ decided he'd leave Taylor to decide when and if she should stop teaching. She knew her own limits. He'd rather she quit, but he'd learned that Taylor was her own woman.

"Mom and Dad," Taylor said, slipping her arm around Russ's waist, "this is my husband, Russ Palmer."

Russ stepped forward and extended his hand to Taylor's father. The older man muttered something unintelligible, and the two exchanged hearty handshakes.

"Come inside," Russ invited, ushering everyone into the warmth of the kitchen. He took their coats and hung them in the hall closet while Taylor settled her parents in the living room.

There had been lots of small changes in the house since Taylor had moved in. She had a natural flair for decorating and had rearranged the furniture and done several other small things that gave the living room a fresh, comfortable feel.

"Would you like some coffee?" she asked.

"We just had some, honey. Thanks," her mother said.

Elizabeth Manning was an older version of her daughter. They both had the same intense blue eyes and long, thick dark hair. Eric Manning was something of a surprise. He was as big as a lumberjack, tall and muscular. It didn't take much to understand how he could intimidate someone. It was important to Russ to win over this man. Important for Taylor. She'd battled with her father most of her life. She'd gone against his will often, but she loved her father, and his approval was important to her.

"Eric," Elizabeth Manning said softly, looking at her husband.

The older man cleared his throat. "Before I do or say anything more to get myself in hot water, I want to apologize for the way I behaved when we last spoke. It's just that finding out my daughter had married without a word to either of her parents came as something of a surprise."

"I understand," Russ said, "and I can't say that I blame you. If she were my daughter, I don't think I would have behaved any differently."

The two men shared a meaningful look.

"There's something you both should know," Taylor said, easing herself down onto the arm of Russ's chair. She gave him a small smile, her eyes round and slightly stricken. "I'm pregnant. Now, Daddy, before you assume the worst," she added in a rush, "this baby was conceived in love with a wedding band on my finger. I swear to you it's the truth."

Russ stared up at his wife with wide-eyed shock. For days she'd been schooling him on the importance of keeping their secret until the Christmas holidays. Again and again she'd insisted the worst thing they could do was announce her pregnancy the moment her parents rolled into the Lazy P. Then, with barely a moment's notice, Taylor had spilled it all.

"Oh, Taylor, that's absolutely wonderful news." Her mother was clearly delighted. One look told Russ that wasn't the case with her father.

"Daddy?" Taylor looked expectantly at her father. She took Russ's hand and held it tightly. "I love him, Dad, more than I ever dreamed it was possible to love a man."

"He's good to you?"

"You're damn right I'm good to her," Russ muttered. He wasn't entirely sure what was going on between father and daughter, but he resented like hell being left out of the conversation.

"That true?" Eric asked, tilting his head toward Russ.

"Yes, Dad."

Eric opened his arms to her, and Taylor flew across the room, to be wrapped in a bear hug with her robust father. The older man's gaze searched for and found Russ's. "She's more trouble than a barrel of monkeys. Opinionated and strong-willed to boot, and has been from the day she was born. I suggest you keep her barefoot and pregnant."

"Daddy!" Taylor tore herself away from her father and braced her hands on her hips.

"I was thinking the same thing myself," Russ said, and chuckled boisterously when Taylor whirled around to glare at him.

The two men smiled at each other; they understood each other well.

"If the two of you think you can order my life, I want you both to know right now that—"

She was never allowed to finish. Russ gently turned her around, draped her over his arm and kissed her soundly.

"I can see our daughter married well," Russ heard Eric Manning inform his wife. "Very well indeed."

* * * * *

Silhouette Special Edition

Now appearing
in a special return engagement, Nora Roberts's
bestselling 1988 miniseries featuring

THE O'HURLEYS!
Nora Roberts

Book 1   **THE LAST HONEST WOMAN**   *Abby's Story*

Book 2   **DANCE TO THE PIPER**   *Maddy's Story*

Book 3   **SKIN DEEP**   *Chantel's Story*

And making his debut in a brand-new title, a very special
leading man . . . Trace O'Hurley!

Book 4   **WITHOUT A TRACE**   *Trace's Tale*

In 1988, Nora Roberts introduced THE O'HURLEYS!—a close-knit
family of entertainers whose early travels spanned the country. The
beautiful triplet sisters and their mysterious brother each experience
the triumphant joy and passion only true love can bring, in four books
you will remember long after the last pages are turned.

Don't miss this captivating miniseries—a special collector's edition
available now wherever paperbacks are sold.

OHUR-1A

The tradition continues in November as Silhouette presents its fifth annual Christmas collection

The romance of Christmas sparkles in four enchanting stories written by some of your favorite Silhouette authors:

Ann Major * SANTA'S SPECIAL MIRACLE
Rita Rainville * LIGHTS OUT!
Lindsay McKenna * ALWAYS AND FOREVER
Kathleen Creighton * THE MYSTERIOUS GIFT

Spend the holidays with Silhouette and discover the special magic of falling in love in this heartwarming Christmas collection.

**From *New York Times* Bestselling author
Penny Jordan, a compelling novel of ruthless passion
that will mesmerize readers everywhere!**

Penny Jordan

Silver

Real power, true power came from
Rothwell. And Charles vowed to have it,
the earldom and all that went with it.

Silver vowed to destroy Charles, just as surely and
uncaringly as he had destroyed her father; just as he had
intended to destroy her. She needed him to want her . . .
to desire her . . . until he'd do anything to have her.

But first she needed a tutor: a man who wanted no one.
He would help her bait the trap.

**Played out on a glittering international stage,
Silver's story leads her from the luxurious comfort of
British aristocracy into the depths of adventure,
passion and danger.**

AVAILABLE NOW!

 HARLEQUIN

PASSPORT TO ROMANCE VACATION SWEEPSTAKES

OFFICIAL RULES

SWEEPSTAKES RULES AND REGULATIONS. NO PURCHASE NECESSARY.

HOW TO ENTER:

1. To enter, complete this official entry form and return with your invoice in the envelope provided, or print your name, address, telephone number and age on a plain piece of paper and mail to: Passport to Romance, P.O. Box #1397, Buffalo, N.Y. 14269-1397. No mechanically reproduced entries accepted.
2. All entries must be received by the Contest Closing Date, midnight, December 31, 1990 to be eligible.
3. Prizes: There will be ten (10) Grand Prizes awarded, each consisting of a choice of a trip for two people to: i) London, England (approximate retail value $5,050 U.S.); ii) England, Wales and Scotland (approximate retail value $6,400 U.S.); iii) Caribbean Cruise (approximate retail value $7,300 U.S.); iv) Hawaii (approximate retail value $ 9,550 U.S.); v) Greek Island Cruise in the Mediterranean (approximate retail value $12,250 U.S.); vi) France (approximate retail value $7,300 U.S.).
4. Any winner may choose to receive any trip or a cash alternative prize of $5,000.00 U.S. in lieu of the trip.
5. Odds of winning depend on number of entries received.
6. A random draw will be made by Nielsen Promotion Services, an independent judging organization on January 29, 1991, in Buffalo, N.Y., at 11:30 a.m. from all eligible entries received on or before the Contest Closing Date. Any Canadian entrants who are selected must correctly answer a time-limited, mathematical skill-testing question in order to win. Quebec residents may submit any litigation respecting the conduct and awarding of a prize in this contest to the Régie des loteries et courses du Quebec.
7. Full contest rules may be obtained by sending a stamped, self-addressed envelope to: "Passport to Romance Rules Request", P.O. Box 9998, Saint John, New Brunswick, E2L 4N4.
8. Payment of taxes other than air and hotel taxes is the sole responsibility of the winner.
9. Void where prohibited by law.

PASSPORT TO ROMANCE VACATION SWEEPSTAKES

OFFICIAL RULES

SWEEPSTAKES RULES AND REGULATIONS. NO PURCHASE NECESSARY.

HOW TO ENTER:

1. To enter, complete this official entry form and return with your invoice in the envelope provided, or print your name, address, telephone number and age on a plain piece of paper and mail to: Passport to Romance, P.O. Box #1397, Buffalo, N.Y. 14269-1397. No mechanically reproduced entries accepted.
2. All entries must be received by the Contest Closing Date, midnight, December 31, 1990 to be eligible.
3. Prizes: There will be ten (10) Grand Prizes awarded, each consisting of a choice of a trip for two people to: i) London, England (approximate retail value $5,050 U.S.); ii) England, Wales and Scotland (approximate retail value $6,400 U.S.); iii) Caribbean Cruise (approximate retail value $7,300 U.S.); iv) Hawaii (approximate retail value $ 9,550 U.S.); v) Greek Island Cruise in the Mediterranean (approximate retail value $12,250 U.S.); vi) France (approximate retail value $7,300 U.S.).
4. Any winner may choose to receive any trip or a cash alternative prize of $5,000.00 U.S. in lieu of the trip.
5. Odds of winning depend on number of entries received.
6. A random draw will be made by Nielsen Promotion Services, an independent judging organization on January 29, 1991, in Buffalo, N.Y., at 11:30 a.m. from all eligible entries received on or before the Contest Closing Date. Any Canadian entrants who are selected must correctly answer a time-limited, mathematical skill-testing question in order to win. Quebec residents may submit any litigation respecting the conduct and awarding of a prize in this contest to the Régie des loteries et courses du Quebec.
7. Full contest rules may be obtained by sending a stamped, self-addressed envelope to: "Passport to Romance Rules Request", P.O. Box 9998, Saint John, New Brunswick, E2L 4N4.
8. Payment of taxes other than air and hotel taxes is the sole responsibility of the winner.
9. Void where prohibited by law.

VACATION SWEEPSTAKES

Official Entry Form

Yes, enter me in the drawing for one of ten Vacations-for-Two! If I'm a winner, I'll get my choice of any of the six different destinations being offered — and I won't have to decide until after I'm notified!

Return entries with invoice in envelope provided along with Daily Travel Allowance Voucher. Each book in your shipment has two entry forms — and the more you enter, the better your chance of winning!

Name _____

Address _____ Apt. _____

City _____ State/Prov. _____ Zip/Postal Code _____

Daytime phone number _____
                              Area Code

☐ I am enclosing a Daily Travel
   Allowance Voucher in the amount of **$**_____ Write in amount
                                                   revealed beneath scratch-off

© 1990 HARLEQUIN ENTERPRISES LTD.

- -

VACATION SWEEPSTAKES

Official Entry Form

PASSPORT **WIN** 1 of 10 Vacations SEE INSIDE TO ROMANCE

MONTH 2 ENTRY

Yes, enter me in the drawing for one of ten Vacations-for-Two! If I'm a winner, I'll get my choice of any of the six different destinations being offered — and I won't have to decide until after I'm notified!

Return entries with invoice in envelope provided along with Daily Travel Allowance Voucher. Each book in your shipment has two entry forms — and the more you enter, the better your chance of winning!

Name _____

Address _____ Apt. _____

City _____ State/Prov. _____ Zip/Postal Code _____

Daytime phone number _____
                              Area Code

☐ I am enclosing a Daily Travel
   Allowance Voucher in the amount of **$**_____ Write in amount
                                                   revealed beneath scratch-off

CPS-TWO